PROPERTY

'You're proving yourself to be a liability,' Brandon proclaimed. 'You can't cook. You can't clean. And now it
seems like you're some lesbian vampire who wants to prey
on my innocent, defenceless staff.'

Cassie tried to tell him it wasn't like that; Laura had
been lying and the kiss had been forced on her; but
Brandon wasn't listening.

'It looks like you only have one purpose around here,'
he continued, 'and I think we should go and exploit that
now.'

PROPERTY

Lisette Ashton

This book is a work of fiction.
In real life, make sure you practise safe sex.

First published in 2002 by
Nexus
Thames Wharf Studios
Rainville Road
London W6 9HA

www.nexus-books.co.uk

Typeset by TW Typesetting, Plymouth, Devon

Printed and bound by
Clays Ltd, St Ives PLC

ISBN 0 352 33744 3

Prologue

'You're here at last. About bloody time.'

Cassie was going to protest but she held her tongue. It wasn't the first time John had spoken to her so brusquely, nor was it the first time he had done it in front of strangers. Ordinarily she might have rebuked him; demanded an apology; or told him that he couldn't speak to her so sharply. But, even with a cursory glance, she could tell these circumstances were different. She could see this was a situation like nothing she had encountered before and her frightened mind insisted it would be best if she turned around and ran away.

'Well, don't just stand there,' John growled. 'Give me the keys and sit down.'

Unnerved, and more than a little intimidated, Cassie remained at the door.

It was close to three in the morning and she had driven quickly through the night after getting his phone call. John had said he *needed her urgently*, and those words had been enough to make Cassie climb out of bed and drive to the office to get the keys for his Porsche.

A part of her – the naïve and optimistic part – had expected to be met by his gratitude. But her pessimistic side had warned her to expect this typical rudeness. However, nothing had prepared her for the other things that were going on.

'Hurry up.' John's voice was sharp with impatience. He snapped his fingers and the resounding clicks sounded like bones breaking. 'Give me the keys and sit down. We haven't got all night.'

Walking hesitantly, reluctance obvious in each step, Cassie started towards him.

The room was thick with the reek of cigars, the acrid stench somehow comforting and sickening at the same time. Coupled with the gloom of a solitary candle's light, the smoky fog turned everything into a sea of shifting shadows.

But Cassie was able to see more than enough.

She could see the other two players sitting at the card table with John, and the half-naked blonde who had been dealing for them. She could also see the other woman behind them but her mind wasn't ready to cope with that sight yet. If she had allowed her thoughts to linger on that image, Cassie knew she wouldn't have stayed a moment longer; she would have simply fled.

'What is this?' she asked. 'What's happening here?' She had wanted her voice to ring with authority but it came out as a nervous squeak. With growing unease she became aware that everyone had turned to look at her.

'Who's she?' asked one player.

'That's John's office girl,' supplied the other.

Cassie bristled at the slur. She wondered if she should explain that she was John's business partner, and point out that she was the 'C' in J & C Property Developments. Certain this was neither the time nor the place for such pedantry, she glared at John and said, 'What's happening here?'

'We're trying to play five card draw,' he told her. 'And, as you'll see, we're almost out of time.' He was holding a fat Havana and used it to point behind the table.

Cassie was loathe to look but her gaze was drawn by macabre curiosity. The woman John had indicated was naked and suspended upside down. Her hands were tied behind her back and her feet were secured wide apart

2

somewhere in the smoky shadows at the ceiling. The base of a fat candle penetrated her sex and Cassie saw this was the same candle that provided the room's only light. Its spluttering flame danced lethargically and licked at the bare flesh between her thighs. Rivulets of spent wax daubed her body. Some had trickled down, over her abdomen and between her breasts, but the majority caked her cleft like a thick deposit of semen. The sight was disturbing and, more than anything else, it increased Cassie's need to escape from the room.

'Sit yourself down lass. Do like your man says.'

The instruction came from the bald man at the card table – the same one who had described her as 'John's office girl'. His words seemed kind enough but his voice had a gruff Scots drawl that made the sentence sound like a command. He used his own Havana to point at an empty chair and Cassie obeyed before she realised what she was doing. Numb with mounting dread, she handed the car keys to John.

'About bloody time,' he grumbled, snatching them from her.

He dangled the keys in front of the other two players and flexed an amiable grin. 'These are the keys to my 911. There's no finance on it – it's bought and paid for. It's also taxed and tested and comes with a full tank of petrol. I should also point out that it's not your run-of-the-mill GT3. I've had it converted to a Gemballa, GTR 600. I don't want to place a financial value on something so desirable but I'm sure you'll both agree that it more than matches the current call.'

'Go on then,' the bald man agreed. 'I could use a runabout.'

The third player, a swarthy looking man with a Havana clenched between his teeth, seemed hesitant. 'What colour is it?'

John shook his head looking pained by the question. 'Don't go and fold on me, Stephen.'

'I'm not folding. I'm just asking what colour is it?'

'It's guard's red.'

Stephen shook his head and threw his cards towards the dealer. 'It's not worth the bet,' he grumbled. 'I've already got a red one.'

John snorted unhappily.

Cassie watched and listened but she couldn't pay attention to what was going on. She knew they were playing poker, and it was obvious the stakes were high, but all of that seemed unimportant compared to the other things that were happening. Ghoulish curiosity kept drawing her gaze back to the woman behind the table. Her head was shrouded by darkness but Cassie didn't need to see her face to know she was in the throes of some extreme emotion. Every muscle in her body was taut and a mixture of shivers and spasms repeatedly buffeted her. Each time she thrashed she caused a fresh flurry of wax to dribble from beneath the candle's wick. When the molten droplets touched bare flesh, she renewed her tortured writhing. The spluttering flame was so close to her sex Cassie wondered how she could choose to tolerate such a heat. It was only as an afterthought that she guessed the woman probably hadn't had any choice in the matter.

'Well, Brandon?' John turned to the bald man. 'Are you still in?'

'I'm still in,' Brandon replied. 'And, I have to congratulate you on a truly magnificent bluff.'

'It's no bluff,' John assured him. 'I'm quietly confident that I can beat whatever you're holding. I just wish Stephen had stayed in so I could have taken the pair of you to the cleaners.'

Stephen ignored them both, his concern seemingly focused on the unlit end of his cigar. With a deepening frown he tapped the pockets of his jacket then pushed himself out of his chair. Stooping to re-light his cigar from the room's only candle, he placed his face close to

4

the suspended woman's sex. As he puffed fresh clouds of smoke into the room, the candle's flame grew broader. Droplets of wax spat from beneath the wick and the long, yellow flame licked at her inner thighs. Cassie watched as the restrained woman thrashed madly to escape the renewed heat.

Brandon blew a plume of smoke through his nostrils and studied John coolly. 'If you're not bluffing, then put the keys on the tray.'

Shrugging as though the matter was of no importance, John snapped his fingers for the dealer's attention. The sound was enough to make Cassie look in his direction and she recoiled in horror. She had only given the dealer a cursory glance on entering the room but, when the woman moved closer to John's side, Cassie was shocked by the sight of another atrocity. Of course she had seen the blonde was topless but, while her nudity had been apparent, it hadn't seemed out of place in this den of perversion. However, Cassie hadn't seen the woman's nipples were both pierced with silver rings and she hadn't noticed the chains that dangled from those piercings. The chains were linked to a small tray, suspending it over the card table. The contents of the tray – a watch that looked like a Rolex, a chunky ID bracelet and a collection of gold sovereigns – all looked to be weighing heavily on the blonde. They dragged the chains down and pulled mercilessly at the silver rings piercing her breasts.

But – and this was the part Cassie couldn't understand – the blonde seemed unmoved by her torture. Her large brown eyes bore a tranquil expression which remained in spite of the torment she was clearly suffering. She blinked lazily into Cassie's shocked features and, when John dropped the 911's keys onto the tray, she didn't even flinch.

'I think you're bluffing,' Brandon said thoughtfully.

John was a composition of indifference. 'Then match the call, and I'll show you what I've got.' He sounded as though he didn't care one way or the other. 'It's your shout, Brandon. You're in the chair.'

Brandon shook his head. 'Why don't we raise the stakes a little higher first? Why don't I meet the value of your car and raise it to the value of my database?'

John sneered. 'And what might that be worth to me?'

'It includes a breakdown of all my major contracts from the past five years. It contains contact names, personal details and the necessary bribes I used to win the biggest deals. A smart man like yourself might be able to make something from it.'

For the first time since she had entered the room, Cassie began to understand some of what was going on. The name Brandon should have been distinctive enough to jog her memory but, because of the other distractions, it hadn't dawned on her this was Brandon McPherson, head of McPherson Developments, their main competitor in the local market. She had heard John talk about Brandon – usually calling him a cheating, bald-headed, Scots bastard – but this was the first time she had met him in person.

Of course none of that went any way to explaining who Stephen was, why two half-tortured women were in attendance, or why John was playing cards with the local competition. But, following the same argument, Cassie couldn't completely understand why she was still sitting there when every instinct in her body was demanding she should run away.

The thought prompted her into action and she placed a hand on John's arm and put her mouth close to his ear. 'I think I should go,' she whispered. Not waiting for his reply, she started to stand.

He grabbed her wrist, squeezing painfully and forcing her back into her chair. 'I think you should stay,' he growled.

Cassie shook her head. 'I don't want to be here, John. This is scaring me and –'

He didn't let her finish. Pulling her close – so close Cassie could inhale the tang of cigars and whisky on his breath – he glared at her with an expression of anger and contempt. 'You're staying here. We leave when I say we leave. Until then, you sit quietly and do as you're told. Do I make myself clear?'

'But I don't want to –'

His fingers pressed hard against her wrist. The pain was unexpected and enormous.

'If you leave now, I'll dissolve our partnership. Is that what you want?'

Cassie wasn't sure what she wanted but she could see his threat was an earnest one. She didn't want to stay at the card table: the room was scary and disturbing, but she didn't want to lose her business either. J & C Property Developments had built up an enviable reputation, using the combined efforts of her acumen and John's capital. If he decided to end the partnership she knew she would have to start building her career from scratch and that wasn't an option she wanted to consider. Assuring herself the card game couldn't go on for ever, and believing he would allow them to leave soon, Cassie tried to convince herself that staying wasn't such a hateful option.

John's eyes remained on her until she nodded her grudging acceptance. He took his hand from her wrist and turned back to Brandon and the card table. 'All right,' he agreed. 'I'll accept your database. But what are you wanting from me?'

'How about a promise?'

'What promise?'

'How about your promise that, when Stephen gets the Harwood property, you leave me to deal with the contract?'

John seemed to consider this. 'Are you close to getting the Harwood property, Stephen?' he called.

'I'm close,' Stephen said cautiously.

John stared at Brandon and shook his head. 'I don't think I could make such a promise and honour it. The Harwood contract is going to be lucrative and I already have some brilliant ideas that Stephen is going to find irresistible. Suggest something else.'

'What about your business?'

Cassie stared at John, terrified he might gamble their business on the game. She opened her mouth to say something, then decided she would only worsen the situation if she did.

'I'm not putting the business in,' John said firmly. 'Try again.'

Brandon glanced at Cassie. 'Then what about your office girl?'

John glanced at Cassie. His smile grew broader and he seemed ignorant to the refusal that widened her eyes. 'You want me to put her in the pot? What possible use could she be to you?'

Brandon shrugged indifferently. He was staring at Cassie and his smile grew lewd with anticipation. He wafted his cigar towards the woman behind the table and said, 'I can always use a spare candleholder for the poker games. Some of the new ones burn out too quickly and too easily.' Nodding at the dealer, he added, 'Perhaps I could get her pierced and teach her how to deal. Faye could use the occasional night off to catch up with her other duties.' Still scrutinising Cassie with his smile, he said, 'I could even use her in one of the other rooms. There's never a shortage of things to do around here for another warm and willing body.'

Cassie shook her head from side to side, too frightened to find her voice. The intimation of what Brandon wanted from her was all too clear. She glanced at John, silently begging him to refuse the suggestion and let her escape from this madness.

'I take it you wouldn't just want her as an office girl.'

Brandon laughed. It was a malicious sound that made Cassie shiver.

'She's quite pretty,' he told John. 'Why on earth would I waste her abilities in the office?' Speaking quickly, allowing his accent to make his words almost indecipherable, he said, 'If you put her in the pot, I'll match the call with the keys to my 355. Do that, and then we can show.'

'You're betting the Ferrari?' John sounded eager. 'Go on then. You're on.'

Cassie stared from one player to the other but they were both ignoring her. She tried to understand the situation but it was impossible to work out exactly what they had agreed. She thought that John had just offered her as a prize in the card game but the idea was so unbelievable she wouldn't let her mind use it as a starting point.

Brandon placed a floppy disc on the tray. 'That's my database,' he said solemnly. 'Put your ante in.'

John turned to Cassie and took hold of her hand. For an instant she thought he was going to reassure her. She thought he was going to squeeze her fingers, tell her she had misunderstood what was happening, and let her laugh about the ludicrous idea that had been gnawing at her thoughts.

Instead, he snatched the watch from her wrist and dropped it on the tray.

Brandon plucked a set of keys from his pocket, placed them on the growing pot, then settled himself back in his chair. 'Go on then, Johnny,' he said. 'You show me yours and I'll show you mine.'

John smiled around the base of his Havana. His eyes gleamed with unashamed triumph. 'I told you I wasn't bluffing,' he said, turning his cards over one by one. 'A quartet of ladies, all bearing a strikingly regal resemblance.' As he spoke he turned over the fourth and final queen. 'Read 'em and weep, Brandon. I've just cleaned you out.'

Cassie wanted to sigh with relief. She didn't know much about poker but she felt sure four queens had to be a good, possibly unbeatable hand. It had been a tense moment but, now it was all over, she felt sure John would allow them to leave and perhaps tomorrow they might even laugh about the whole ordeal.

John chuckled softly to himself and started reaching for the contents of the tray. His fingers had just circled the keys to the Ferrari when Brandon stopped him.

'That is a good hand,' Brandon said amiably. 'If I'd had that hand I might have bet as much as you just did. But instead, I only had these.' Slowly, drawing obvious pleasure from the tension, he laid two aces on the table.

John began to frown.

As his consternation deepened, Cassie's own worries returned.

'I only had two pairs,' Brandon explained. 'Those two aces, and these two.' He placed another two aces beside the first pair.

John groaned.

'John?' Cassie asked. She didn't understand what the problem was. John had put down four queens and all Brandon had was four ones. It seemed obvious that queens had to be better than ones because they had pictures on them. And yet John was acting as though he had lost the game. 'He hasn't beaten you, has he, John?' When he didn't answer immediately she repeated the question, aware her voice was rising with mounting panic. 'He hasn't beaten you, has he?'

Brandon reached over the table and placed his hand on hers. 'You shouldn't be asking him any more questions,' he told her. 'You belong to me now.'

One

A shriek like a warning siren tore through the room. Cassie turned towards the noise and saw the suspended woman thrashing madly. Before she could see what had caused her to cry out the candle was extinguished. The room was plunged into a darkness broken only by the cherry glow of three cigar stubs. Cassie was engulfed by her own need to scream but she contained the urge.

'It looks like the poker's over for tonight,' Brandon said calmly. 'Same time next Friday, gentlemen?'

It was difficult to hear their replies. The woman's shriek had subsided but her anguished sobs rode over every other noise. On top of that, Cassie's heartbeat pounded louder than the dragging chairs and shuffling footsteps that echoed around her. She strained to hear what was being said but, even though she caught every word, she couldn't understand any of it.

'Why don't we find one more candle?' John suggested. 'Even if it's just a stub. You can give me a chance to win back my Gemballa.'

Brandon answered flatly. 'It's my Gemballa now. You know the rules, Johnny. You'll have to try and win it back next Friday.'

'Next Friday,' John grunted. He didn't sound happy. 'What the fuck am I supposed to drive until then?'

Stephen asked John if he needed a lift and John grudgingly accepted.

For Cassie, hearing them speak was like listening to strangers in a dream: their words were out of place and made no sense. She knew what should really have been happening and it seemed insane that no one else in the room was aware of it. John should have been telling Brandon he had been joking when he bet her in the game. John should have been taking hold of her hand, firmly removing her from Brandon's clutches, and escorting her out of the horrible room.

Yet none of those things happened.

Instead, she heard footsteps padding into the furthest corners of the darkness. The cherry eyes of the cigar stubs disappeared until there was only one remaining. Because that one was so close to her face, and because it hadn't moved since the lights had gone out, Cassie knew it belonged to Brandon. It had wavered each time he spoke and there was no doubt in her mind she was alone in the room with him and the two naked women.

The slam of an unseen door punctuated her fears.

'Light a candle, Faye. Let me see what I've won.'

Instantaneously, a match fluttered to life and Faye was caught in the painfully bright illumination. She blinked her eyes at the sudden eruption of light while touching the flame to a candle's wick.

Cassie scoured the darkened corners of the room, hoping John might be lurking there, ready to tell her this was all a prank. It was a facile idea, and she knew she was only fooling herself, but it was better to think that than try to come to terms with the notion John had left her at the mercy of this unsettling stranger.

When she had finally accepted John was gone, Cassie turned to Brandon. He was an imposing figure, broad shouldered and clearly capable. The muted glow of the candle reflected from his bald head, accentuating the frown lines that creased his brow. He scowled unhappily and the expression twisted his features into something frightening. Even though she wanted to draw his

12

attention, and needed to talk to him so they could discuss how she was going to get home, a part of her was thankful he didn't deign to look at her.

His gaze was fixed on the tray suspended from Faye's breasts. 'What a piss poor haul,' he grunted. His thick accent turned the words into a melancholy complaint. 'This could have been much better. This could have been much, much better.'

He finally turned his attention to Cassie and she wanted to swoon with relief. Common sense told her he was going to suggest she phone a taxi and start her journey home. No one could really expect to play cards for a woman and keep her as their prize. She had been insane to think she was dealing with such uncivilised behaviour and she quietly rebuked herself for giving in to such a fanciful idea. She supposed part of her frenzy had come from the peculiarity of the situation. The naked women; the allusion to torture and misogyny; it had all gone a long way to convincing her that John and Brandon had both been serious about using her as a prize. Feeling giddy with relief she found her legs and started to rise out of her seat so she could thank him and leave.

'Stay where you are,' Brandon said firmly. His strict voice smacked of unarguable authority. 'Stay sitting. Stay quiet and wait until you're spoken to before you speak.'

When Cassie opened her mouth he raised a warning finger. In the candlelight his eyes smouldered like coals. 'I'll repeat those instructions if you want me to. But I'll do it while I'm using a tawse to paint stripes across your arse. Do you want me to repeat those instructions?'

All her arguments disappeared before she could give them voice. Feeling deflated, she shook her head and lowered her gaze to the table.

Brandon turned to Faye and reached for the chains that dangled from her nipple piercings. His fingers worked clumsily with the small clips as he tried to remove the tray and his frown deepened with concentration.

As he grumbled and cursed at the nuisance of the chore, Faye's features remained tranquil. She maintained her composure while her breasts were dragged and pulled. The rings that pierced her nipples were pushed roughly this way and that but there was never a moment when she gave expression to the embarrassment or discomfort that she had to be suffering. All the time Brandon worked on the clips, she calmly studied him, untroubled by the torment being wrought upon her.

Brandon finally released the tray and Cassie thought she heard Faye sigh. Her eyes flashed in the blonde's direction but there was no sign of pain or relief breaking her composed features. The only change Cassie could discern was that Faye's smile seemed ever so slightly broader.

Brandon began to pick through his winnings. 'Let's see what we've got here,' he growled. He removed his own car keys from the top of the pile and stuffed them in his trouser pocket. After studying the set that belonged to the Gemballa, he slammed them down in front of Faye. 'Call Johnny's office tomorrow morning and get the paperwork for this thing,' he told her. 'I want it insured by the end of the day.'

'Yes, master,' she nodded, quietly whispering the words.

Brandon ignored her. He glanced disdainfully at the Rolex before tossing it to one side. After regarding the rest of the jewellery with the same contempt he reached Cassie's wristwatch. His obvious distaste was briefly etched by the candlelight. 'A second-hand car and a handful of unwanted trinkets,' he muttered. His voice was edged with frustration and anger. 'What a disappointing end to an evening where I could have had so much more.'

Seeming suddenly angry, he glared at Faye and clutched both of her nipples.

'I had the chance to win it all tonight,' he told her. 'I had the chance to win everything. But that chance was taken away from me.'

Faye gasped but she tolerated the abuse without trying to pull away. Her jaw trembled lightly but it was the only physical sign of the effort she was using to contain her response.

'Johnny was on the verge of betting his entire business,' Brandon told her. 'He could have given me an open shot at the Harwood contract. But instead, all I end up with is a second-hand car and unwanted rubbish.'

He glanced briefly at Cassie and she was sure he was talking about her. The idea that she could be categorised as 'unwanted rubbish' was galling, but she didn't think it was inaccurate. She was currently between boyfriends, as she had been for the past three years. A part of her kept hoping John might eventually fill that gap in her life but she secretly knew that was never going to happen. He hadn't looked at her twice in the twelve months they had worked together and, unless she suddenly started to resemble an Italian sports car, she doubted she would ever draw his interest. Weighing those facts against Brandon's harsh words made her feel as though 'unwanted rubbish' described her perfectly. The truth of the sentiment had her close to releasing a flood of tears. The only reason she was able to stay quiet was for fear of prolonging Brandon's interest.

He turned back to Faye, renewing his efforts to squeeze the fat buds of her breasts. The tendons on his wrist began to cord as his grip tightened. 'I was playing well this evening,' he said solemnly. 'I had a shot at a really big win. And three people conspired to take that chance away from me.'

Faye shook her head. 'No, master. No one conspired against you.'

Cassie stared on in horror. She had thought Faye looked to be suffering enough when the weighted tray had dangled from her nipple piercings. But that looked like nothing compared to the deliberate torment Brandon now inflicted. Her sensitive flesh was squeezed between his thumbs and index fingers. He tugged harshly, distending the shape of her breasts as he pulled and twisted.

'Three people conspired to rob me of my chance for glory,' he grunted. 'You were one of them.'

'No, master.'

'Your shuffling was ponderous and lazy.'

'I was trying to do it thoroughly.'

'Your dealing was clumsy and slow.'

'It was the best I could do.'

He spoke over her arguments as though he hadn't heard them. 'Because you weren't doing your job properly, I didn't get time for a final game. One more game would have done it. One good hand and Johnny would have given me everything I wanted. One more hand and I would have had the Harwood contract.'

Faye's composure remained sanguine. Her nipples were being squeezed mercilessly, the flesh already beginning to look bruised and purple, while Brandon tugged so hard he looked on the verge of dragging her from her chair. And yet she maintained eye contact with him and never flinched as he intensified his efforts. 'I'm sorry you feel that way, master,' she said calmly. 'I tried to do your bidding to the best of my abilities. If it wasn't good enough, then I'm truly sorry.'

He grunted. 'You will be truly sorry,' he assured her. He released his hold with an angry thrust that pushed her back in the chair. 'Bend over,' he demanded. 'Bend over and let me make you truly sorry.'

Cassie glanced towards the shadows where she thought the door was and wondered if she dared try to run. The idea had been repeatedly pestering her thoughts but she was scared to make the attempt. She wanted to get out of the room – she wanted that more than anything she had ever wanted – but she was petrified she wouldn't find her way out. Panic had made her disoriented and she was unfamiliar with the layout of where she was. She was also scared of how Brandon might punish her if she tried to escape and failed. Her fear of his wrath kept her sitting at the table.

Faye rose from her chair and Cassie realised she had been wrong to think of the woman as half naked. When the blonde stood up she revealed that the only thing she was wearing were the two silver rings that pierced her nipples. Cassie caught a glimpse of the neatly trimmed triangle of her pubic mound, with dark blonde curls so short they resembled razor stubble, and then she looked quickly away. Even when she was staring into the darkened corners of the room, her thoughts lingered over the memory of Faye's slender figure and her inviting curves. Quite why another woman's nudity should seem so appealing was a question she didn't want to explore, especially not in such unnerving circumstances. With a determined effort, Cassie shut the notion from her thoughts. She was almost thankful for the distraction that came when Brandon walked to Faye's side of the table.

'Didn't I tell you to bend over?' he growled.

Obediently, Faye did as he instructed. She turned away from Cassie and bent forwards until she was almost touching her toes.

The idea of running had never been stronger and Cassie almost gave into the urge without caring about the consequences. She was being presented with an unfettered view of Faye's sex. The blonde's arse cheeks were two perfectly rounded moons. They were so close that, had she wanted to, Cassie could have reached out and touched them.

Telling herself she was repulsed by that idea, Cassie shivered.

Candlelight glinted against the pale tufts of hair that edged Faye's sex. Beneath the downy blonde curls, the pussy lips glistened wetly. Cassie didn't want to dwell on that image, unable to comprehend how anyone could suffer such degradation and still show signs of arousal. But her mind kept turning back to the sight, as though it was the key to a greater understanding.

'If you'd done your job properly, there would have been time for one more hand,' Brandon told Faye.

For the first time, Cassie noticed he was holding a tawse. She didn't know where it had come from, or how he had been able to locate it in the gloomy half-shadows of the room, but it dangled limply from his hand as he took his place behind the blonde.

'If there'd been time for one more hand, I could have cleaned him out.'

'I'm sorry, master,' Faye murmured. 'I'm truly sorry.'

Brandon raised the tawse high, then sliced it sharply down. There was the brittle sound of leather scoring flesh and the blonde stiffened.

Cassie drew shocked breath. Other than the sharp crack of the tawse marking its target, her gasp was the only sound in the room.

'Your apology doesn't turn back time, does it?' Brandon demanded.

'No, master.'

Brandon landed the tawse for a second time. It striped the flesh of one buttock, leaving a wavering red line in its wake.

'Your apology doesn't win me the Harwood contract, does it?'

'No, master.'

'Then stop apologising and stay quiet while I punish you.'

Without any further warning, Brandon delivered six stinging smacks. He slapped the tawse hard against Faye, switching his aim from one cheek to the other. He used enough force to make the leather whistle with each descent and every crack sounded more loudly than the last. When he had placed the final blow, Brandon stepped back and told Faye to stand up.

She turned to face him, still without any real emotion spoiling her features. 'I'm sorry that my inadequacies caused your lack of success, master.'

Brandon scowled at her. 'Kneel.'

Obediently, Faye fell to her knees.

Brandon raised the tawse again. When he swiped his arm down, the first blow scored Faye's right breast. His aim was good and a single red line erupted across the circle of her areola. The silver ring that pierced her nipple trembled from side to side.

Faye caught a startled breath and fixed him with a pleading expression.

Ignoring her unspoken request, Brandon slapped the tawse against her left breast. He landed this blow with uncompromising force. The leather scored so crisply its afterecho rang musically from the walls.

Although she made no sound, a solitary tear rolled onto Faye's cheek. In the candlelight it sparkled like a diamond.

'Now you're sorry,' Brandon grunted.

Faye lowered her gaze. 'Yes, master,' she whispered. 'Now I'm sorry.'

He turned away from her and briefly glanced at Cassie. The limp length of the tawse remained in his hand and he half-heartedly brandished it at her.

Fearful he might now try to punish her, Cassie cowered back in her chair. She didn't know whether to be relieved or upset when he sneered and turned away. She was still puzzling over her body's unsettling response as Brandon walked to the side of the suspended woman.

'Three of you conspired to rob me of my victory,' Brandon growled. 'Faye's just suffered for her part, but what about you, Marion? What do you think you deserve?'

Since her initial, terrifying shriek, Marion's sobs had tapered to a flow of miserable tears. However, as soon as Brandon started speaking to her, she began to moan again. 'I haven't conspired against you, master,' she told him. 'The candle was burning me and there was a dribble of wax that –'

He cut off her words with a flick of the tawse. The tip bit sharply against her breast. 'Another five minutes would have been enough,' Brandon said solemnly. 'You could have tolerated your discomfort for that much longer, couldn't you?'

'I'm sorry, master.'

He raised the crop and striped her for a second time. 'No,' he said stiffly. 'You aren't sorry yet. That's the lesson I'm about to teach you.'

Cassie watched on, wishing she could intervene but petrified by the idea of even trying. Marion was cloaked by shadows, on the farthest edges of the room's darkness, but Cassie was able to see the trickles of wax glinting on her bare flesh. She could make out the woman was a brunette, and guessed she might have appeared tall, athletic and beautiful under other circumstances. But, because she was dangling upside down, and being subjected to unimaginable torment, she looked dishevelled, unattractive and broken.

'I blame you for tonight being such a waste of time,' Brandon grunted. 'I blame you more than I blamed Faye.'

Marion shook her head.

'If you could have kept the candle burning for a little while longer, I might have won Johnny's business. One more game and he would have been gambling first crack at the Harwood contract. If he'd done that, I could have raised him to betting his business, and then I would really have won.'

20

Marion sobbed. 'I'm sorry, master,' she whispered. 'I really am sorry.'

He snorted. 'And I can put your apology in the bank the same time that I deposit Faye's there, can't I?'

Cassie half expected him to strike the brunette with his tawse but, instead, Brandon reached for her leg. His fingers traced down one thigh until they reached the hard mess of wax that was caked onto her cleft.

'You candleholders normally take a hot bath after the game, don't you?'

Sniffing to get the words through her tears, Marion told him that was right.

'Perhaps that's how I should punish you?' he suggested. 'Maybe I should take away the privilege of a hot bath. Maybe I should take away the need for a hot bath.'

Cassie didn't understand his threat but it was obvious Marion knew what was being implied. She thrashed viciously against her restraints and begged him for mercy.

'Stay still,' he snapped. 'Stay still or I'll make this far, far worse.'

Reluctantly, Marion obeyed.

Cassie stared on with a combination of intrigue and disgust. Realisation of what was happening only came as she watched Brandon pluck at a strip of the hardened wax. Unmindful of the pain he might inflict, he tore it away from Marion's flesh.

The brunette wailed.

Brandon flicked the tawse, silencing her exclamation with another shot to her breast. Unhurriedly, he ripped another sliver of wax from her sex. This time, Marion contained her cry and the only sound she released was a pitiable whimper.

Cassie didn't want to watch but she couldn't tear her gaze away. The concept of Marion's suffering was an extreme she had never had to think about before. The woman had been humiliated, casually abused and now she was being subjected to having hardened wax stripped from her cleft. Cassie tried to imagine the pain and anguish but her mind recoiled from the prospect.

'You robbed me of my chance for success,' Brandon grunted.

As he spoke he tore another strip of wax from her hole. Unlike the smooth, backhand swipes he had made earlier there seemed to be some resistance this time.

Watching every detail intently, Cassie knew exactly what had caused it.

Brandon had snatched at one of the lines of wax that had dripped into Marion's pubic triangle. The molten spend had entangled itself into her curls and the resistance came as the hairs strained at their follicles. When he lowered his hand, Cassie could see a wavering line of freshly depilated pubic mound.

Marion shrieked. Her cries sang from every corner of the room as she screamed again and again. She shook viciously against her bondage, rattling the chains that suspended her from the ceiling. When she eventually had control over her responses, she drew a quivering breath and said, 'I'm sorry, master.'

'You conspired to do it, didn't you?'

'No, master.' She sounded pathetic and broken. Her words were carried by a mournful undercurrent. 'I didn't conspire against you. I just failed you,' she whispered. 'I didn't mean to fail you. But I . . . I . . . I just failed you.'

He was reaching for her sex again, and then stopped himself. 'That's right,' he agreed. 'You have failed me. I'm truly disappointed in you Marion. So disappointed I'm going to leave your punishment until tomorrow. I'm going to spend the night thinking how best to make you realise that I don't tolerate failure.'

She started to protest, assuring him she hadn't done it deliberately, and that she would never do it again, but Brandon wasn't listening.

He turned to face Cassie.

'And so we come to the third person responsible for my losses this evening.'

She shook her head, the power of speech momentarily escaping her.

'There would have been more games if Faye had dealt faster,' he said, stepping closer. 'There would have been time for another hand if Marion had done her duty less selfishly. And Johnny would have bet the Harwood contract if you hadn't turned up.'

He raised the tawse as he came nearer. Cassie thought the length of leather should have looked harmless but Brandon managed to wield it as though it was a vicious implement of torture. She shrank back in her chair, shaking her head from side to side.

'Instead,' Brandon continued, 'because he had you to use in that last game, things didn't go how I'd planned. Because he had you to use in that last game, Johnny managed to escape from here with his business, and he still has a fair shot at winning Stephen's contract.'

Cassie wanted to tell him none of that was her fault, and that he couldn't blame her for any of it. She wanted to explain that she would never have willingly given consent to be used as one of the prizes in a hand of poker. But the words refused to come. Instead of saying anything she simply cowered beneath Brandon's frown and prayed he wouldn't hurt her.

'Undress, girl,' he commanded. 'Let me see what I've won.'

'I want to leave,' she whispered.

He nodded. 'I imagine you do. But that option hasn't been available to you for a while now. That option hasn't been available since I won you. Now, do as I say and undress.'

She tried to meet his imposing figure with defiance. 'I'll scream.'

The threat made Brandon smile. 'You can scream if you want to,' he told her. Pointing behind himself with

23

the tawse, he said, 'Marion screamed, and see how much good it did her.'

'I don't want to be here,' Cassie insisted.

He shook his head. 'That's a shame, because you are here. And you're staying here until I say otherwise. You can try and escape but I'll warn you now, no one has ever managed it. A handful have tried and that same handful have been made to regret their actions. Do you want to join their number?'

Cassie glanced at Faye and met a silent communication from the woman's eyes. With the slightest shake of her head Faye seemed to be telling her not to try and escape. Without saying a word she managed to impart that it would be a grave mistake.

'Now,' Brandon continued. 'This is the last time I'm going to ask nicely. Are you going to undress and show me what I've won? Are you going to undress, or do I have to do it for you?'

She didn't want to obey him. The idea of exposing herself to this cruel and unpleasant stranger made her feel sick. But she was repulsed by the idea of letting him do it for her and she could see there was no other option. With shaking fingers, she reached for the buttons at the front of her blouse and began to unfasten them.

'Do it faster,' he barked. 'If I want to watch a slow striptease I've got others who are trained for that chore.'

Sniffing back tears, Cassie tried to work her fingers more quickly. She was aware all three of them were watching her and their attention caused her blushes to deepen. Nevertheless, she managed to release all the buttons and then started to unzip her skirt.

'I want to see more flesh,' Brandon snapped. His voice was quick with impatience.

From the corner of her eye Cassie could see he was raising the tawse. She shrugged the blouse from her shoulders and allowed her skirt to drop to her ankles.

24

Feeling exposed and vulnerable in her bra and panties she began to shiver. Hesitantly, she lifted her gaze to meet Brandon's. It was impossible to read the emotions that may have lurked behind his frown.

'Continue,' he barked.

Swallowing down her fears, and almost crippled by the somersaults that were folding through her stomach, Cassie crossed her arms over her chest.

'Continue,' Brandon repeated, 'or I really will do it for you.'

The threat was enough to spur her into action. She turned her back to the three of them and reached behind herself to unfasten the bra's clasp. Feeling more vulnerable than ever she allowed the straps to slip from her shoulders and dropped the garment to the floor. Still trying to contain her modesty, she cupped her hands over her breasts before turning back to face him.

'While coyness may excite some men, it doesn't excite me,' he growled. 'Are you going to move your hands?'

'I don't want to be doing this,' she whispered. 'I don't even want to be here.'

'I'd realised that much,' he agreed. 'And I'm sure that you've realised that I don't really care what you want. Remove your panties and put your hands behind your back.'

'I –'

'Remove your panties and put your hands behind your back.'

He started towards her and Cassie took a step back. Knowing there was no other choice, she turned her back on him again and eased her panties down. The embarrassment she had suffered before had been bad but this time it was unbearable. She had never known a humiliation so strong. A nauseating swell of shame left her struggling for breath. Her cheeks burnt with mortified blushes and her head pounded with a rush of shame-induced adrenaline.

'Now turn around,' Brandon instructed, 'and, if your hands aren't behind your back, I'll come over there and handcuff them.'

Trembling, Cassie did as he asked. She clutched her hands together above her buttocks, trying not to think of the display she was presenting. Not wanting to see him looking at her she lowered her gaze but that only made things worse. Staring down, she could see the length of her own naked body, the shape of her plump breasts and the dark thatch of pubic curls. She could also see her nipples were standing upright and she tried to convince herself that was a symptom of the room's chill. The argument wasn't a strong one but she was happier to accept that explanation over any other.

Brandon was still studying her when Cassie wrenched her gaze from her own nudity. She wanted to look at something that didn't remind her of the terrible situation she was in but everything in the room reinforced the hopeless predicament she was facing. She briefly met Faye's cool interest but that only made her feel more exposed and vulnerable and she quickly turned to look elsewhere. Seeing Marion reminded Cassie there could be worse suffering to come and her nervousness increased. Instead of looking at anything, she closed her eyes and tried to wish the moment away.

'Turn around,' Brandon snapped.

She obeyed, thankful to be able to turn her back on him, but hating the knowledge he was lecherously admiring her rear. When he instructed her to face him again she finally found the courage to meet his gaze. The lack of compassion she saw there made her feel more defeated than ever.

'I think you're the worst culprit of this evening's conspiracy,' he told her.

Cassie wanted to shake her head but she didn't dare. She knew that if she started, the tremors would course through her body until she collapsed in a gibbering heap.

'I think you're the worst culprit, and I hold you chiefly responsible for my upset.'

'No,' she whispered.

He held up a silencing finger. 'Don't argue with me. As I'm sure you've already guessed, this isn't a discussion group.'

He reached for her breast and, while she wanted to pull away, she knew there would be repercussions if she did. Loathing the torment of his caress, she stood motionless. His fingers traced the swell of one orb, making their way down to the thrust of her nipple. The traitorous bud grew larger with his attention and Cassie bristled from a shock of pleasure. The response seemed so out of place in the circumstances of shame and abuse that her first thought was that he had hurt her.

'You've earned the real punishment tonight,' he decided. 'Faye's had her discipline, and Marion will be brought to book tomorrow. But for tonight I think I need to make you aware of my unhappiness.'

Cassie shook her head but Brandon wasn't looking.

He slapped the tawse against the card table, summoning Faye's attention. 'Release Marion, then I want the pair of you to take this one into the cellar. I'll join you shortly.'

Faye remained in her seat, gracing him with a worried frown. She glanced quickly at Cassie, then back to Brandon. 'Are you sure that's wise, master?'

His eyes narrowed to disapproving slits and it was clear he wasn't used to having his orders questioned. 'Explain yourself,' he growled.

Faye swallowed twice. Spitting the words out quickly, clearly fearful she was about to be punished for speaking out of place, she said, 'She's an outsider. She's a free woman by the looks of her and I don't think John had any right to gamble her in the card game. I don't think it would be wise to keep her here against her will. I think it could jeopardise everything we have.'

Cassie could have wept with gratitude. With the hope of a reprieve she mentally thanked the gods that had decided to answer her prayers. Not wanting to show signs of relief that might antagonise Brandon, she kept her reaction contained.

'You think she's a free woman?' Brandon grunted. He switched his gaze from Faye to Cassie, then back to Faye. 'Is that what you're telling me? You think I'm abusing the civil liberties of a free woman?'

Warily, Faye nodded.

Brandon shook his head and turned back to Cassie. Throwing the words back over his shoulder, he said, 'You have your instructions, Faye. Release Marion and then take this one to the cellar.' His smile glinted like a cutting blade as he studied Cassie's nudity. 'She might have been a free woman when she came in here,' he started, 'but she isn't any longer. She's property now. She's my property. And she stays that way until I say different.'

Two

Cassie allowed them to lead her away without making any protest.

The evening had taken on such a surreal quality she didn't bother to voice her reservations. She was stark naked, held by two unknown women, and being led by candlelight through a strange house. The only explanation to make sense was that she had to be dreaming and she latched onto that idea like a drowning woman grasping a life preserver. She comforted herself with the same belief as she was taken through unlit corridors, down a long flight of stone stairs, and into the gloom of a cellar.

Marion took a candle and began to light the sconces on the walls.

Faye continued holding Cassie, untroubled by the fact that their naked bodies kept touching. She was strong, capability apparent in the way her fingers buried into Cassie's arm, but Cassie was more aware of Faye's beauty than her strength. She was quietly grateful her subconscious had put her at the mercy of such an attractive gaoler and, secure in the belief this was all a fantasy, she admired the woman's inviting curves. A bared breast pressed against her own and she was touched by the cool ring of metal that penetrated Faye's nipple. Excited and intrigued, she reached out to examine the cruel decoration.

Faye slapped her hand away before it could make contact.

Cassie frowned but the expression went unnoticed in the darkness. A metallic jingle broke the silence and she realised the sound was made by a pair of handcuffs. She had only just made the association when her hands were pushed behind her back and the cold bracelets encircled her wrists.

Faye encouraged her to get down on the floor and, still convinced she was asleep and imagining all of this, Cassie obliged. As soon as her knees had touched the cold stone, a second pair of cuffs were fixed around her ankles. After making an exploratory tug on her bondage, she discovered her wrists and ankles were linked together. Cassie was limited to remaining on her knees and knew she would have to stay like that until someone released her, or until she finally woke up.

'Stay servile,' Faye hissed. 'Stay servile. Apologise when necessary, and don't talk back to the master. Do that and you might stand a chance of getting out of here.'

Marion continued to make her way around the room, lighting candles that revealed the hidden walls of the cellar. In the first corner a huddled figure blinked her eyes used to the wavering light. She was a freckle-faced redhead, naked and secured on her knees in the same position. Her bondage left her breasts exposed and revealed a thatch of ginger curls covering her sex. Cassie was unsettled because she realised she was being displayed in the same shameless way.

The second corner was unoccupied, save for an empty set of manacles but, when Marion reached the third, the candlelight illuminated another woman. As naked as the rest, she had dark brown hair and a surly expression. Her features were well defined and attractive but her beauty was marred by a scowl. Her upper lip was curled into a sneer and her eyes were narrow slits that glowered with distrust. She gave Cassie a cursory glance and her sneer deepened. Lowering her eyes, Cassie noticed the woman's pubic mound had been trimmed into an exclamation mark. She decided it was more detail than she was used to in her dreams and wondered why her mind was torturing her with such lurid visions.

Faye shook her shoulder and Cassie looked up at her.

'Did you hear me? Did you hear what I said?'

Cassie smiled blithely. 'It doesn't matter whether I heard you or not. You're a dream,' she explained. 'She's a dream,' she said, nodding at Marion, 'and they're a dream,' she added, glancing quickly at the other two women. If her hand had been free she would have used it to indicate the cellar and the house above them. 'This is all a dream.'

Faye slapped her cheek, the blow landing viciously. There was enough force to almost knock her over and, because her hands and feet were effectively bound together, Cassie came close to falling on her side. She only managed to stay upright because Faye grabbed a fistful of hair to steady her. An explosion of bright agony tore through her scalp and, unable to stop herself, Cassie moaned.

'If you want to get away from here you have to stop thinking like that. This is no dream. This is really happening. Do you want another slap just to prove it?'

She raised her hand again and Cassie cowered from the threat. Her cheek stung where she had been struck and she didn't want to revisit that pain. The anguish in her scalp began to subside but that was only because Faye had released the hold on her hair. Cassie met the woman's stern gaze and shook her head. The reality of the situation was finally beginning to strike home and with it came waves of dread and apprehension. 'OK,' she agreed. 'It's not a dream.'

'No,' Faye agreed. 'And you're not going to escape unless you realise that. You're not going to escape unless you do as I said. Stay servile. Apologise when necessary. And don't upset the master.'

A thousand questions rushed to the front of her mind, the importance of each threatening to drown her with a rising tide of panic. She wanted to know what was going to happen to her, why Faye had secured her in such a way, and who the other women were. She wanted to know all of those things and more but, before she could ask a single question, the cellar door opened.

Every eye turned to look upwards.

Brandon stood at the top of the stairs as imposing and menacing as a fairy tale giant. Cassie assured herself it was only a trick of perspective – she was kneeling and he was standing at the top of a flight of stairs above her – but that knowledge didn't leave her feeling any less intimidated.

'Are you inducting her to her new life here, Faye?' His voice resounded from the stone walls.

Faye blushed and lowered her gaze.

Brandon made a slow descent, slapping the tawse against his thigh with every other step. When he reached the cellar floor he walked towards Cassie until he was almost standing on top of her. She was on eye level with his crotch and couldn't help but notice the groin of his trousers was distended by a thick bulge.

'Marion,' he called.

The brunette glanced fearfully from the task of lighting the final candle.

'Go and clean yourself up,' he commanded. 'I've decided I want you resplendent for your punishment tomorrow. You can start preparing yourself now.'

Marion rushed to obey. She started to glide past him, headed towards the stairs.

Brandon caught her arm and forced her to stand still. Taking the candle from her hand, he held it close to her face. 'I believe you could have tolerated a lot more hot wax this evening, couldn't you?'

Marion shook her head. Her eyes gaped widely. 'No master. I stood it for as long as I could.'

He nodded but looked as though he wasn't listening. 'You could have tolerated a lot more hot wax, and tomorrow I'm going to prove you can.'

With a silent refusal lighting her eyes, Marion tried to step away.

Brandon maintained his grip, pulling her closer. He tilted the candle and a trickle of wax dribbled from beneath its wick. With devastating accuracy it landed against the tip of her breast. The liquid stuck to her flesh and turned immediately solid and white, capping her areola with a handful of thick spatters.

Marion drew startled breath. She seemed to shrink away from him without moving. Her features stretched into a muted scream of surprise and, despite her obvious reluctance, she remained where she was as Brandon poured a second line of wax over her other breast. She made no sound as he forced her to endure the punishment. The only indication she gave of her suffering was the unspoken plea for leniency that flickered in her eyes.

Brandon returned the candle to her hand and then dismissed her from the cellar. He frowned at Faye and said, 'Go to your corner. I'll summon you when you're required.'

Defiantly, Faye remained standing by Cassie's side. Her features maintained their sanguine composure but there was a glimmer of steel shining in her eyes. 'I think you should reconsider this, master. I think you're in danger of making a grave mistake with this one.'

His glare was full of foreboding and Cassie couldn't understand how Faye dared to challenge him. She knew that if she had been in the blonde's position she would have accepted every opportunity to escape from Brandon's intimidating presence. It seemed unthinkable that anyone could have the courage to stand up to such an ogre and she didn't know what Faye thought she could possibly achieve.

'John had no right to put this one in the card game,' Faye told him. 'You saw what was going on. You must have seen he had no right to –'

'No right?' Brandon broke in. He sounded as though he was testing the idea. 'You'd be familiar with the concept of someone having no rights, wouldn't you?'

Faye's blushes darkened but she maintained eye contact.

'You'd be familiar with that,' he continued, 'because you're aware you have no rights. No rights at all.'

'But, master –' Faye began.

He raised his tawse. Its presence silenced her arguments. 'You have no rights as an individual,' he said stiffly, 'and you have no right to challenge me. You know your position here, Faye. Kindly remember it and do as I've instructed.'

The tawse trembled as though he was on the verge of hurling it against her.

Faye switched her gaze between the length of leather and Brandon's face. She looked as though she was going to continue with her defiance and Cassie couldn't decide whether she wanted the woman to carry on or stay silent. She was grateful the blonde was being brave enough to speak against him, especially as it was being done on her behalf, but she was scared the confrontation might worsen Brandon's already volatile temper. As the pair silently contemplated one another, Cassie switched her gaze from one face to the other and prayed for the moment to pass without incident.

'Return to your place, Faye,' Brandon told her. 'Do it now. And do it without questioning my authority further.'

With a frustrated sigh, Faye did as she was told.

Brandon continued watching her until she had backstepped all the way to one corner and lowered herself to her knees. She folded her hands behind her buttocks, assuming the same position as the other women. The challenge was gone from her eyes, replaced by an expression of acceptance.

Satisfied with her return to obedience, Brandon turned to Cassie. 'Stay where you are. Stay quiet, and speak only when you're spoken to.'

She thought it was a ridiculous thing for him to say because the cuffs held her immobile and her fear had rendered her mute. Staring wordlessly up at him she tried to imagine the fate that was lying ahead. Considering what she had already seen she imagined it would be something inhumane and perverse.

Brandon reached for her breast and stroked the orb. His caress was subtle and she was aware of her nipple thickening to his touch. Cassie was as surprised by her body's response as she was disgusted. She stared from the nipple to Brandon's growing smile, unable to mask her disbelief.

'Six stripes should be enough to make you aware of my upset,' he said darkly.

She tried to pull away but he held her nipple tight between his finger and thumb. When he finally let go she was only able to stare at the fat bud and wonder why it had responded so traitorously.

'Six stripes ought to do it,' he decided. 'Then we can discuss your position here.'

'No,' Cassie started. 'I –'

She got no further.

He slapped the tawse against her bared breast, stunning her with a bolt of pure pain. The leather caught her nipple and she was branded by a burning weal. The sensation was so total that for an instant it enveloped her entire universe. Nothing else existed except the searing agony in her breast.

'Master!' Faye gasped.

'Silence,' he grunted. He said the word as he struck Cassie for a second time. His aim faltered and the tawse struck the swell of her orb rather than catching the nub.

Nevertheless, Cassie thought the pain couldn't have been more excruciating. She sucked lungfuls of air, then released them in a gasp that sounded close to being a sob. Shivering with nervous energy, she considered begging him to stop, then realised it would do no good.

He smacked the tawse down again and again, inflicting bright bolts that scorched through her breasts. The anguish was immense, immediate and unarguable. But Cassie was disturbed to discover that pain wasn't the sole response her body endured. Each punishing blow fired her with arousal. She shunned that thought, knowing it was alien and wrong. When he had delivered the sixth blow she allowed her tears to flow unchecked.

'You're my property now,' he growled. 'Accept that fact, or suffer.'

Caught between tears and refusal, Cassie shook her head. 'I don't want to be your property,' she sobbed. 'You can't make me stay here.'

'I think you'll find I can make you stay here,' he said smugly. 'And I think you should come to terms with your position before I grow bored with your whining.'

She opened her mouth to deny him again but he raised the tawse. The threat of more suffering made her fall silent.

'Defiance will only make your position here more difficult,' he growled. 'You've just experienced a demonstration of the punishment I mete out. Perhaps you'd like a demonstration of the things you can look forward to if you continue to defy me?'

Cassie didn't want to see any of the things he was proposing. She stared helplessly up at him and allowed the tears to stream freely down her cheeks.

Taking her silence as consent, Brandon straightened his shoulders and began to strut around the cellar. 'I keep an extensive staff here,' he began. Using the tawse as a limp pointer he gestured towards Faye. 'You've already seen her in action. Faye deals cards for me, and she's uncommonly proficient. I keep staff for a variety of specialised chores, from polishing and cleaning through to cooking and tending the bedrooms.' He walked to one corner and stroked his fingers through the luxuriant raven tresses of the dark-haired woman. 'Sarah, over there, is one of my entertainment staff,' he said, using his tawse to point at the redhead. 'Laura here makes herself useful by cleaning.'

Laura sneered at this remark but the challenge of her eyes never dared to meet Brandon's. Instead, she remained motionless as he stroked and pulled on her hair and fixed her scowl on Cassie.

There was such animosity in her expression that Cassie felt as though she was encountering a dangerous enemy. She couldn't understand why Laura might have taken an instant dislike to her, but she knew it was a fact as clearly as she knew she was naked and chained in a stranger's cellar.

'Everyone here has their own position to fulfil,' Brandon continued, 'and that's what we need to work out for you. Where are you going to fit in? What service can you provide for me?'

Cassie willed herself to find the courage to answer back. 'I don't want to be here,' she whispered. 'I don't want to fulfil a position.'

'Can you cook?'

'No.'

'Can you clean?'

She shook her head.

'Have you any experience of waiting-on?'

'No. And it wouldn't matter if I could do any of those things.' She heard Faye's shocked gasp from the corner and Cassie remembered the warning the blonde had given. Faye had said not to upset Brandon – to remain servile and apologetic – but those were difficult instructions to obey now she had found the courage to talk back to him. Ignoring the memory of Faye's warning, and trying not to think of the punishing sting that still burnt in her breasts, she met his gaze and dared to carry on. 'It wouldn't matter if I could do any of those things,' she told him. 'I'm not your property. I'm not your property and I'm not staying here.'

He released an impatient sigh through his nostrils. Clutching a fistful of Laura's hair, he pulled until she squealed. He held the tawse in his other hand and it trembled like a warning of his mounting annoyance. 'I'm going to show you the services Sarah and Laura provide for me,' he told her. 'It might help you understand the regime we have here. It might help you see how I deal with difficult property. And it might make you less prone to speak out of place.'

'Master –' Faye began.

'Save it,' he growled.

The two words silenced her.

Uncaringly, Brandon pushed Laura away and stormed towards Sarah.

The redhead's eyes sparkled and she didn't cower away from him. Even when Brandon grabbed her by the shoulder, and started dragging her across the floor, she didn't give voice to any desire to escape. Sarah allowed him to pull her to the centre of the room and let him deposit her in front of Cassie.

'I keep Sarah here for entertainment purposes,' Brandon explained. 'Watch carefully and you'll see how I like to be entertained.' As he spoke, he began to step out of his trousers.

Transfixed by her own disbelief, Cassie stared on.

The rest of Brandon's body was as smooth and hairless as his shaved skull. He sported a thick erection and, because there were no pubic hairs at the base, Cassie thought his shaft looked impossibly long. She saw his scrotum was a tight, bulging sac, then decided this was more detail than she was comfortable with. Hurriedly, she turned her head away and studied the cellar's stone floor.

'I told you to watch this,' Brandon snarled. His tawse caressed Cassie's cheek, chilling her with the implication of punishment. 'I told you to watch this because I'm demonstrating an important point.'

Knowing there was no choice other than to obey, Cassie turned to watch.

Like the rest of them, Sarah had her hands secured to her feet. Brandon had pushed her face to the floor and the bondage spread her legs and lifted her ankles so they hung over her back. Obscenely, the position exposed every intimate aspect of the woman.

Kneeling between her thighs, Brandon placed his shaft against her hole. The end of his length nuzzled her pussy lips as he held himself on the brink of penetration. The sight was sickeningly exciting but Cassie told herself it wasn't inspiring any arousal. Nevertheless, she empathised with the redhead's sigh when Brandon plunged into her.

He clutched her hips, pulling her onto his shaft and filling her with his thickness. As he rode in and out, Sarah's breathing deepened and her cries turned into ragged moans. She balled her cuffed hands into fists and strained against her bondage but it was clear her exertion didn't come from a desire to escape. She looked like a woman in the throes of rapture.

Madly, Cassie thought it would have been easier to watch if Sarah had shown signs of suffering or displeasure. Because the redhead looked to be revelling in this public exhibition, Cassie didn't know how to respond. She couldn't deny there was excitement in the display but she didn't want to acknowledge it. The sex was raw, charged with passion and being enjoyed by both participants. Along with everything she could see, there was also the fragrance of Sarah's intimate musk and the tang of Brandon's clean, fresh sweat. But Cassie was uncomfortable with the sight and she turned her eyes to Faye.

'Look away once more and I might decide you're thinking you can do this better than Sarah,' Brandon growled. 'Look away once more and I'll use you instead.'

It was enough of a threat to rivet Cassie's attention. She blinked away miserable tears and continued watching.

Brandon kept glancing in her direction as he rode in and out and Cassie thought it made the whole ordeal even more unacceptable. He was using another woman's pussy while smiling at her and it made her feel as though she was an active participant in his sordid act.

Brandon's thrusts became urgent. At first he had languidly drawn himself back and forth, filling the redhead completely, then pulling his shaft so it almost escaped her confines. But, as the moment of his climax approached, he pounded in and out with a brutal, greedy haste. Slipping his hands from Sarah's hips, he reached beneath her and began to knead her breasts. There was no tenderness in his touch and he tugged with scant regard for her feelings.

Finally, as he turned to Cassie with a cruel smile, he forced his shaft deep into the redhead's sex. He held himself steady as his groin convulsed. Sarah seemed to enjoy her own brief orgasm but Brandon clearly regarded that as peripheral. He held her by the waist and kept himself inside until his climax was fully spent. After he had released a satisfied groan he withdrew his flailing shaft and turned his smile away from Cassie. Standing up, he idly slapped the tawse against Sarah's backside, encouraging her to wriggle away.

With a snap of his fingers, he summoned Laura.

She hobbled along the floor as best as her bondage would allow. She knew what was expected of her because she made straight for Brandon's limp shaft and began to lick him. Her tongue lapped the rivulets of spent semen from his stiffening length and chased away the remnants of Sarah's excitement. Painfully attuned to every detail, Cassie saw Laura did all of this without once losing the scowl from her face.

Brandon tugged Laura by the hair, forcing her to tend to the base of his shaft.

His wet length daubed a smear of glistening white against her cheek and, because she was unable to use her hands to wipe herself clean, it remained on Laura's face like a battle-scar.

'This is the point behind my demonstration,' Brandon began calmly.

Cassie thought it was unreal a man could stand in front of her and have his shaft licked while he tried to engage her with casual conversation. The situation seemed so bizarre it was a struggle to concentrate on what he was saying. Scared of the consequences that would come if she didn't listen, she forced herself to focus on everything he said.

'When Laura first came here, she was as defiant as you,' Brandon went on. 'She was quite willing to tell me she shouldn't be here, and she disobeyed my implicit instructions about staying silent until spoken to. But, since then, I've spent time training her for special cleaning duties. I don't think she enjoys this chore, but I'm sure she prefers it to the alternatives.'

He raised his tawse to emphasise the threat.

Cassie struggled to shrink away from him.

'Continue to defy me – continue to tell me you shouldn't be here, and that you're not my property – and I'll see you relieving Laura of her position. Do you understand?'

Cassie nodded.

Brandon glanced down at his spent length and seemed to decide Laura had cleaned him sufficiently. He slipped his shaft away from her mouth and pointed at Sarah's exposed cleft. Cassie saw the white flow of his ejaculate was leaking from the redhead's pussy and the sight filled her with a rising tide of nausea.

'Clean her,' Brandon told Laura.

Laura looked set to refuse, then thought better of it. Lowering herself awkwardly between Sarah's legs, she began to work her tongue against the intimate flesh. She nuzzled and lapped greedily, drinking his seed from the redhead's gaping sex lips.

Brandon seemed satisfied he had made his point because his manner became businesslike and almost genial. 'Faye deals the cards, Sarah is here for my entertainment, and Laura cleans up afterwards. How are you going to fit in?'

Cassie didn't know what answer he expected but she was surprised to discover she was seriously cataloguing her abilities. The idea of continuing to defy him seemed as far away as her life as a partner at J & C Property Developments. 'I don't know how I'm going to fit in,' she said quietly.

He nodded. 'I don't suppose there's any rush. We have all the time in the world to work out the niche you can fill.' Grinning lecherously, assailing her with the same smile he had used while he had pounded his shaft into the redhead, he said, 'We have all the time in the world. And I think it's going to be a voyage of discovery for both of us.'

The words seemed to conclude his interest because he turned away and started towards the stairs. As soon as he had slammed the cellar door closed, Laura lifted her face from Sarah's sex and spat a wad of semen onto the cellar's floor.

'Congratulations,' she said thickly. 'You've done it now.'

Cassie frowned. 'I've done what now?'

'Don't you know?' Her sneer turned into a cruel smile. 'Are you really so thick that you can't see it? You've just consigned yourself to being his property.'

Three

Vicky's pulse pounded like a freight train. If she could have seen her reflection she knew her normally wan cheeks would be rouged with guilt and her hazel eyes would be sparkling. Not that she was doing anything wrong, she reminded herself. She was only entering Cassie's empty office and she was expected to do that a dozen times or more in the course of a week. But, even in her own mind, the rationalisation sounded hollow and unconvincing.

Telling herself she had to hurry if she wanted everything in place before John arrived, Vicky ignored her nerves and slipped her svelte frame through the door. The room was compact and functional, its corner view overlooking the car park and neighbouring industrial estate. Its bland walls were hidden behind uniform shelves, each stacked neatly with row upon row of lever arch files. Most of the threadbare carpet was concealed by Cassie's huge mahogany desk and the oversized leather chair that sat behind it.

Closing the door behind herself, Vicky felt like an intruder.

Cassie's desk looked cluttered and untidy, more so than usual because the work had been building up for the last six days. If Vicky had thought about that, she might have begun to consider Cassie's absence suspicious. Because she wasn't thinking beyond her own career development, she simply saw the situation as a golden opportunity.

Reaching towards the brimming in-tray she removed two thirds of the waiting paperwork. Not looking at what she was holding, she dropped it all into Cassie's out-tray, then took the top file and opened the first page. Glancing through the scribbled notes, she familiarised herself with the basics of the contract, while jotting imaginary appointments in the desk diary. She had scheduled a fortnight's random meetings before deciding the stage was sufficiently set.

She started guiltily when the telephone began to ring. Its shrill bell was an alarm, telling everyone within earshot that she was up to no good and had no right to be there. Laughing off her momentary panic – assuring herself no one knew what she was planning, and that her goals remained a closely guarded secret – Vicky answered the call.

'J & V Property Developments,' she drawled. 'How may I help you?' She paused and frowned at the voice coming through the handset. 'No,' she told the caller. '*It is J & C*. That's what I said. Why on earth would I say *J & V*?'

Scared she might have given something away, Vicky slammed the receiver back into its cradle. She glanced fretfully around the office, thankful no one had been around to catch her Freudian slip. Her heart was hammering and she sat down before her legs could give out. She was too wound up to appreciate the sumptuous feel of leather against the backs of her thighs and, acting on autopilot, she took a novel from her bag.

Defying her nerves and deliberately trying to make herself comfortable, Vicky kicked her feet onto the desk and prepared to delve into the paperback. Whenever she was stressed or fraught, reading usually managed to calm her. The briefest indulgence in a fantasy world had often been enough to help her forget her worries from the real one and she hoped that was how it would work now. Her heel caught Cassie's deskplate and sent it tumbling to the floor. Deciding that was the best place for it, she left the brass plaque where it had fallen. Before she had located her place in the novel, she thought better about the idea of reading and folded the book closed.

She didn't make the decision because John was headed for the office, and probably only moments away. Cassie's office window was open and Vicky knew she would hear the deafening roar of his Gemballa when he arrived. The car's thunderous engine would give her enough warning and leave plenty of time to conceal the book.

But memories of what had happened the last time made her hesitate.

She stared longingly at the cover of the paperback, trying to find the courage to read another chapter and knowing that she wasn't going to. She had been caught reading a novel in the office before and the consequences had been painfully embarrassing.

Vicky had been engrossed in a copy of *Slave Girl* and, as she read about the sexual punishment being inflicted on the story's heroine, the text had inspired her with a burning, unarguable arousal. Alone at the time, she had snaked a hand to her crotch and started to relieve her frustration. Lost in the story's pages, she had begun frigging herself briskly and efficiently. Oblivious to her surroundings, she had soon been hurtling towards a swift and potentially powerful climax.

And that was when Cassie had walked in.

Thinking back to that moment, Vicky remembered the look of horror and revulsion on Cassie's face. She grudgingly conceded there might have been some cause for her shock. Vicky had been caught in a compromising position, with her legs wide apart and the gusset of her panties pushed to one side. At the time of Cassie's arrival she had three fingers thrust deep into her hole and was struggling to insert a fourth. But, even though she had been presenting an indecorous image, Vicky still thought the junior partner's reaction had been extreme.

She had no problem remembering Cassie's loathsome expression, just as she could recall every word of the pious lecture that had been given afterwards. Trite phrases continued to ring in her ears and seemed to return every time she felt a rush of guilt or embarrassment.

'. . . *a time and a place for everything but the office is never the place for* . . .'

'. . . *private behaviour* . . .'

'. . . *and as your employer, it's not my duty to enforce morals on you, but* . . .'

Vicky shut off the memory of the sanctimonious reprimand, hating the way the incident continued to haunt her. She cursed the bad luck that had made Cassie return when she did, and the worse misfortune that had made it Cassie who had discovered her rather than John.

Vicky felt sure that if John had walked in he would have been far more understanding about her drives. He might have still wanted to reprimand her but she thought it would have been a more enjoyable experience than Cassie's scathing rhetoric. Part of her wanted to believe it would have been like one of the dressing-downs that happened in her favourite novels, but she knew that was too much to hope for and didn't allow her imagination to follow that idea. If she let her thoughts continue in that vein Vicky knew there was a danger of repeating that same embarrassment.

Unhappily, she tucked the book back into her bag and removed her feet from the desk. She had just lifted a pen, so she could doodle on the open file, when John burst into the room.

'Oh!' he grunted. His face was a composite of disgust and disappointment. 'It's only you.'

Surprised he had managed to enter the office so quietly, Vicky glanced at the open office window. 'I didn't hear your Gemballa.'

For an instant she thought he was blushing. His cheeks darkened and his eyes refused to meet hers. 'Did you come in here just to listen for my car?' he asked angrily.

She shook her head. 'No.'

'Then what the hell are you doing?' he demanded. 'Don't you know this is Cassie's office?'

His gruff tone heightened her nerves and she struggled to remember her prepared speech. The enormity of what she was trying to do left her mind blank and she willed herself not to stammer and appear foolish. 'Cassie hasn't been in all week,' she began.

'I'm quite aware Cassie hasn't been in,' he growled.

'Her work has been piling up and –'

'I'm aware of that.'

'– and there's a danger that we could lose some of her clients.'

Stone-faced and silent, he stared at her without speaking. Eventually, after the moment had dragged out to an interminable degree, he said, 'So?'

His manner mixed contempt with derision and Vicky knew it didn't bode well for her chances of success. Nevertheless, knowing this would probably be her only opportunity to show her potential, she said, 'So, I've been going through her contracts and seeing what I could deal with.'

'You've been going through Cassie's work?'

His expression couldn't have looked more scornful and she could see her goal moving further and further away. 'Yes,' she mumbled.

'That should make for an interesting paragraph on the liquidator's report.'

Vicky wasn't sure what he meant but she could tell by his tone that he lacked faith in her abilities. Still, she continued to smile, determined to prove herself to him.

'What makes you think you can manage Cassie's work?' John demanded.

Vicky shrugged, forcing the gesture to look carefree and matter-of-fact. She had spent the last few days preparing herself for this moment and, now it was upon her, she wanted to look professional in spite of John's obvious doubts. She used her pen to casually point at the over-burdened out-tray. 'I think I've managed all right with those. But I suppose you'll want Cassie to go over them when she gets back.'

His frown began to melt as he studied the huge pile of work she was claiming to have done. Making no attempt to hide his scepticism he said, 'You did all that?'

'Yes,' she lied. 'I've also pencilled in a handful of appointments in her diary and I dealt with one of them today.' This was another lie and she lowered her gaze as she spoke, fearful John might see the truth in her eyes. 'What I've done seems fairly straightforward,' she continued, 'but you'll want Cassie to go over the files when she gets back, won't you?'

He glanced towards the window. 'Cassie won't be coming back.'

Vicky was momentarily speechless. It was the news she had been hoping to hear and she struggled to keep the delight from showing on her face or appearing in her voice. 'Cassie's not coming back?' she repeated. 'Why? What's happened? Where's she gone?'

'The last time I saw Cassie she was taking orders from that bald-headed bastard, McPherson,' John growled. 'I was a little tipsy at the time, but I'm beginning to think my Gemballa might be with her as well.'

Vicky placed a hand over her mouth. The gesture made her look shocked and it had the added advantage of hiding her triumphant smile. She knew, if Cassie had stolen John's car and gone to work for the opposition, that meant the junior partner's position at J & C Property Developments was almost certainly up for grabs. This was better news than she had hoped for. 'McPherson of McPherson Developments?' she asked.

'I don't know any other McPherson,' John snapped.

Vicky shook her head. Trying not to let the words sound like a well-practised line, she said, 'But, if Cassie's not coming back, who's going to do her work?'

He shrugged, looking uncomfortable with the topic. His cheeks were reddened by the same blush of guilt Vicky had noticed when she mentioned his Gemballa and he seemed to make a deliberate effort to steer the conversation in a different direction. Glancing at the over-laden out-tray John said, 'You've typed enough of Cassie's work to know how she does things. If you're happy with what you've done this morning, maybe you should carry on.'

Vicky's heart beat faster. These were all the responses she had been hoping for but they were coming so quickly she felt sure she was missing something. Forcing herself not to get too excited, she tried to look hesitant. 'What are you saying to me? Are you asking me to do Cassie's job?'

He shrugged off his jacket and sat down in the chair facing hers. His guilt, if that was what it had been, had evaporated. In its place was John's familiar arrogant smile. 'Do you want to take Cassie's job?'

She didn't hesitate to reply. 'Of course. Yes.'

He nodded and, for the first time since she had worked for J & C Property Developments, Vicky realised John was looking at her with predatory interest. He tilted his head, so he could glance under the desk, and she was sure he was trying to see beneath the hem of her short skirt. When he raised his eyes they flashed briefly in the direction of her breasts and his smile grew broader. 'Of course I should probably interview a few others who might fill her position more ably,' he began. 'But it looks like you've already started to make things happen.'

A knot of unease tightened inside her stomach. Vicky had thought she was in control of the situation – she had prepared the office so it looked like she had been busy and had tried to give the impression she was able to do everything Cassie could – but there was an undercurrent to John's tone that said he knew it was all a charade. She told herself she was just hearing the paranoid voice of her anxiety but, as she dwelt on the idea, she began to feel sure he had seen through her act.

'Cassie had a certain way of doing things in the office,' he expanded. 'Whoever takes over from her, will have to work exactly the same way she did.'

'Of course,' Vicky agreed quickly. 'And how exactly would I do that?'

His grin turned salacious and his gaze locked on hers. 'Cassie never wore panties in the office.'

Vicky was sure he was lying, but didn't dare to tell him so. She had experience of Cassie's prudishness and knew the junior partner would never have done anything so brazen as arriving at work without panties. Almost certainly, Cassie would consider such indecency as 'private behaviour', but Vicky knew she couldn't point that out to John.

'If you want to take over Cassie's job, you're going to have to do the same,' he told her. 'If you want me to consider you for the position, you'll have to take your panties off.'

Part of her had been prepared to flirt with John if it gave her the chance of Cassie's job but she hadn't expected his approach to be this bold. She struggled to think how best to respond but her mind was too stunned to think properly.

'The choice is yours,' he said quietly. 'But I'm going to stand firm on this point for every woman I interview. Anyone who wants the job will have to work without their panties.'

She considered him warily. 'How will that improve the work I do?'

'I don't know. Take them off and let's find out.'

It was a demand and she couldn't think of a way to politely decline. He was offering her a chance for the job she had dreamt of having and all she needed to do was remove her panties. Her hesitation was so brief it didn't even feel as though she had given the matter any thought. She started to reach below the desk and then hesitated. 'Are you going to turn your back?'

'I'd rather not.'

'You might see something you shouldn't.'

'Maybe that's what I'm hoping for.'

Shifting uncomfortably in her seat, Vicky knew she was only prolonging the inevitable. It was difficult to do as he asked without harbouring some doubts and it was only when she thought of the opportunity she might lose that the last of her reservations slipped away. She inched a hand beneath the desk, reached under her skirt, and pulled at the elasticated waistband of her panties.

John continued to study her, his eyes sparkling with lecherous amusement.

She couldn't decide if it was the heat, her nerves or the leather seat. Whatever the cause, her underwear was slick with sweat and stuck to her buttocks and cleft. Peeling the fabric away from the flesh, she continued to meet John's eyes as she slipped the garment off. His constant gaze was unnerving and exciting. The silence that filled the office was so thick it hurt. Eventually, she found she had to speak just to break the tension. 'Why has Cassie gone to McPherson?'

John shrugged. 'Who knows? She might have done it for a bet.'

For some reason he seemed to find the glib remark funny and snorted back laughter. His mirth disappeared when she placed her panties on the desk between them.

The pink tangas were mottled with moisture and her cheeks turned crimson when she realised John might think the wetness had been caused by something other than perspiration.

'There,' she said boldly. The skin around her sex felt strangely cool and flushed at the same time. She was more aware of that sensation than the mortified burning of her cheeks. 'Am I ready to take over where Cassie left off now?'

He shook his head slowly. 'That's not all Cassie would do to win a contract.'

Vicky told herself she should leave the office. He was lying, and doing it solely to exploit her, and she knew it would be sensible to take the first opportunity and leave. The idea was tempting but, if she walked away now, she would never have another chance to achieve this goal. Making a silent promise not to degrade herself further, she cocked her jaw defiantly and asked, 'What else would Cassie do?'

'Cassie would always kiss a contract for good luck.'

Relief made her want to sigh.

She had expected him to make some sexual demand, possibly ask her to do something for him, or maybe insist she take her top off. Compared to what he might have asked, kissing the contract seemed innocent enough. She picked up the document that lay open before her and placed her lips against it. She smacked wetly against the first page and was pleased with the scarlet lipstick imprint she left at the top. Smiling, she turned the folder so John could see what she had done.

He shook his head. 'Cassie used to kiss the contracts for luck. But she never did it with her mouth.'

'She ... I don't ...' Vicky stopped herself from completing the sentence as understanding washed over her. Her blushes had burnt badly before but this time they were red hot coals against her cheeks. She scrutinised his face to see if he was teasing then looked away from the honest lechery of his smile. 'She used to kiss them with her –' Instead of saying the words, Vicky pointed beneath the desk. '– with those lips?' she finished lamely.

John nodded.

Realising she had already committed herself to the debasement, Vicky decided this final sacrifice wouldn't be asking too much. If it gave her the chance of having Cassie's job then she supposed it was a price worth paying. Repeating those thoughts inside her mind, trying to believe them in spite of their unconvincing ring, she took the contract and started to push it beneath the desk.

John leant over the desk and placed a hand on her arm to stop her. His touch was firm and masculine and Vicky couldn't help but respond to a small thrill of electric frisson.

'Cassie used to kiss it on the desk,' he explained solemnly. 'If you're going to take over where she left off you'll have to do it properly. If you're going to take over from Cassie, you'll have to kiss the contract on the desk.'

Her eyes grew wider and she tried to silently beseech him for an escape route. Seeing nothing but steely defiance in his expression, Vicky resigned herself to her fate and placed the contract back between them. Sliding out of the chair, she climbed onto the desk and placed a foot on either side of the open contract.

John kept his gaze fixed on her all the time.

It was embarrassing to be in a position where she towered over him, and not just because she was wearing a short skirt with no panties beneath. Even though she was above him, and should have been enjoying a superior position, Vicky knew he had control over her. The idea was simultaneously worrying and exhilarating.

John watched as she hitched the skirt up over her thighs and he maintained eye contact as she bent her knees and lowered herself to the table.

The position was demeaning, degrading and filled with excitement. She could see the gleam in his eyes when his gaze flicked to her sex and she wondered if he

53

was aware of the effect his interest was inspiring. The thrill of doing something so tawdry left her insides twisted with a thick cord of arousal. The excitement heightened as she dropped to her haunches and, when her bared pussy lips graced the open page of the contract, she felt close to the point of climax.

The dry paper should have been an asexual caress but, because of the electric atmosphere building between them, Vicky thought it was like having a lover's tongue brush against her cleft. A tingle of excitement bristled from her sex and she struggled to contain her shivers.

'That's not how Cassie would have done it,' John murmured.

Vicky frowned at him, unhappy that she had apparently done something wrong. 'How should I have done it?'

'You just rubbed your crotch against it,' he complained. 'Cassie would have kissed it fully. Cassie would have got the page wet.'

Vicky shook her head, not understanding and anxious to know where she had gone wrong.

'You're not kissing it properly,' he told her. There was a shrill note of impatience in his voice. 'Aren't you capable of doing Cassie's job? Is that what you're telling me?'

'I can't see how else I can kiss it.'

'Do you want me to help?'

Before she could reply, John was climbing out of his chair and reaching for her. Allowing him to move his hand nearer she closed her eyes as he touched between her legs.

His fingers were cool against her burning flesh and she was aware of her sex lips melting for him. A spike of arousal penetrated her and she opened her eyes to stare at him with surprise.

'You need to kiss the contract while these lips are open,' he whispered.

He held her inner labia between his index fingers and thumbs. His grip was firm as he pulled the slivers of flesh apart. His touch seemed to linger for an unnecessary length of time while he gently pulled and stretched her open. John's brow was furrowed by a frown of concentration and he seemed unaware of the response he was provoking. When he finally returned to his seat, Vicky was breathless with need and had all but forgotten why she was squatting on Cassie's desk in such an obscene pose.

'Kiss the contract now,' John instructed.

Eagerly, Vicky squashed her pussy against the desk. She knew her sex was leaving a sticky residue against the page and could feel the viscous smear of arousal slipping over the paper. The thrill she had felt before was a pale shadow of the sensations that coursed through her body this time. Excitement scorched every pore and left her dizzied by need. She struggled to keep her tone even as she levered herself away from the desk and asked, 'Was that how Cassie would have done it?'

'You have to do it twice for good luck,' he replied.

She started to squat back down, then stopped herself. Licking two fingers on her right hand she splayed her sex open and teased the lips apart. The atmosphere had been charged since John had asked her to remove her panties but this moment went far beyond that. Teasing herself to a point where she was close to orgasm, Vicky squatted back down and pressed her sex against the open page.

The pressure sparked her climax. The explosion started somewhere at the centre of her sex then flourished through every inch of her body. She shivered and would have fallen off the table if John hadn't climbed out of his chair and placed a steadying hand on her arm.

His nearness, and the knowledge she had allowed him to watch her perform such an intimate act, made for a debilitating combination. His mouth was close enough so their lips could touch and Vicky pouted expectantly.

'What's the contract that you've just been kissing?' he asked.

The question was so unexpected that for a moment she almost faltered. Racking her brains, trying to think past the burden of arousal that coloured her thoughts, she said, 'Harwood. I think it's the Harwood contract.'

His mood changed with bewildering swiftness. He snatched the contract from beneath her and began to leaf through the pages.

'The bloody Harwood contract,' he exclaimed. 'When did this come in?'

For a moment she was unable to think. John's interest in her had disappeared so suddenly Vicky felt alone and out of place. She half expected him to start reprimanding her for exposing herself in the office and, as her guilt and embarrassment began to make themselves known, she could almost hear the words he would use.

'There's a time and a place for everything, but the office is never the place for that sort of private behaviour . . .'

'When did this come in?' John repeated.

The anger in his voice was enough to cut through her mounting panic. Looking over his shoulder, seeing the date stamp on the top page, she said, 'That came in on Monday.'

He rolled his eyes and rubbed a hand over his face.

Vicky was left to climb unceremoniously from the desk and straighten her clothes back to some semblance of modesty. She wriggled her hips back into her skirt and stepped back into her panties.

John didn't notice her.

He flicked through the pages of the document and his annoyance became more profound as he read various lines. 'It's a listed building,' he mumbled. 'And what the fuck does "access rights for ramblers" mean?'

'It means that there's going to be a lot of complicated paperwork if the new proprietor wants to make money from his investment,' Vicky said quietly.

John turned on her. 'You can stop trying to pretend you know what you're talking about. I think you exceeded your skills by kissing the contract.'

The words struck her like a slap to the face. She opened her mouth to argue but no sounds came out.

'Call McPherson,' John demanded. 'Tell him I want Cassie back.'

Vicky shook her head. 'I thought I was going to take over from Cassie.'

He grunted and this time she didn't miss the disparaging note in his voice. 'Maybe in your wildest and wettest dreams,' he mumbled, 'but not in this reality.' He turned back to the paperwork, reading further and seeming to grow more despondent. 'Bloody hell! There's a site meeting this Saturday! Why didn't Stephen mention any of this the other night?' He raked his fingers through his fringe, dishevelling his usually well-groomed coiffure. 'I need Cassie to work through this contract for me. You wouldn't know where to begin.'

'It's simply a matter of getting the right planning permissions,' Vicky said stiffly. 'It's going to be complicated, granted. But it's not something I couldn't do.'

He studied her and his expression gave Vicky a renewed burst of hope. Something in his eyes told her he was seriously weighing up her potential as Cassie's replacement.

'If we include a little bit of ambiguous phrasing in our proposals,' she started, 'and use a couple of helpful clerical errors, we should be able to force the local planning committees to accept almost anything. There shouldn't be any problem at all in converting the Harwood property into a private leisure facility.'

His smile shone with wry amusement. 'Perhaps I've been underestimating you,' he grinned. 'Perhaps you might be able to manage this contract.'

'And take over Cassie's job?' Vicky pressed hopefully.

John pushed the document into her hands. In spite of his smile, his face remained deliberately noncommittal. 'We can talk about your job title once you've sealed this contract,' he told her. 'But the way things are looking right now, I don't think we need to get Cassie away from McPherson. I don't think we need her at all.'

Four

'That's it, you filthy slut! You know you want it.'

Cassie closed her eyes and tried to ignore the sound of his voice. Throughout the week she had been imprisoned against her will; forced to dress like the worst sort of slattern; and borne witness to disciplines that were cruel, inhumane and unjust. Those torments alone would have been bad enough but – and this was the worst part – each experience had been accompanied by a loathsome arousal. For some reason she couldn't fathom, her body responded to every warped or sadistic stimulus and the sound of Brandon's voice was only serving to make that final humiliation cut worse than ever.

'Bend over so I can go deeper into you, bitch. And don't wriggle that much or I'll have to stripe your arse again.'

As much as she didn't want to hear what was happening in the other room, it was impossible not to listen. Brandon's barbaric cries were underscored by moans of feminine ecstasy and it took little imagination to picture the scene within his private office. He had instructed her to sit at the reception desk while Faye and Laura were summoned to the seclusion of his inner sanctum. The trio's obvious and passionate throes had been going on for the best part of an hour and, although she wanted to distance herself from those events, Cassie couldn't stop taunting herself with images of their unclothed bodies writhing together.

She knew Brandon would be naked, his smooth hairless body powerfully dominating the women, and she expected Faye and Laura would have stripped to accommodate him. In her mind's eye she could see their bared breasts – Brandon greedily mauling them – and she expected the two women would be gorging on his length. Their legs would be wrapped around him as their supine bodies joined and the mental picture was obscene and sickly exciting.

'Go on!' Brandon roared.

His words were carried on a shriek of euphoria and Cassie was familiar enough with the tone to know he had finally reached his climax. She had heard it so often over the past seven days she could easily associate the cry with his satisfied smile.

'Yes! That's it. Swallow it all, you whore! Swallow it all.' His voice tapered off to a sated growl that was drowned by Faye's shriek of delight.

Cassie squirmed uncomfortably against her seat. In a deliberate effort to shut all thoughts of pleasure from her mind she desperately tried to focus on her plans to escape. If she wanted to retain any hope of deliverance from McPherson's house, Cassie knew she couldn't lose sight of that one goal.

The week had sped past in a haze of torments and humiliation.

Brandon kept his tawse close to hand and never hesitated before using it to express his displeasure. He had an ability to stripe bare flesh with what looked like the most casual of backhand flicks and he could deliver a blow with crippling intensity. She had seen him chastise Marion for not being a more capable candle-holder and she had watched as he punished Sarah for a seemingly minor misdemeanour. Noting how cruelly he exacted those disciplines – not missing the sadistic pleasure he gleaned from his victims' suffering – Cassie had vowed to avoid receiving the same treatment. And it was a vow she intended to keep.

Brandon hadn't punished her since her first evening at the house but Cassie thought it was only a combination of circumstances and good luck that had stopped her from suffering his wrath. Common sense told her, if she remained in the house much longer, she would undoubtedly be chastised again. Having noticed the avaricious glint in his eyes she knew, the next time Brandon punished her, he would make it extremely memorable.

The telephone on the desk before her rang. Its shrill bell shocked Cassie from her musings and she quickly snatched the handset from its cradle. 'McPherson Developments. How may I help you?'

Part of her wanted to cry out for help and explain to the unknown caller she was being held prisoner but she knew there would be no advantage in trying such a tactic. During Cassie's induction, Faye had explained the telephone was Brandon's private line: a number reserved exclusively for the benefit of his most important clients. It only accepted incoming calls, with no option to dial out and, as if she was trying to pre-empt Cassie's plans, Faye had told her the only callers who used that number were aware of the master's lifestyle.

'Stephen Price for Brandon McPherson. I need to talk to him about the Harwood contract.'

Cassie paused, wondering why the name sounded familiar and important. It wasn't difficult to remember because Brandon had given her a copy of the Harwood contract earlier in the week and the details of that document were indelibly etched in her memory. By profession she was a property developer and used to dealing with a variety of proposals for potential businesses but the Harwood contract had been something disturbingly new. Stephen Price was wanting to convert a listed building into what he coyly described as an adult leisure facility. His suggestions for torture chambers, bondage rooms, group sex parlours and sex play areas had been unnervingly graphic and Cassie had refused to do anything with the contract other than threaten to throw it in the bin.

Not wanting to talk to the man any more than was necessary, and fearing there might be repercussions if she didn't transfer the call as quickly as she was able, Cassie put Stephen on hold. She called through to Brandon's office and told him the name of the caller.

Brandon accepted the line without a word of thanks.

In the thickening silence of her solitude Cassie glanced down at herself. Offended by what she saw, she quickly looked away from the vulgar display she was presenting. Brandon had provided her with a uniform and told her it was the only clothing she would be allowed to wear as long as she remained his property. The fishnet body stocking, disgustingly tight and outrageously revealing, exposed every curve and crease. The sheer fabric was virtually transparent and left nothing to the imagination. The thrust of her nipples was clearly discernible above the swell of each breast while the shadow of her pubic thatch darkened the gusset. When she first caught a glimpse of her reflection, she had been shocked to see the body stocking was tight enough to outline the shape of her pussy lips. The whole ensemble was so garish Cassie still couldn't look at herself without being crippled by a pang of humiliation.

The door to Brandon's office opened and Laura walked majestically out of the room. Behind her Faye and Brandon remained naked but, struck as always by Laura's aristocratic beauty, Cassie barely noticed the couple. The brunette was dressed in an identical body stocking to Cassie's, although somehow she managed to wear the garment without seeming troubled by its exhibitionist cut. It exposed the tantalising length of her legs, the exquisite perfection of her figure and the fullness of her shapely breasts. Glancing furtively at Laura, Cassie watched the woman wipe the side of her face and lick something from the back of her hand. With an air of cultivated deportment, she made herself comfortable in one of the reception chairs and crossed her ankles demurely.

Cassie nodded to acknowledge her presence.

Laura held her with a haughty gaze. 'I know what you're planning.'

Cassie blinked. She was so startled Laura had finally deigned to talk to her that, for an instant, she wasn't sure how to respond. Since her first night at McPherson's – almost a full week earlier she realised glumly – the brunette had deliberately rebuffed all of Cassie's attempts to strike up a conversation. Her constant scowl and expression of superiority had never wavered. In spite of Cassie's politeness, Laura had made it obvious she wanted nothing to do with her. Yet now, she leant forward in the chair and lowered her voice to a conspiratorial whisper.

'I know what you're trying to do and I can tell you now: it's not going to work.'

Fearful her intentions had been written on her face, Cassie contained a guilty blush. Trying to conceal her embarrassment behind a show of defiance she asked, 'And what am I trying to do?'

'You're trying to escape.'

Cassie glanced towards the closed door of Brandon's office, worried Laura's words might have been overheard. Without thinking about what she was doing, she placed a finger over her lips and tried to shush Laura into silence.

Escape had been at the forefront of her mind ever since she realised John wasn't coming back for her. The windows of McPherson's house were barred; the doors were constantly locked; and she spent her nights handcuffed to the stone floor of the cellar. There weren't many hours in the day when she had the chance to make an escape but Cassie knew the time was going to come soon and, when it did, she intended to take full advantage of the opportunity. If her assessment of the situation was right she expected to be out of the house by the end of the evening. Friday night was poker night and, from what Faye had told her about the necessary arrangements, Cassie thought McPherson might be too involved in his game to worry about something as inconsequential as security. From the little she remembered of the previous Friday everyone's attention had been too focused on the card game to worry about anything else.

'Of course I'm trying to escape,' Cassie hissed quietly. 'Can you blame me?'

Laura sneered and sat back in her chair. 'Bitches like you make me sick,' she spat. 'Bitches like you – with all your pious morals and your stupid ideals about what's right and wrong – you really make me want to throw up.'

Cassie glared at her. She was too stunned by the outburst to think of a reply.

'You look down your nose at the staff here in the house,' Laura continued. 'Yet, when it comes down to it, you're driven by the same urges that govern us all. You're just as bad as the rest of us.'

'I don't think so,' Cassie sniffed loftily. 'I don't think so at all.'

Laura moved with lightning speed, jumping out of her chair and pinning Cassie to her seat. She placed a hand on each of her arms and pressed her face close. The caress of her a leg stroked against Cassie's outer thigh and she brought with her a fragrance of warm musk. 'You don't think so?' Laura repeated.

She was disturbingly near, her breath whispering against Cassie's cheek. The mint fresh aroma of each exhalation was tainted by the memory of Brandon's semen. Cassie couldn't decide whether she was excited or repulsed by the scent but she knew she had to get away from it. Despite her attempts to struggle free, Laura kept her fixed.

'Are you telling me you weren't getting aroused when Brandon striped your tits last Friday?' Laura demanded. 'Are you saying you didn't get wet between your legs when you watched the master fuck Sarah, then had me lick her clean? Are you telling me none of that happened?'

Cassie closed her eyes and turned her face away. 'Brandon's sick for what he does to you,' she whispered. 'And you're sick for allowing him to do it.'

'And are you sick for being excited by everything that happens around here?'

Cassie was preparing to refute the allegation when she glanced up at the woman. For the first time she noted Laura had stopped sneering. She wore a smile that was simultaneously beautiful and threatening. The pleasure she was exacting from Cassie's unhappiness was obvious but that didn't stop Cassie from thinking Laura was the most attractive woman she had ever seen. Firmly she stifled her admiration, willing herself to remember the woman was physically dominating her.

'I haven't been excited by anything while I've been here.' Trying to sound indignant she added, 'It's a sick and twisted set-up you have. I can't understand why you might think otherwise.'

Laura laughed mirthlessly. 'Isn't it obvious?' Without hesitating she reached for the front of Cassie's uniform and cupped one breast. The nub beneath the sheer fabric was hard and it sat between them like an inarguable fact. As Laura rolled her thumb over the rigid nipple, Cassie was brushed by a whisper of arousal.

It crossed her mind to rebuke the woman – push her away or tell her to stop touching – but instead she allowed the contact to continue. There was something seductive about the intimacy that she knew her body craved. As her breast was washed by a flood of dawning sensations, Cassie released a soft, exalted breath.

'Are you beginning to see my point of view? Are you beginning to realise I might be right? Or do you need more convincing?'

Unable to think of a way to extricate herself, not sure that was what she really wanted, Cassie remained immobile as Laura teased the body stocking away from her shoulder. She pulled the fabric down, exposed Cassie's ripe breast, then lowered her head. Her lips edged closer to the orb and encircled the shape of the nipple.

The moment stung with its poignancy. Laura's kiss charged the responsive flesh with an unprecedented thrill. She trilled her tongue against the nub, nibbling lightly to add untold facets to the stimulation, before gently sucking. The whisper of arousal Cassie had felt when Laura touched her was transformed into a moan of pleasure. Hardly aware she was doing it, Cassie ground her thighs dryly together.

With a cruel smile, Laura moved her head away. 'You're governed by the same impulses that drive the rest of us,' she sneered. 'You're just as sick and twisted as we are.'

Cassie shook her head but she was too breathless to deny the allegation. She caught sight of Laura's disapproving frown and then realised the woman was bearing down on her for a second time. Without any hesitation Laura reached down and pushed her legs apart. The caress of her fingertips brushed against Cassie's thighs before she realised what was happening. With a sickening lurch she saw Laura was tugging the crotch of the body stocking to one side. By the time the fact had registered the brunette was already touching her.

The frisson of Laura's hand against her pussy was tantalising. Cassie bit back a cry of excitement as the woman teased her labia apart and slipped two, then three fingers into her sex. They entered her with an ease that was both glorious and nauseating.

'You're still dripping at the memory of what happened on your first night here,' Laura growled. 'You're absolutely sodden.' It was impossible to work out if she was pleased or disgusted by the discovery. She pushed her fingers deeper, squirming them against the clenching inner muscles of Cassie's pussy. 'You're wetter than I would have expected, and I thought you'd be sopping. How dare you look down your nose on the rest of us when you're driven by the same impulses.'

'I'm not driven by those impulses!' Cassie wailed miserably. She wanted to believe the words, even though Laura's argument seemed irrefutable. 'I'm not driven by the same impulses as the rest of you perverts. I'm –'

She got no further. Laura silenced the remainder of what she had to say by placing her lips over Cassie's.

The kiss was enveloping, unexpected and arousing. Cassie was aware of a tongue plundering her mouth and then realised she was responding avariciously to the intrusion. She used her own tongue to explore Laura, not hesitating in her urgency to turn the kiss into a two-way exchange.

Laura continued to wriggle her penetrating fingers as she moved her other hand back to Cassie's exposed breast. While their mouths continued to meld she teased one nipple between her finger and thumb then squeezed it with only a little more force than was necessary. If Cassie had been able to see what was happening, she wouldn't have been surprised to see Laura's manicured nails pressing wickedly into the fat bud of flesh. Because the woman's face filled her vision, she could only marvel over the aesthetic perfection of Laura's beauty and the pleasure she was delivering.

Without breaking contact, making the move a subtle addition to the slow frigging of her right hand, Laura slipped a fourth finger inside Cassie's pussy.

Elated by the experience Cassie melted and allowed the brunette to dominate her. She was wallowing in the burgeoning throes of ecstasy when Laura finally broke the kiss and sneered.

'You're as bad as the rest of us,' she scoffed. 'Worse, most probably because you can't even be honest with yourself. You make me sick.'

The words struck like a slap to the face and finally made Cassie retaliate. She pulled herself from Laura's loose embrace and tried to adjust her clothing to some semblance of modesty. She tugged the body stocking so her breast was covered by its flimsy denier, then pulled the gusset back into place to hide the throbbing lips of her sex. Flushing crimson, not knowing what had possessed her to let Laura touch her, she started trying to run out of the room.

'The master will be cross if you're not waiting here when he gets back,' Laura taunted. 'The master will be *very* cross.'

Not listening, Cassie tried to turn the handle on the door. It was slipping through her fingers when she felt Laura reach for her shoulder. Not thinking about her actions, only desperate to escape the claustrophobic atmosphere of the reception, she brushed the hand away.

Laura caught her fingers and turned her around. She was quick and strong and the combination left Cassie helpless. She was powerless to resist as Laura enveloped her in an inescapable embrace.

The excitement Cassie had felt before was nothing compared to the surge of arousal that tormented her as Laura pressed closer. The nearness of her body, and the sensation of the brunette's breasts pressing lewdly against her, were an unbearable combination. One of Laura's bare legs snaked behind Cassie's and the friction was enough to make her dizzy with need. The brunette grabbed her by the back of the neck and held her head rigid as she lowered her mouth. Cassie surrendered to the kiss with an inevitability that was frightening and warming. She allowed the woman to stroke and caress her, unmindful of whether her actions could be construed as right or wrong. The only thought she was aware of was that Laura had awoken an urge inside her and it needed satisfying.

'What the hell is going on here?'

Brandon's cry dragged Cassie quickly back to the real world. She started guiltily as Laura lowered her gaze, stepped backwards and swiftly put distance between them.

'I asked a question and I expect an answer,' Brandon insisted. 'What the hell is going on here?'

He stood in the doorway to his private office, Faye by his side and, as ever, the hateful length of the tawse in his hand. Cassie had forgotten how ineffectual the length of leather could look but she still remembered how cruelly it could bite.

'One of you will answer me, or I'll thrash my way to a reply. What's going on here?'

'I'm sorry, master,' Laura mumbled. Stepping further away, raising an accusatory finger, she pointed at Cassie and said, 'She made me do it. She led me on and told me it would be all right for us to kiss.'

Too dumbfounded to reply, Cassie stared at her. She shook her head but it was the closest she could come to denying the accusation.

Faye placed a hand on Brandon's arm but he brushed it aside. Marching angrily around the desk he bore down on Cassie and Laura with his tawse raised high in the air. 'I should have known something like this was going to happen. I should have know you were trouble from the minute I first saw you.'

'No –' Cassie began. She would have said more but Brandon was towering over her. The threat of punishment was enough to make her stand rigid and simply shake her head by way of argument.

'You know how I feel about my charges fraternising together,' Brandon told Laura. 'What the hell were you thinking?'

Laura feigned a tear and lowered her gaze to her feet. 'She led me on,' she said, pointing a wavering finger at Cassie. 'I didn't want to do anything with her but she said you'd be all right about it.'

Cassie started to object but Brandon only had to snap his fingers and she fell obediently silent. 'You're an embarrassment to me at times, Laura,' he said thickly. 'I trust you won't be this much trouble for the next few days.'

Laura lifted her gaze, her eyes narrowed to untrusting slits. Watching her, Cassie knew the woman wanted to ask what was so important about the next few days but she clearly didn't dare to question her master so directly. The brunette's consternation seemed to grow more severe as Brandon's smile widened.

'Go and pack a travelling bag,' he commanded. 'You'll be spending the next few days in the employ of Stephen Price.'

Laura shook her head, looking genuinely horrified at the prospect. 'Don't make me go and work under him,' Laura begged. She fell to her knees and clawed the ankle of Brandon's trousers. 'Please, master. I don't like him and, whenever you've loaned me out to others in the past they always demand more than I'm willing to –'

He sliced his tawse through the air, cutting off the rest of her protests. 'You're going to work under Price until I say otherwise. You'll oblige his every instruction and, in return, I expect he will award me the Harwood contract. Upset him, and the suffering I'll put you through will be legendary.'

It was enough of a threat to make Laura defer. She climbed from her knees, apologised humbly and started out of the reception. As she walked past Cassie her dark eyes sparkled triumphantly and the corners of her lips twisted into a jubilant grin.

'And, as for you!' Brandon exclaimed.

Cassie turned meekly towards him, uncomfortable with the idea of facing his displeasure. His cheeks were flushed, his mood looked thunderous, and he still held the tawse in his right hand.

'I think this is ill-advised, master,' Faye broke in. She placed a hand on his shoulder but he shrugged it away and silenced her with a glare.

Speaking to Cassie he said, 'Laura's being punished by spending the next few days away from this sanctuary. Do you know how I'm going to punish you?'

Shaking her head, blinking back the tears that wanted to spill down her cheeks, she waited for him to tell her.

'Your punishment starts now,' Brandon announced. He snapped his fingers for Faye to follow, then he grabbed Cassie by the shoulder and dragged her out of the reception.

Five

'You're proving yourself to be a liability,' Brandon proclaimed. 'You can't cook. You can't clean. I ask you to go over one measly contract and you go all pious on me. And now it seems like you're some lesbian vampire who wants to prey on my innocent, defenceless staff.'

Cassie tried to tell him it wasn't like that; Laura had been lying and the kiss had been forced on her; but Brandon wasn't listening.

'It looks like you only have one purpose around here,' he continued, 'and I think we should go and exploit that now.'

As much as Cassie tried to resist, Brandon had a firm hold and he hauled her effortlessly along the corridor. His fingers were buried beneath the swell of her scapula and his thumb held her shoulder in an inescapable lock. Faye hurried behind them, constantly trying to get Brandon's attention and repeatedly being ignored.

Cassie wanted to remain oblivious to what was happening, reminding herself that her escape plans would soon be reaching fruition and it would only be a matter of hours before she was able to get away. Faye had told her preparations for the poker game began early in the afternoon and she intimated it would leave the opportunity for Cassie to break free. There was an hour prior to the guests' arrival when Brandon's charges were permitted to eat and Faye had said the main doors were usually left unlocked in case anyone arrived early. All Cassie needed to do was wait for the appropriate time, miss her meal, carefully make her way down the corridor and then, once she had slipped out of the front door, she could leave Brandon McPherson behind her. But, as much as she wanted to dream about that moment, she couldn't think past the fear for her immediate future.

Brandon tugged her past the front doorway and up the central staircase. Cassie almost stumbled as she tried to keep up with him, sure if she did fall he would only drag her in his wake. The frantic clip of Faye's high heels against each step matched the quickening pace of Cassie's heartbeat.

'Master!' Faye cried. 'I wish you'd listen to me. I don't think she's one of us and I don't think she ever will be. I really wish you'd hear what I'm saying.'

Brandon stopped and turned to glare at Faye. He held his tawse as though ready to strike and his frown looked to have been carved from granite. Staring up at him Cassie thought she had never seen anyone who looked so intimidating. 'You'll come with us to the punishment floor,' he snapped. 'I think you're long overdue for a visit to one of the second-floor rooms.' Before Faye could reply he turned his back on her and continued to drag Cassie up the stairs.

They reached the first landing. Cassie almost found her footing and thought she had a chance to break free, until Brandon turned and led her up a second flight of stairs. As Cassie stumbled to keep up with him she hoped she hadn't heard correctly when Brandon had mentioned a punishment floor. It was depressing to think the concept somehow sounded right amongst the perversity of everything else in McPherson's home.

Early evening had begun to encroach, giving the upper landings a dismal and menacing air. Cassie had never been permitted to venture to this floor of the house but, rather than study her surroundings with curiosity or interest, she continued to struggle against his grip. She gained a vague impression of stately elegance around her, but nothing more. Brandon took her past one door, hesitated outside another, then seemed to think the next room would be more suitable.

'Master,' Faye protested. 'Not room number three. You can't take her in there. You simply can't.'

Brandon's smile was a cruel slit. 'Stop telling me what I can and can't do,' he growled. 'You've already earned your punishment. All of us are going in room three.' Without hesitating, he pushed the door open and hurled Cassie inside. He waited outside for a moment and, as she struggled to find her feet, Cassie watched him direct a reluctant Faye into the room before he locked the door.

She took in her surroundings at a glance, and was relieved to find they were more innocuous than she had anticipated. One mirrored wall gave an impression of space that was augmented by the lines of polished floorboarding. Two milking stools stood in the centre of the room but, aside from the sink in the corner, there were no other furnishings. This was nowhere near as bad as she had feared.

'Forget your place and you'll make me an angry master,' Brandon warned Faye.

The authority in his voice made Cassie turn to watch the pair.

'Forget your place and I'll make you spend a day in room number five.'

Although he was speaking to her in a menacing growl Faye stood defiant. 'I'm not forgetting my place,' she insisted. 'I'm just trying to point out –'

'Enough!'

He raised his tawse and Cassie looked away, not wanting to watch what he might do to the blonde. She found herself staring out of the room's picture window at the landscaped greenery behind Brandon's house. Her eye was caught by the brilliant guards' red of John's Gemballa and she stifled a gasp of delight at the hope he had finally come to her rescue. Her joy began to evaporate when she remembered Brandon had won the car on the same evening she had been lost. Her mounting desperation heightened when she noticed the other features of the desolate view.

Beyond the stables the greenery stretched for miles and Cassie wondered what sort of trek she would have to endure to make her escape. She knew it had been a long drive to Brandon's the previous Friday but she hoped the house didn't prove to be as remote as she remembered.

'This room isn't right for her,' Faye told Brandon. Her voice was lowered to a hissed whisper but the acoustics of the polished floor and lack of furnishings amplified every syllable. 'I don't think any punishment room is right for her,' Faye continued, 'but this one certainly isn't.'

Instead of responding angrily, Brandon's reply came in an understanding lilt. 'You're not convinced she's a submissive, are you?'

'I'm sure she's not,' Faye said firmly.

'Then I'm going to prove you wrong,' Brandon decided. 'I'm going to prove you both wrong.' Faye looked set to interrupt but Brandon hadn't finished speaking. 'I could see she was a sub from the moment she first entered the games room. There was a glint in her eyes that said she was excited by what she saw and I could see she wanted to be a part of it.'

'That expression in her eyes was pure terror,' Faye told him. 'You may have been right about this sort of thing in the past but you're wrong on this occasion. You're terribly, terribly wrong.'

'We'll see,' Brandon scowled. If he had been prepared to address Faye's arguments rationally it seemed clear that time had now passed. The briskness of his tone said he wasn't going to trouble himself with further discussions.

He snapped his fingers and Cassie found herself responding to the command like a well-trained dog. She turned away from the window and took two tentative steps towards him.

'Have my other charges told you about these punishment rooms?' he asked.

Cassie shook her head.

He looked sceptical, as though doubting she was telling the truth. 'I have half a dozen rooms on this floor, each one tailored to a specific form of chastisement. Room number one is strictly for CP and I keep a variety of canes there. Room number two is slightly crueller.' His smile turned wicked as he glanced at Faye and said, 'I had you pierced in room two, didn't I?'

Blushing lightly, Faye lowered her gaze and nodded.

'I won't bore you with explanations about the other rooms – you'll probably find out about them in your own good time – but I will tell you what happens in here. This is room number three.'

In the silence that followed, Cassie could feel her stomach churning with nerves. Her mouth was dry, her palms had begun to sweat and she switched her gaze uneasily between Brandon and Faye. Whatever he was going to say she knew it would be unpleasant and she wished she could think of a way to escape the impending ordeal.

'Don't put her through this,' Faye begged. 'If you're wanting to find a use for her let me teach her how to deal. I've seen her handle a deck of cards and she seems like she'd be quite capable. Let me train her to do something useful rather than torturing her with –'

'You've noticed the milking stool,' Brandon said. He talked over Faye and pointed at the furniture. 'And I take it you've noticed the sink over in the corner. Have

77

you been very observant since you came in here? Have you seen what's in the sink? Have you noticed the enema bag and pipe?'

Cassie moaned softly and began to shake her head. She started to tell him she wanted no more of his domination but Brandon flicked his tawse. The crack of leather breaking air was enough to silence her. Without thinking, she closed her eyes as she flinched from the sound.

'Take off your uniform and bend over that stool, facing the mirror,' Brandon snapped. 'Do it now girl. I don't have any time to waste.'

Cassie opened her eyes, ready to beg with him rather than suffer this embarrassment. When she saw he wasn't talking to her she was speechless.

Under Brandon's watchful eye, Faye reluctantly obeyed his command. She removed her uniform, dropped it to the floor and began to stride defiantly towards the milking stool.

The sight of the woman's nudity was enough to make Cassie feel uneasy. Faye's hourglass figure was breathtakingly arousing and it was difficult to wrench her gaze from the woman's pierced nipples and the neatly trimmed triangle of her pubic mound. She wondered why her mind was rebelling against her common sense and finding excitement in images that should have been unsettling. But, rather than try to solve the mystery, Cassie decided it wasn't an avenue she was keen to explore. She suspected the answers might reveal an aspect to her personality that she didn't want to discover.

With all the dignity she could maintain, Faye bent over the milking stool. This was clearly a position she had assumed before because she looked perfectly at ease with the awkward posture. Drawing her ankles up to the stool's feet, she pressed her stomach against the seat.

Cassie could see the split of the woman's backside and the pouting lips of her pussy. The labia glistened slickly and Cassie wondered if that wetness came from perspiration, or if Faye had been aroused by Brandon's brusque domination.

Wilfully, she tore her gaze away from the sight.

'Secure her,' Brandon snapped.

Cassie saw he was tossing something through the air and she had to act quickly to catch the handcuffs he was throwing. She hesitated briefly, not sure if she ought to be doing as he asked, then decided he would only bully her into obeying if she refused. Kneeling on the wooden floor she placed a metal bracelet around Faye's left wrist, looped the chain behind one of the stool's legs, then fastened the remaining cuff around the blonde's right wrist. Keeping her voice low, fearful Brandon would hear any exchange that rose above a whisper, she said, 'I'm sorry. I wish I wasn't doing this. I really am sorry.'

'It could have been worse,' Faye muttered. 'The master could have taken us to room number five.'

'No more talking,' Brandon barked. He punctuated his command by throwing a second pair of cuffs on the floor. They landed with a metallic clatter and skated along the polished wood until they struck Cassie's foot. 'Fasten her ankles together and then we can begin. Do it quickly girl. I don't have time to waste this evening. The Friday night game is due to start shortly.'

The words spurred her into action. Hearing that the beginning of the poker game was so close she realised the moment for her escape was getting nearer. She mumbled another apology to Faye and clipped the metal bracelets around her ankles. It meant having to hold her face against the swell of one buttock as she secured the final cuff and she was disturbed to find herself responding to the warmth of the woman's nearness. Hurriedly, she made sure the handcuffs were fastened then backed away.

'Not so fast,' Brandon said, settling himself comfortably on the second milking stool. 'You have to prepare her for her enema now.'

Cassie's cheeks blazed crimson as she glared at him. She wanted to make an outright refusal but courage failed her. Instead of telling him she wasn't going to do it, she said, 'I wouldn't know how to begin.'

'It's very simple,' Brandon smiled. 'You just have to make sure she's properly lubricated.'

Cassie shook her head as tears of reluctance spilt down her cheeks. Despite her silent refusal she knew she had no option but to obey.

'You'll be able to draw warm, soapy water from the sink,' Brandon explained patiently. 'Use that to get her ready for the enema. And never forget, time is against us this evening.'

Blushing angrily Cassie went to the corner of the room and began to wash her hands under a stream of lukewarm water. Her fingers were shaking and she wished she could steady her nerves. She supposed that escaping from Brandon's control would certainly help her with that problem and she prayed for the moments to pass quickly so she could leave the punishment room and make her break for freedom. She took a sponge from the side of the sink and soaked it in the tepid flow. Then she walked back to Faye's secured figure.

Brandon watched her with a predatory smile.

Doing her best to ignore his lascivious interest, Cassie patted the sodden sponge against the blonde's backside. Dribbles of warm water wetted Faye's cheeks and trickled over both her anus and her pussy lips before spilling down her legs.

'Lubricate her properly,' Brandon drawled wearily. 'She's having an enema, not a sponge bath.'

'I am doing it properly,' Cassie told him. She could hear insurrection in her voice and half expected Brandon to challenge her for speaking with such a lack of respect. Not wanting to cause a confrontation, aware she would have a better chance of getting out of the room quicker if she behaved with servility, Cassie

80

repeated the words in a meek voice. 'I am doing it properly.'

'You have to make sure her hole is good and soapy,' Brandon commanded. 'Push a couple of wet fingers in there if you have to.'

Unable to stop herself, Cassie glared at him with venomous fury. The expression melted when she saw he had made the remark in earnest and she struggled not to show her disgust. 'I can't do that,' she gasped. 'I can't possibly do that.'

Brandon shrugged. 'You have two choices,' he said easily. 'You can either do as I'm telling you, or I can unfasten Faye and you can change places with her.'

Cassie's eyes widened in horror. Without thinking, she took a backward step away from him.

'The choice is yours,' Brandon went on. 'But, I'm warning you now: if you change places with Faye, she won't be the one preparing you for the enema. I'll take great pleasure in doing that myself.'

Shrinking from the idea of Brandon touching her in such a way, Cassie turned quickly back to Faye. Wetting the end of one finger, making it soapy with the sponge, Cassie touched the puckered ring of Faye's anus. Trying not to think about what she was doing, she traced a gentle circle against the blonde's forbidden muscle.

Faye sighed.

'You need to push your finger inside her anus,' Brandon said gleefully. 'It wouldn't be fair to cause Faye any more suffering than she's already going to have to put up with. Push a wet finger into her anus and get her hole good and soapy.'

Despising him for enjoying her misery, Cassie did as she was told. She pressed the tip of her index finger against Faye's backside and watched it start to slip inside. There was a brief moment of resistance – a tautening of muscles and a stiffening of the blonde's posture – then Cassie's finger was pushing deeper.

Bent over the milking stool, Faye sighed more deeply.

Cassie was mesmerised by the vision of her finger sliding into the blonde's behind. She could feel the unnatural warmth of the woman's sphincter; the clenching of her muscles; and a dark exciting pulse. The rush of sensations was so acute she quickly tried to work out what she was doing and why she was doing it.

Frightened, she snatched her hand away.

Brandon laughed and Cassie glared at him wondering if he knew how unsettling she had found the experience.

'You might want to use two fingers on her,' he grinned happily. 'It's vital you make sure she's slippery and open. Carry on now.'

Steeling herself to complete the task, Cassie wet her fingers again and pressed at the yielding centre of Faye's anus. The muscle parted slightly and this time she was able to enter easily. Her finger slid all the way up to the knuckle before Cassie stopped the penetration from going further.

Faye's growl from the floor was a cry of unmistakable encouragement.

Warming to her chore, surprised to find the intimacy darkly exciting, Cassie slipped a second finger alongside the first. Initially, Faye's anus resisted the increased girth but, because Cassie was pushing firmly, the sphincter finally relented. Cassie smiled to herself as she rubbed back and forth along Faye's anal canal enjoying the forbidden sensation in a way she would never have imagined. Her smile faltered when she realised Brandon was grinning triumphantly. The expression on his face seemed to say that he thought he had scored some twisted victory.

'Do you think she's prepared for the enema?' Brandon asked sweetly.

'I wouldn't know,' she mumbled thickly. 'I've never done anything like this before.'

'You surprise me,' he smirked. 'You were handling that as though you were born to be an enema girl.

Perhaps that's the role you can fill while you're residing here.'

Flushing hotly, Cassie shook her head and said, 'I've never done anything like this before. Never ever.'

'Of course you haven't,' Brandon agreed. 'So, if you don't know whether you've done it properly, why don't you ask Faye?'

Cassie glanced down at the mop of gold-coloured ringlets concealing the back of Faye's head. 'Faye?' she asked hesitantly. 'Have I done it properly yet?'

'Not yet,' Faye breathed. Her voice was a guttural whisper. 'Use three.'

Cassie could feel the tremor of each word tingling through the tips of her fingers. She didn't know why the sensation was so arousing but she couldn't deny the thrill it gave her. Pulling her hand free, wetting it thoroughly with the soapy sponge, she eased three fingers into Faye's tight, forbidden hole. This time it was more of a struggle to penetrate her but, because she had made her hand properly slippery, and because Faye's anus was already gaping hungrily, Cassie managed to enter her. She squeezed her fingers into the woman, taking great satisfaction from pushing them as deep as they would go.

'You look to be enjoying that,' Brandon observed.

Cassie tried to remain unmoved by what he was suggesting and met his sneer with defiance. 'You didn't tell me I wasn't allowed to enjoy it.'

'That's true,' Brandon agreed. 'I just hope you get as much pleasure when you give Faye her enema.'

Cassie pulled her hand away and began shaking her head. 'I'm not doing that,' she whispered. 'You can't make me do that and I won't.'

Brandon shrugged. 'You don't have to if you don't want,' he agreed affably. 'But we still have the same arrangement that we had before: if you don't do as I ask, then I'll make you change places with Faye. It's your choice. Are you sure you don't want to give her the enema?'

Glaring impotently, knowing there was no way she could win, Cassie stormed back to the sink. She snatched the enema bag and the pipe from the bowl and began to run the tap.

'Don't make the water too soapy,' Brandon called, 'and try not to let the water get uncomfortably warm.'

Cassie thought of telling him to do it himself if he was so damned particular but she refrained from issuing the challenge, fearful of his response. Heeding everything he had said she filled the bag with a strongly diluted mixture of soapy, warm water.

Walking back to Faye's secured figure she didn't dare to look at her reflection in the mirror. She remained nervous about what she was doing, yet a bizarre calmness had overtaken her. She wanted to get the ordeal over with as quickly as possible and she didn't want to see herself participating in this perverted act. She suspected the woman who would stare back at her might be a different person to the one who had been lost in last Friday night's poker game.

Brandon stood up as she approached, and placed a hand on her wrist.

Cassie glared at him.

'You know you have to be gentle with Faye, don't you?' he asked. 'I might have her doing this to you later and you wouldn't want to give her any reason to carry a grudge.'

Cassie stared at him, trying to work out if he was serious or if this was just another twisted facet of his sense of mirth. When he began to laugh, she guessed the comment had only been made to intimidate her and she berated herself for being such easy prey.

Still chuckling, Brandon settled himself back on his stool and indicated for Cassie to continue.

Putting aside her reservations, she stepped behind Faye and drew a deep breath. Allowing water to spill from the tip of the nozzle, she let a light spray douse Faye's buttocks and cleft. Content the stream was flowing freely, Cassie guided the end of the pipe towards the blonde's backside. It was a struggle to insert the nozzle at first and, when she finally managed, she and Faye both released a sigh. Faye's was a long drawn out cry that bordered on elation. The sound unnerved Cassie because it was as though the woman was in the throes of extreme pleasure. She rested one hand against the blonde's taut, peachlike buttock. The flesh trembled beneath her touch and, as she had when she was fingering the woman's anus, Cassie found herself caught by an unexpected thrill. She didn't know where the emotion came from and couldn't work out how to deal with it. But she couldn't deny it was as real as every aspect of the perversion she was being forced to commit.

'Raise that bag slightly higher,' Brandon instructed. His clipped commands echoed dramatically around the room. 'Don't take it above her waist level or the water will flow too fast, but she needs it higher than that.'

Obediently, Cassie lifted the bag higher.

Faye growled with satisfaction.

Glancing down at her, Cassie saw the woman's fingers were spreading out, then flexing into fists, before stretching fully back out again. She could hear the rising pitch of Faye's respiration and each ragged breath had the same husky quality Cassie associated with arousal.

The enema continued to flow slowly, its steady trickle barely audible beneath Faye's mounting sighs and Cassie's own deafening heartbeat. She couldn't believe what she was doing and she tried holding onto that sense of disbelief. At the back of her mind Cassie knew, if she let her thoughts wander in any other direction, she might start to dwell on the pleasure she was getting from Faye's predicament.

'No more!' Faye whispered. 'I can't take any more.'

Cassie turned to Brandon for guidance but he simply waved for her to carry on. Not wanting to go against his wishes, but reluctant to continue, Cassie vacillated between the pair. She attempted to give Faye's buttock a reassuring squeeze but the gesture seemed more forceful than she intended. There was a sultry intimacy to the caress that felt disturbingly sexual, and Cassie wondered what had possessed her to do something so foolish. She heard the woman moan and was struck by the electrical charge of contact from the blonde's bare flesh.

'Please stop!' Faye begged. 'I really can't take any more. Make her stop, master. Please make her stop.' When she began to beat her fists against the floor, Cassie turned to ask Brandon what she should do next.

He was already standing and gesturing for her to step aside.

His nearness, and the disturbing way he was studying her body, unnerved Cassie and she lowered her gaze from his commanding stare. She saw his erection pressing forcibly against the front of his trousers. Not wanting to witness his excitement, she deliberately looked away.

'You can remove the enema now,' he growled. 'It's my turn to deal with Faye.'

Thankful to be relieved from her duty, Cassie stepped away from the pair and took the drained enema bag back to the sink. She remained there watching Brandon and Faye's exchange from the furthest distance the room would allow.

'You should have remembered your place in the order of things,' Brandon declared. The tawse was in his hand and he aimed at the blonde's exposed buttocks. 'You should have remembered not to question my authority.'

'I'm sorry, master,' Faye sobbed.

'Sorry won't help you now,' he growled. He struck down hard against her backside; the blow landed fiercely, and left a blazing red line. 'Sorry won't help you one bit.'

Faye writhed against her restraints but it was impossible for Cassie to decide if she was watching the throes of agony or ecstasy. There was a frown of consternation on her lips but her face was flushed with excitement and her eyes shone brightly.

'You won't tell me how to deal with my property again, will you?' Brandon demanded. He slashed the tawse down twice: a stripe for each buttock. 'You won't be so presumptuous in future, will you?'

Cassie flinched as each blow landed.

'I'm sorry, master,' Faye moaned. 'It won't happen again.'

Brandon slapped the leather twice more against her buttocks. The blows were short, sharp and merciless, leaving Faye writhing in response. Brandon knelt down beside her and whispered something in her ear as he unfastened the restraints.

Cassie strained to hear what was being said but he kept his voice deliberately low and this time the acoustics in the room worked against her. When he finally moved his lips away from the blonde's ear, Cassie had no idea what he had said.

'Go on,' Brandon called, releasing the final clasp from Faye's ankle. 'Do as you've been instructed and stand by the door.'

Walking with measured slowness, clearly suffering from the effects of the enema, Faye made her way to the door. Her cheeks were florid with exertion and she held a hand over her stomach as though the weight of her palm was affording relief. Sweat gleamed against her bare body and made her look as though she had been cast from molten silver.

Watching her, Cassie wanted to sigh with gratitude. She was thankful the day's excursion into madness was finally drawing to a close and relieved she hadn't had to physically participate in too much of the unseemliness. Her thoughts had moved onto her intended escape and she wondered how much longer she would have to remain in Brandon's hateful house before she could finally make her break for freedom. She suspected the remaining time could be measured in minutes and that thought managed to banish the last vestiges of her desperation. Anxious to get her plan underway, desperate to leave Brandon and his army of obscenely willing subordinates, she started making her way to the door.

'Come here, girl,' Brandon snapped. 'I want you bent over this stool now.'

Unable to stop herself, Cassie shook her head.

'You won't be receiving the enema,' he coaxed. 'I just want you to know a small measure of the humiliation Faye's just had to endure. After all you've put her through, you can't refuse that, can you?'

Turning to look at Faye, Cassie was disappointed to find the blonde silently beseeching her. She didn't want to submit to Brandon but because Faye wasn't trying to argue her corner, Cassie couldn't see any way to resist.

'Come here and bend over the stool,' Brandon repeated. 'None of us are leaving this room until you've done that much.'

Faye opened her mouth as if to say something then stopped herself abruptly. Her thighs were squeezed tightly together and the hand she held against her stomach clawed viciously at the flesh as though she was trying to stave off impending cramps.

Not wanting to make her suffer any more than was necessary, and aware an argument with Brandon was likely to prolong their torment, Cassie went to the milking stool and assumed the same position. Trying to remain calm about what was happening, she made no protest as Brandon fastened the handcuffs around her wrists and ankles.

'What are you going to do with me?' Cassie whispered. She wasn't sure she wanted an answer but a part of her needed to know if he really did mean to make her suffer the same fate as Faye. Reluctant to voice that fear, scared it might put the idea into his head, she fought back the threat of tears and said the words again. 'Please tell me. What are you going to do with me?'

'Do with you?' Brandon repeated. He stood up and laughed before slapping her gently on the backside. The weight of his hand wasn't heavy but the playful blow was infuriatingly condescending. 'I don't think I'm going to do anything with you this evening. I've got a poker game to attend.'

She strained her neck in an effort to stare up at him. 'But . . .' she began. 'But, you can't leave me like this.'

'I'm always worried about the safety of new acquisitions when I can't watch over them,' Brandon explained. 'I think you should be secure in here while I have my game of poker.'

'You can't leave me like this,' Cassie wailed. She could see her hopes of escape were rapidly dwindling and all she could think to do was shout to try and get her opinion across. 'You can't leave me like this,' she insisted. 'You can't.'

'I think you'll find I can,' Brandon countered.

He reached down and stroked a stray lock of hair away from her cheek. The gesture was disturbingly close to affection and Cassie cringed at the thought of being the recipient of his fondness.

'Don't worry,' he assured her. 'I don't intend to leave you all night. If I'm in a good mood after the card game, I might come back up here.' Solicitously he asked, 'What do you think we could do if I did that?'

Not trusting herself to reply, not allowing herself to think about that horrific outcome, Cassie said nothing. Laughing, Brandon escorted Faye out of the room. Cassie heard him lock the door. She glanced at her reflection in the mirror and the sight of her bound, helpless body was enough to make her cry.

Six

Vicky walked at the back of the group, her despondency increasing with every step. Stephen Price led the tour of Harwood Manor telling John and the small team of executives how he expected them to develop his property. At first it had sounded like he wanted an exciting pleasure palace: something reminiscent of the exotic and erotic places Vicky had read about in the most adventurous of her favourite novels. Stephen mentioned themed torture chambers, group sex play areas and plans for a BDSM dungeon and Vicky felt thrilled and excited he was talking on a wavelength she could comprehend. But, as the tour progressed – and as Stephen started moaning on about building regulations, planning permissions and viable loopholes in the listed building consents – her enthusiasm began to wane. By the time he was leading them off the ground floor, discussing room layouts, soundproofing and period refurbishment, she wondered if she wasn't well and truly out of her depth. Her hopes of creating a proposal that allowed for so many complicated factors were looking more and more unlikely and she wondered what had ever possessed her to think she could do Cassie's job.

'Can you hear clearly enough back there?' John barked. 'This is very important stuff that Stephen's saying.'

Glumly, Vicky nodded. 'I can hear clearly enough.'

'You don't look like you're taking notes or anything,' John pressed. 'Are you listening to what he wants so you can iron out all the details for our proposal?'

'That's what I'm here for, isn't it?' she replied, shaping the words so she wasn't actually lying. 'That's why you asked me to come here today, isn't it?'

Seemingly satisfied, John turned his back on her and returned to the group as they made their way up the stairs. Not wanting to listen to any more of Stephen's prattling, uncomfortable with the interest she was cultivating from the bald-headed Scotsman in the party, and depressed by the discovery of her limitations, Vicky slipped through the open front doors and stepped out into the afternoon's sunshine.

She tried to console herself with the knowledge that she had almost taken Cassie's position as junior partner, but it wasn't enough to fend off her growing depression. All she could focus on was the fact she had only been asked to prepare one proposal and she had already realised it was more than she could manage. It made her feel like an incompetent failure.

Reaching for her purse, Vicky withdrew a packet of cigarettes and lit one. Greedily inhaling she allowed the smoke to calm her before bothering to take in her surroundings. Towering poplars lined the drive and the boundaries. A majestic fountain, either broken or simply not switched on, stood directly opposite the manor's main doors. Once the grounds had been properly landscaped the greenery would make for a pleasant, secluded vista and the fountain would become an elegant feature. But Vicky noticed none of this.

She was more startled to see a brunette standing beside the house's main door.

The woman watched her guardedly.

When their gazes connected Vicky felt like a switch had been flicked. The brunette had looked as still as a mannequin but, on meeting Vicky's eyes, she pushed herself from the wall and stepped boldly forward. 'May I have one of those?' she asked, pointing at Vicky's cigarettes.

She would have been strikingly attractive if not for the scowl that kinked her upper lip and wrinkled her nose. Wearing a black leather catsuit – its clinging cut accentuating her long legs and narrow waist, and the fabric stretched and shiny over her buttocks and breasts – she looked as though she was dressed for the Harwood Manor that Stephen wanted rather than the one he currently owned. Stepping from the shadows at the door, she moved closer to Vicky and held out her hand expectantly. 'May I have one of those cigarettes?' she repeated. 'Or, are you expecting me to say please?'

Intimidated, but trying not to show it, Vicky tested a carefree shrug and passed the pack. The brunette took one, placed it between her lips, then took the lit cigarette from Vicky's fingers. Lighting her own smoke from the tip of Vicky's she maintained eye contact and exhaled through her nose.

Vicky was unnerved by the woman's commanding presence and gingerly accepted the return of her own cigarette before releasing a pent-up breath. Held by the brunette's mesmerising gaze she realised her staring could easily be misconstrued as some sort of interest and quickly lowered her eyes. The woman wore a pair of stiletto sandals with cripplingly high heels and tight straps that disappeared beneath the cuffs of her catsuit's trousers. Vicky thought they were the sort of shoes a woman would leave on while making love and, because that idea was so explicit and conjured up such vivid imagery, she hurriedly looked away.

Silently, they both contemplated the dry fountain.

'Are you another property developer?' Vicky asked eventually.

The brunette snorted mirthless laughter. 'I'm not a property developer,' she said. 'I'm just property.' She wafted her half-smoked cigarette by way of greeting and said, 'My name's Laura. I've been watching you since you arrived and I think I know your secret.'

Vicky felt her smile falter. 'What secret? I don't have any secrets.'

'You're not a property developer, are you?'

Vicky bristled with indignation. 'That's why I'm here,' she said defensively. 'I'm the "V" in J & C Property Developments.'

Laura's brow tightened into a puzzled frown before she dismissed what Vicky had said as being irrelevant. 'You may be here as a property developer but I'll bet that's the secret you're keeping. You're no more a property developer than I am a bricklayer.'

Vicky blushed, contemplated arguing, then decided there would be no point. Laura spoke with such confidence that Vicky knew any lie would be seen. 'Maybe you're right,' she conceded grudgingly. 'But what business is it to you?'

'You're trying to impress that man you're with, aren't you? Is his name John?'

The burning at her cheeks turned crimson. Vicky drew on her cigarette and said, 'Do you make a point of watching everyone who comes here? You must have been looking at me quite intently to notice so much.'

Laura shook her head. 'Not really. You smile for him. You quicken your pace for him. For him you feign knowledge of things that clearly confuse you. I didn't need to watch that intently to notice those details. A cursory glance was enough for me to see that much.'

Vicky stabbed her cigarette against the wall of the manor and contemplated returning to the tour. From inside the house she could hear the constant drone of Stephen's voice and the rise and fall of questions from the rest of the party. They all seemed worlds away and she wondered if any of them had yet noticed she was missing. Although Laura seemed a little disconcerting –

she was uncommonly attractive and clearly trying to make some point that Vicky didn't think she would like – the brunette's chatter was distracting her from thoughts of personal failure. She wondered if she should tell Laura that she wasn't really interested in John, but more the position as his business partner. It crossed her mind there was no need to be defending herself but she didn't want the attractive and intimidating stranger thinking badly of her. She was also reluctant to leave Laura's company now the woman knew she was a fraud. The idea that Laura might go to John and expose Vicky's ignorance was enough to make her stay outside the manor's front doors and continue listening.

'What do you think it would take to win over his interest?' Laura asked thoughtfully. She talked as she smoked, almost as though she was conversing with herself rather than waiting for Vicky's input. 'I take it you've got this far by submitting yourself to him in some way or other. But it seems you think he wants more if he's going to keep you at his side. Are you trying to impress him by being his attentive aide?' She cast a sideways glance at Vicky then shook her head as if dismissing the notion. 'No. Of course not, otherwise you wouldn't be standing here, outside the damned building, and looking so despondent. Do you think landing the contract for developing this property might help?' She raised a speculative eyebrow and seemed encouraged by Vicky's vexed frown. 'Is that what you're doing? Have you come here because you think you have a chance of preparing a winning proposal for the Harwood Manor contract.'

Her observations were infuriatingly accurate and Vicky shook her head. 'I don't know who you are,' she began indignantly, 'but obviously you think you're cleverer than me. Perhaps I'm not the most proficient property developer in the world but I do intend to submit the best proposal I can.' Puffing out her chest with all the pride she could muster, she added, 'And I'll bet my proposal stands as good a chance as any at being accepted.'

Laura studied her sceptically. 'So, you wouldn't be interested if I said I could guarantee you the contract?'

Vicky sniffed dismissively. 'You couldn't manage that.'

Laura shrugged. 'I'm currently seconded to Mr Price's office. I'll be responsible for how he sees each of the proposals. I'm in a position where I can decide whose name to attach to the proposal that wins his interest. I think, considering I'm in such a trusted position, I could quite easily guarantee who's going to be awarded the contract.'

Vicky wanted to tell the woman she was bluffing but even if she had been able to find the words, she lacked the courage to say them. Excited by the idea she might still have a chance to rise to the position of junior partner, Vicky tried to contain her enthusiasm. 'Why would you do that? What would you expect in return?'

'I'd expect your co-operation on a couple of matters,' Laura replied. 'Why? Do you think this is an arrangement in which you might be interested?'

Vicky's thoughts came in a tumultuous rush. She had believed her chances of succeeding were gone but now Laura offered her the hope of securing the elusive Harwood contract. Unable to believe her luck had changed so dramatically, she shook her head giddily and said, 'Are you sure you can really do that?'

Laura sighed and dropped her cigarette to the floor, while stamping on it the muscle of her thigh was perfectly defined by the clinging leather of her catsuit. 'I've already answered that question once. I'm not one for repeating myself. If you're not prepared to discuss this properly, I might as well go back inside.' Without waiting for Vicky's response she started to walk through the main doors and into the manor.

Vicky placed a hand on the woman's arm. 'Please,' she begged. 'What do you want in exchange? I'm sure we can come to some arrangement. Just tell me and we can start to negotiate.'

Laura considered her with a twisted grin. If her expression had seemed haughty before it had only been a shadow of the superiority that now etched her features. 'I don't think you're ready to negotiate yet.'

'Of course I am,' Vicky insisted. She was speaking quickly, rushing the words together in her haste to make Laura see that she wanted to come to a deal. This was an opportunity she had never expected and she was determined to do whatever it took to make Laura see she was serious. 'What would you expect in return for doing this for me? A bribe? A percentage of the profit? I could organise whatever you want if you'd just tell me.'

Laura's smile shifted into something sly and unpleasant. She brushed Vicky's hand from her arm and pulled down the zip on her catsuit. Her cleavage was revealed and the swell of bare flesh was immediate and obvious. Both breasts spilled from their confines as though they had been straining to escape. 'Suck my nipple,' Laura growled thickly. 'Suck my nipple and show me you're serious about meeting my demands.'

Vicky took a step back. She was shocked by the woman's words and not sure how to respond. Laura's breasts were disturbingly inviting: round, swollen orbs tipped by dusky pink nipples that stood proud and erect. The temptation to do as she asked was profound but, nervous as to where it might lead, Vicky hesitated.

'Suck my nipple,' Laura insisted, 'or should I go back in there and see if anyone else is interested in taking up my generous offer? Your business partner will not want to continue with your services if he sees I can deliver more effectively than you.' Glancing at Vicky's unremarkable chest she sneered and added, 'There might be several areas where I can offer him more than you're able to provide.'

Vicky's hesitation continued, but only briefly. She didn't doubt John would show plenty of interest in Laura and she couldn't bear the idea of losing this last chance at success. Pushing her reservations aside she studied the woman's eyes for a hint of leniency. Seeing nothing but an expectant challenge, Vicky drew a nervous breath and stepped closer. Warily, she lowered her head to Laura's breast.

She could hear Stephen inside the house, droning on about the necessary renovations to the structure of the roof. The building's acoustics transported every syllable and she could even hear the Scotsman asking something about the listed building's greenback folder. Their conversation was monotonous and humdrum and a million miles away from the excitement flooding her veins.

Her bowels twisted deliciously and she shivered with apprehension. She was torn between the fear of discovery and the daring of what she was actually doing. As her mouth pressed around Laura's bare flesh the woman released a sigh of obvious pleasure. Her nipple stiffened against Vicky's tongue and this was enough to make Vicky's arousal heighten. Loosely embracing her, enjoying the sensation of placing her hands against Laura's narrow waist, Vicky suckled gently.

'Harder,' Laura barked. 'Suck harder.'

Anxious to do anything that would keep Laura in a mood for negotiation, Vicky did as she was told. She wanted to press her tongue against the alien flesh in her mouth – feel its dark pulse and savour its rigidity with her lips – but she knew Laura's instruction had to be obeyed. With infinite care, she sucked at the areola.

'I told you to do it harder,' Laura growled. 'Are you deaf or stupid?'

Vicky complied without thinking about what she was doing. She sucked so hard her cheeks dimpled. The nipple swelled inside her mouth and throbbed with a quivering undulation, as Laura released a sigh that sounded like a breath of relief.

'Stroke your tongue against it,' Laura whispered. 'Then catch the tip between your teeth and nibble.'

Her instructions were clipped and brooked no argument. Vicky did as she was told, hurrying so she didn't upset the tenuous balance of the brunette's mood. As much as she was trying not to think about what she was doing, she wished Laura wasn't making her rush. Ideally she would have taken the time to savour this forbidden indulgence, and the wickedness of that thought made her want to squirm. Her cleft was fetid with excitement and she could feel the familiar discomfort of her own nipples stiffening inside the restraints of her bra. The pulse behind her temples pounded with a familiar surge of anticipation and arousal.

'Now put your mouth over the other one,' Laura barked. 'Don't you know how to turn a woman on?'

Vicky moved her head to the other breast and continued to follow the orders. She tasted the fresh bud, suckled against it, then gnawed lightly as the bead of flesh thickened. Laura responded with a series of breathy sighs and Vicky wondered if the woman was enjoying the experience as much as she was. Clearly Laura had enjoyed female lovers before but this was something new to Vicky and the discovery that a woman's body could be so much fun was a startling revelation.

'Good girl,' Laura sighed. 'Just that little bit harder. Perhaps this will help you get closer to where I need you.'

Vicky was disquieted to see Laura pulling the zipper on her catsuit further down. The woman's breasts were already free and Vicky wondered why the brunette was exposing herself so obviously. It crossed her mind that Laura might be getting ready to make more daring instructions but, because she couldn't decide how she would respond to such demands, Vicky refused to speculate further.

'You seem like you might be able to discuss this on my terms,' Laura conceded. She only sounded slightly breathless but her eyes shone with a mixture of cruelty and excitement. 'Let's see if you're properly on my wavelength.'

She pulled the zipper of her catsuit down a further two inches until it reached her crotch. Both breasts were exposed and she was showing the flat expanse of her stomach. Beneath that, framed at the bottom of the V left by the zipper, lay a neatly trimmed thatch of dark curls.

Vicky frowned uncertainly. Her gaze faltered between Laura's commanding expression and the jet-black pubic hairs she was revealing. 'What are you asking me to do?'

'I'm asking you to eat my pussy,' Laura replied. 'You don't have an issue with that, do you?'

Vicky did have issues with the request but she couldn't picture herself raising any of them. She racked her brains, trying to think of a way to politely decline, but she knew inspiration wasn't going to come. Silently begging Laura, beseeching her cold expression with the most pitiful plea she could manage, Vicky chewed on her lower lip and hoped the woman would give her a reprieve.

'You don't have an issue with doing that, do you?' Laura repeated. She shrugged her shoulders from the catsuit and allowed it to fall to her ankles. She was disturbingly confident of the figure she presented and unmindful of the openness of their position. The tantalising length of her legs made her figure striking and, with the rounded swell of her breasts and the narrowness of her waist, Vicky had to admit Laura's suggestion made a very tempting offer.

Without hesitation she stepped closer and stroked one orb while sucking the other. Her fingertips teased the

100

shape and thrust of Laura's rigid nipple. Warming to what she was doing, Vicky began to press a series of kisses down the brunette's abdomen. She lowered herself to her knees and, as her lips got closer to the thatch of curls, she realised her heart had begun to beat faster. Exhilaration and a sense of discovery stopped her from judging whether she was right or wrong to be submitting. The only thought she was aware of was that this afternoon had proved far more exciting than she would ever have believed.

'Go on, you little tease,' Laura demanded. She sounded torn between anger and arousal. 'Go on and kiss me. You know you want to.'

Vicky's nose nuzzled through the curly hairs. She could detect the scent of musk and she was aware of Laura's pulse beating as frantically as her own.

'Go on,' Laura urged.

She was beginning to sound desperate with need and Vicky sympathised with her plight. She was just as eager to do Laura's bidding and in the thrall of the same powerful arousal. The fear of discovery remained at the forefront of her thoughts but, rather than hampering her excitement it was proving to be an additional spur. The idea of John, or any of the developers, coming out and discovering her and Laura was such a strong possibility she felt sure it was bound to happen. Picturing that moment she knew it would be wonderfully humiliating and didn't doubt it would prove to be a cathartic experience. Vicky felt certain that if John caught her with the brunette he would find the indiscretion exciting and might possibly try to involve himself in what was happening. He certainly wouldn't berate her with a diatribe that included the disparaging words, 'a time and a place for everything'.

'Kiss me, you tease,' Laura insisted. 'Go on and kiss me.'

Vicky knew, if she had chosen that moment to touch herself, she would have exploded with pleasure. She was kneeling on the floor, and it would only have taken a fraction of a second to raise the hem of her skirt and satisfy the gnawing ache of her throbbing clitoris, but she resisted the urge. As much as she craved the release an orgasm would give her, the thought of giving in to that need was dwarfed by the knowledge she had to satisfy Laura.

Tentatively, she placed her tongue against the brunette's sex lips.

Laura pushed herself back against the manor's wall. The muscles in her legs stiffened and she placed a fist inside her mouth. With her other hand she clapped non-rhythmically against the masonry.

Vicky saw all this from her place between the woman's legs. It was an unusual perspective and infinitely exciting. Laura's beautiful face, framed between her breasts, was flushed with the first throes of climax. Pleased with the effect she had generated, Vicky lapped more forcefully at her. The delicate lips bristled to her touch and the musk was a sweet and unexpected bonus. Relishing every nuance of the discovery, Vicky pressed a series of gentle kisses against the woman's sweat scented hole.

'Tongue me,' Laura gasped. The words were wrenched from her throat and spoken without care for anyone overhearing. 'Push your tongue deep inside. I want to feel how deep you can go.'

Only waiting for the instruction, Vicky eagerly strained her neck to do as she was asked. She had to place her hands on Laura's buttocks for balance and the sensation of the peachlike orbs against her fingertips was another indulgence in forbidden pleasures that threatened to prove too exciting. Daringly, she eased her tongue between the pussy lips and plundered the fragrant wetness of her sex.

A tight ring of muscle gripped her tongue, making the kiss a two-way exchange that was more exquisite than Vicky could have imagined.

'Deeper,' Laura growled.

Vicky ignored the instruction. She wanted to obey, and could have plunged her tongue deeper, but the thrust of Laura's clitoris kept pulsing against her upper lip. Knowing it was how she would want to be pleasured if their roles were reversed, knowing how much she now longed to have a woman's mouth between her legs, Vicky tested the tip of her tongue against the bead of flesh.

Laura drew startled breath.

Her gasp came so quickly it almost sounded like a shriek of pain. Encouraged, Vicky licked the bud for a second time and coaxed it from beneath its hood. She rubbed her lower lip against the sensitive bead and was delighted to feel its pulse shiver through her mouth.

Laura had been pressed hard against the wall before but now she seemed to be trying to push herself into the brickwork. The heels of her stiletto sandals ground dust from the stone floor as she held herself taut in reluctant acceptance of the pleasure.

Revelling in the discovery of her ability to please, Vicky gripped the woman's backside tightly and began to devour her sex. She licked greedily at the wettening lips and alternated her kisses from tentative pecks at the clitoris to penetrating lunges with her tongue. Concentrating hard on what she was doing, and savouring every moment, she wasn't surprised to hear Laura stifle a cry of unbridled elation. Her voice spiralled up to a scream of absolute satisfaction that was loud enough to startle a handful of birds from the surrounding poplars.

'Enough!' Laura gasped, pushing Vicky away.

She looked to be in the throes of a pleasure that was both undeniable but only grudgingly accepted. Shivering obviously, losing her ice-maiden composure for the briefest of instants, she stood motionless as the orgasm passed through her. Her cruel smile wavered as she struggled to catch breath and she glared at Vicky as though offended by the pleasure that had been inflicted.

'More than enough,' she said firmly. Her glacial expression melted and, laughing darkly to herself she said, 'You've proved you're willing to discuss this properly. I think we can come to an arrangement.'

Vicky remained on the floor and stared doubtfully up at her. While she had been doing Laura's bidding there had been a pleasure in not thinking about what might be expected of her. Now the moment was passed she wondered if she might have committed herself to give more than she was able. It was a depressing worry and made her wish she could spend her life in sexual servitude rather than having to face all the infuriating problems that life kept throwing at her. 'What is it you want?' she asked warily.

Laura shook her head. 'Don't sound so worried,' she grinned. 'My demands won't be as bad as you're fearing.'

'But –'

Laura held up a silencing finger. 'You'll be awarded the contract. I'll see you receive a copy of the successful proposal so you can pretend to John that it's all your own handiwork. But I'll have it amended to include one small, non-negotiable clause.'

'What clause? What are you talking about?'

Laura shook her head. She fastened the zipper on her catsuit and shook her hair back into place. Staring up at her, Vicky thought the woman looked as resplendent as she had before they became acquainted and she wondered if she could ever carry herself with such composure. She watched Laura light two fresh cigarettes and accepted one as it was passed to her. With something akin to pleasure she saw Laura's scarlet lipstick circled the filtered tip and it gave her a sexual thrill to suck on the end. It was almost as though she was enjoying a kiss with the woman.

'I'll tell you all about it when we next speak,' Laura explained. 'It's nothing that should trouble you to any great deal.'

Vicky nodded as though she understood exactly what Laura was saying even though the woman's words mystified her. Drawing on her cigarette, she found it difficult to think of anything except how pleasant it was staring up and admiring Laura, and how much she wanted to kiss her again.

Laura cocked her head to one side then glanced down at Vicky's kneeling figure. 'I'd suggest you get off your knees now,' she whispered. 'It sounds like your partner is coming down the stairs and I don't think you want him to catch you down there, do you?'

Vicky pulled herself from the floor and brushed the dust and debris from her knees. She had only just managed to straighten herself when John appeared in the doorway. He glanced curiously at Laura, then fixed his glare on Vicky.

'I've been searching every-bloody-where for you,' he exclaimed. 'Did you get lost? Have you missed what Stephen's been saying? This is the contract that will either make or break our business. Haven't I bloody told you that already?'

He sounded on the verge of anger and Vicky contemplated him with growing anxiety. His temper could be volatile and, whenever he was angry, John had a habit of saying the most hurtful things.

'You shouldn't be talking to her that way,' Laura said quietly.

John sneered at the brunette. 'And what the hell would you know about this?'

Laura shrugged. 'Vicky's just been telling me about the proposal she's going to prepare for Stephen. I think she has a good grasp of what's required. The way she's sounded her ideas against me makes me think she's onto a winner.'

John glanced from Laura to Vicky, then back to Laura. He looked unable to accept the idea of Vicky being the subject of praise and made no attempt to disguise his lack of credulity. 'Who the hell are you? And what the hell do you know about this?'

Laura glanced slyly at Vicky then extended a hand. 'My name's Laura. I currently work in Mr Price's office.'

Shaking her hand, unsure he had heard her praise correctly, John said, 'Are you telling me Vicky has got some good ideas?'

'I'm telling you Vicky has some *winning* ideas,' Laura insisted. She smiled with surprising warmth and added, 'Unless I'm very much mistaken, I think her name will be on the proposal that Stephen finally selects.'

Blushing at this praise, Vicky lowered her gaze demurely to the floor. When she dared to risk a sideways glance she was thrilled to find John staring at her with something that looked uncannily like respect.

Seven

The clamp bit hard against Cassie's nipple. It held her flesh with all the delicacy and finesse of a steel bolt. She regarded Faye with wide-eyed horror, and shook her head in an effort to refute the enormity of the pain. Unexpected tears welled in the corners of her eyes and wetted her cheeks as she tried to blink them away.

'Stay still,' Faye warned her tonelessly. 'I need to fasten the other clamp.'

Cassie started to say no but she knew no one was listening. Faye had cupped her orb and spread her palm around the swell of the breast so the nipple peeped from between her thumb and index finger. It should have been an asexual contact and Cassie told herself she wasn't responding to the woman's intimate touch. But it might have been easier to believe if her nipple hadn't stood erect, as though it was excited by Faye's silky caress. Flushing furiously, unable to decide if she was more troubled by pain or embarrassment, Cassie studied the scratched and timeworn surface of the card table.

With practised ease, Faye fastened the second clamp into place. The jaws closed around their prize and tightly gripped the pulsing thrust of Cassie's bud. The pain was unbearably acute; then it grew sharper.

Cassie chugged breath.

Her eyes were open so wide the tears could no longer form but it didn't make the suffering any more tolerable. Her anguish just seemed to get worse until, eventually, it became intolerable. 'I can't go through with this,' she gasped. 'It hurts too much.'

Faye checked the clamps were secure, tested the chains that dangled from each of them, and then returned to her chair. Ignoring Cassie, she glanced at the others and asked, 'Are we all ready to begin?'

The four of them were sitting in the claustrophobic confines of the Friday night retreat. It was an internal room without windows and, because Brandon insisted the electric light fittings weren't allowed to be used, it was perpetually held in midnight shadows. A flickering candle in the centre of the table provided the only illumination and its flame threatened to expire beneath each of Cassie's gasped exhalations. Sharing a cigar, Sarah and Marion sat to Cassie's right while Faye made herself comfortable in the remaining seat to her left. There was an air of thick expectancy around the table and, with Faye's question, all eyes turned to Cassie.

'I can't do this,' she said miserably. 'I just can't.'

'If you're ready to begin you can deal,' Faye told her.

Cassie shook her head and wet her lips so she could voice her denial. The deck of cards was in her hand, where it seemed to have been for the last four days, but she still believed the task was beyond her.

Since the early hours of Saturday morning she had been familiarising herself with the feel of the cards and learning subtle artifices to cover and conceal her intended trickery. Her fingers had begun to ache with the unfamiliar exertion but, once she had overcome that discomfort, Cassie had discovered a surprising skill to deal from the bottom of the deck. Remembering the way her hands had first hurt she realised that ache had been nothing more than a minor irritation compared to the agony she was currently suffering. 'Please take this off,' she said, nodding down at her chest. 'I can't cope with it. I can't cope with any of this. It's too much.'

Beneath the clamps hung a suspended tray. It wasn't the same one she had seen Faye wearing on her first night at Brandon's but Cassie could see it was a similar contraption. Where the original one had been fashioned for someone with pierced nipples, this version was fitted with clamps instead of clips. It was designed to be attached directly to the dealer regardless of whether or not they had appropriate body jewellery. But, the pressure of the merciless jaws, and the weight of the chains and the tray, were proving to be an unbearable combination. As much as Cassie tried to close her mind to the torment, the tugging at her sensitive flesh was an inarguable constant and it was impossible to think beyond the pain.

'Go ahead and deal,' Faye encouraged. 'You need to practise this if you want to get out of here. We only have a couple more days before Friday is on us again and you need to be up to speed by then. We're playing five card draw, and using a straight deck with two jokers.'

Wanting to argue, but knowing the blonde was right, Cassie steeled herself against the discomfort and began to shuffle the cards. The practice had become an integral part of her residence at Brandon's home. In the early hours of Saturday morning Faye had released Cassie from punishment room number three and suggested a plan. Because it seemed like the most promising way of making an escape, Cassie had readily gone along with the idea. But now, as the reality of what she was attempting began to sink in, Cassie wondered if she was trying to do something that went beyond her abilities.

Recognising her defeatist attitude for what it was, and unwilling to submit without a struggle, she forced her features into a mask of equanimity. The sanguine smile remained on her face as she tossed cards to the three women but the expression felt forced and strained. The biting clamps made her nipples poignantly aware of each movement and she couldn't help but feel touched by a shiver of unwanted arousal. The pain was almost a welcome distraction because it stopped her from dwelling on the idea that the experience wasn't wholly unpleasurable.

After dealing the last of the cards she slammed the deck down and groaned. 'I don't think I can do this,' she gasped. The words came out as a depressing revelation but she felt sure it was true. If she couldn't manage this one task she knew she was going to remain as Brandon's property until someone else decided her fate but even that lack of control seemed more appealing than putting herself through the torture she was currently suffering. She shook her head as though disagreeing with her previous statement and said, 'No. I was wrong. I'm *sure* I can't do this.'

'You've been practising palming for hours upon end,' Faye reminded her. 'And I'm not trying to flatter you, but I've never seen anyone pick it up so fast.'

Cassie smiled weakly. She could have told Faye she had probably never met anyone with as strong a motivation as she had but she knew that would have sounded contentious. For some reason Cassie couldn't understand Faye was content with her life as Brandon's property and the blonde took umbrage at any remark directed against the master.

'The three of us have all agreed to help you in one way or another,' Faye continued, 'and we've all taught you our own personal tips and tricks.'

'That's right,' Sarah chimed in.

She passed her cigar to Marion, brushed the ginger flecks of her fringe to one side, and leant across the table. Her breasts were clearly visible through her body stocking and Cassie could see the redhead's nipples were taut and excited. It was an unnerving vision and Cassie couldn't decide if the woman's arousal was symptomatic of being in the poker room, or if she was gleaning pleasure from the torture she was helping to inflict.

'Marion told you Brandon always flicks the ash from his cigar when he has a good hand. I told you how John changes the topic of conversation depending on what he's holding. We've all been trying to help and you've been picking things up ever so well.'

Their praise sounded genuine enough but it was obvious they were missing the point. Gritting her teeth together, Cassie hissed, 'I'm not talking about whether or not I can rig a deal. I've followed everything you've all said and I think I've learnt pretty well. Did anyone see me doing anything untoward during that last deal?'

She glanced around the table to be met by Sarah's puzzled frown. Marion shook her head while Faye shrugged and said, 'No.'

'I didn't see you cheating,' Marion admitted.

Sarah said, 'Me neither.'

Cassie pointed at Sarah. 'You're holding a full house but it's only threes and sixes.' Nodding at Marion she said, 'You've got a pair of kings and I'll be giving you a third when you change cards.' Turning to Faye she grinned with undisguised triumph and said, 'You're holding the king, queen, jack and ten of hearts. I'll throw you a joker once you've put your ante in.'

Sarah and Marion exchanged hesitant glances. They showed each other the hands they had been dealt then laughed delightedly.

Faye didn't bother looking at her cards. 'If it's the pain of the nipple clamps . . .'

Through gritted teeth Cassie said, 'I can put up with the pain.' She didn't want to talk about how the clamps were affecting her.

Faye shook her head and looked mystified. 'Then, if it's not the pain, and if you can deal so adeptly, what makes you think you can't go through with this? It seems to me you have all the skills necessary to cheat yourself out of here.'

Cassie lowered her gaze and studied the surface of the card table. It was a dusky black shadow in the sputtering candlelight but it was preferable to look at that rather than meet the disapproving frown that she knew would twist Faye's features. Taking a deep breath, then speaking so softly it was almost as though she was whispering the words to herself, Cassie said, 'I can't let John see me like this.'

No one said a word and Cassie thought their silence was more damning than any discourse might have been. It was embarrassing enough to be naked in the room in the company of three other women. She had never been an exhibitionist of any description and, even though they had been constant companions for the last eleven days, Cassie still remained uncomfortable sharing her nudity with the rest of Brandon's property. The idea of having to display herself so openly at the poker game was mortifying enough but, when she pictured the scene with John there, Cassie knew she was attempting something she couldn't manage. The knowledge that he would see her nudity, and the fear he might make fun or could even be aroused, were concepts she didn't dare to consider. Her cheeks blazed at the thought of being caught in such a humiliating situation and she shook her head determinedly. 'I simply can't go through with it,' she insisted. 'I simply can't.'

Faye shrugged. She collected the playing cards from Sarah and Marion and pushed them back into Cassie's hand. 'If it's as simple as that then there's no point in us continuing, is there? I have duties I need to conclude and so do the others.' With laconic ease she pushed her seat back and started to walk away from the table.

It wasn't the response Cassie had expected and she stared with slack-jawed incredulity as Faye made for the door. A part of her wondered if the svelte blonde was using some sort of reverse psychology but Cassie could see she wasn't going to get the chance to call the woman's bluff. Knowing she would have to endure the embarrassment of having John see her in this demeaning position, aware that all she could do was try and find some way to cope with the shame, Cassie cleared her throat. 'All right,' she decided. 'We can practise some more and I'll try and get myself in the right frame of mind for the game.'

'Don't bother,' Faye said idly. She stood close to the door, shrouded by shadows and making no attempt to return to her seat. 'If you think you'll have difficulty overcoming the hurdle of having John see you at the card table, you won't be able to manage the other things that will happen during the poker game.'

Cassie frowned. Her bowels twisted with consternation as she tried to understand this new development and a fresh spike of fear twisted in her guts. 'You never mentioned *other things* before,' she said thickly. 'What *other things* are likely to happen during the poker game?'

Faye stepped closer and her grin was illuminated by the candlelight. The wavering flame made her eyes sparkle with malicious glee. 'Most of the players Brandon invites believe it's customary to tease the dealer,' she began. 'Before the game begins they try to arouse her; they try to torment her; and they like to watch her squirm.' She breathed the words in a husky whisper. 'Do you think you can put up with that? Or is that another hurdle that you're going to run away from?'

Cassie was struggling to find a reply when Faye reached out to touch her. Her fingertips traced the lower swell of Cassie's breast before rubbing against the chain that dangled from her left nipple. She didn't tug or pull but the slight shift in the weight of the clamp sent searing bolts of discomfort through Cassie's orb. She stiffened against the rekindled pain and almost dropped the cards she was holding.

From Cassie's right Sarah inched closer.

Cassie was wondering what the woman was doing but the question was answered before she could ask. A hand traced against her inner thigh, stroking gently upwards and pressing more firmly as it crept to the top of her leg. The redhead stretched out one finger and Cassie could feel her pussy lips being lightly brushed. The shock of being touched was augmented by the disturbing tickle of pleasure that shivered through her sex.

She studied Sarah uneasily.

The redhead smiled coolly back at her.

Movement at the corner of her eye made Cassie realise Marion had left the table. The brunette stepped gracefully behind her, then lifted Cassie's ponytail to expose the back of her neck. She placed a whisper soft kiss against the skin and, with leisurely haste, began to touch her lips against the jut of each vertebra. The effect was intense and exciting. Cassie had never been struck by an arousal that hit with such demanding force and the exhilaration left her breathless.

'I don't . . .' she began. The words came out in a husky croak and she swallowed twice before daring to continue. 'I mean, I'm not sure if . . .'

'We're only doing this lightly,' Faye explained. 'But we all know what we're doing.' As she spoke she tugged at the clamp holding Cassie's left nipple. 'Leave us to continue for five minutes and you'll have come.'

Cassie allowed the words to echo through her mind knowing Faye was stating a fact. She wondered if it had been said so she could ask the woman to stop, or if she was expected to wait and see if the prediction was proved correct. While she was dwelling on the choices a fresh burst of pain exploded from the jaws of the nipple clamps. This time it was a seasoning to her pleasure. The sharp discomfort made Cassie aware of sensations that might quickly have become bearable or common-place. Her body was now swathed with a slick coating of sweat and every nerve receptor began to tingle in anticipation of a greater delight.

'We're only teasing you gently,' Sarah agreed.

Her index finger rubbed against the split of Cassie's pussy and the labia began to melt beneath the redhead's touch. The woman's hand was clammy and warm against her thigh and Cassie held herself immobile for fear she might show some reaction that seemed like a wanton response. She wasn't entirely sure why the women were teasing her but she was even more confused about whether or not she wanted them to continue. A part of her was repulsed that she was allowing them to touch her so intimately but that rational voice was drowned out by her need to experience more.

Marion spoke from behind her, whispering between each light kiss. 'There won't be any of this subtlety on Friday night,' she said sadly. Her hair trailed between Cassie's shoulder blades and the light caress tickled exquisitely. 'But that doesn't mean they won't arouse you.'

Cassie swallowed before speaking. Every pore on her body was responding to some sort of stimulus and the distraction made clarity of thought as simple as translating quantum mechanics into Esperanto. She tried to remember what she had been about to say but couldn't think past her need for Sarah to continue sliding a finger against her pussy. The wet friction was a wonderful sensation.

'What are they likely to do with me?' she asked eventually.

Faye shook her head. 'If you don't think you can cope with this much, you don't really want to know.'

'I have to know,' Cassie said. She held herself rigid. 'If I'm going to put myself through it, I have to know. What are they likely to do with me?'

Faye moved her hand from the nipple clamp and gestured for Sarah and Marion to step back. The two women obliged her as eagerly as they would have obeyed Brandon.

Unnerved, Cassie switched her worried gaze from one woman to another.

Faye tugged her arm, encouraging Cassie to leave her seat. 'They'll start with a traditional warning, to stop you from cheating.'

As she spoke, she pointed to the chair and Cassie realised she was expected to kneel on it. The action of standing had made the tray begin to sway and each movement wrought exquisite bolts of agony through her tortured nipples. The pain was almost enough to make her calm at the prospect of bending over the chair's high back to expose herself to the three women.

'They'll spank you,' Sarah said, smacking the palm of her hand against Cassie's backside.

The slap was only light but, because it landed on bare flesh, and because it came from a hand that had been pleasuring her a moment earlier, Cassie thought it was peculiarly effective. She gasped and tried to hold herself still for fear of making the suspended tray move any more than it was already.

'They won't just use their hands,' Faye growled.

To illustrate her point she delivered a stinging blow across Cassie's buttocks. The shock of pain was gigantic and, long after the impact was over, Cassie could feel a burning sting blazing across her rear cheeks. She blinked to clear fresh tears from her eyes and glanced over her shoulder to see what Faye had used. Nonchalantly staring back at her, the blonde held a long leather belt in her hand. She smiled into Cassie's startled features and thrashed the strap against her a second time.

The belt bit hard, striping her with an agony she hadn't expected, but Cassie didn't think that was the worst aspect of the punishment. The most unsettling part was the fact that Faye had continued to smile as she delivered the blow. She was on the verge of protesting, ready to tell them they had convinced her this was truly beyond her abilities, when Faye struck the belt against her for a third time.

'And they won't just be leathering your backside,' Marion added.

With sounds from the outside world lost beneath the onrushing roar of adrenaline that pounded through her temples, Cassie barely heard her. She was trying to hold herself rigid but the torment made her body quiver spasmodically. Each jerk brought her closer to a realm of uncontrollable throes and she feared, if she gave herself over to that void of release, it might prove too tempting for her to want to escape.

'They won't just be leathering your backside,' Marion repeated. 'They'll be taking advantage of you.'

A hand clutched her buttock – fingertips scoured against the blazing red weal Faye had inflicted – and etched fresh pain from each cheek. Cassie thought this was the apex of her torment until slippery fingers teased against her cleft.

Two fingers plundered her sex, pushing the pussy lips aside and sliding easily into her warmth. Her inner muscles clenched hungrily around the intruder and delicious ripples bristled throughout her body.

'I don't –' she started.

'You won't be permitted to speak while you're dealing,' Faye barked.

A second hand clutched Cassie's backside. As before, fingernails were raked over the blazing lines that striped her buttocks. The pain was sudden and all-consuming and, before its burning agony had diminished, Cassie realised it was also making her acutely aware of every sensation.

While the fingers continued squirming inside her pussy another pressed at her anus. She didn't think the muscle was going to relent and she quietly prayed it would resist the pressure but, whoever was trying to slide their finger there was clearly determined. With only a little force they managed to push into her forbidden hole.

Cassie screamed. The cry echoed miserably around the black room and ended abruptly when a hand slapped her face.

'They won't tolerate noises like that,' Faye hissed, 'and neither will we.'

Mumbling an apology, unsure if her tears were caused by misery, confusion or elation, Cassie remained still as the fingers were dragged from her holes. She was pulled from the chair, turned around, and pushed back into a sitting position. At first she thought the candle had been extinguished, then realised she had been closing her eyes in the hope she might be able to shut out the reality of what was happening.

'Do you think you can cope with that?' Faye whispered.

She tapped Cassie's hand and, without needing to be told, Cassie realised she was expected to deal. Blithely, she tossed cards across the table to each of the women.

'Do you think you can cope with that sort of introduction to the evening?' Faye pressed. 'It's important that we know before we begin.'

'I don't know,' Cassie groaned honestly. 'But I have to try, don't I?'

Faye nodded at Sarah and, acting on the silent instruction, the redhead reached for Cassie's right breast. Her fingertips toyed with the clamp and she teased it back and forth. Her smile twisted with malicious glee as Cassie sobbed her way through the remainder of the deal.

'What's your gameplan for Friday night?' Faye pressed.

She was treating Cassie's left nipple to the same torment Sarah was inflicting from her right. Every twist and turn of the clamp sparked new explosions from the aching nub and Cassie wondered how she was managing to cope with the trauma.

'Tell us what you've planned to do, just so we know you haven't forgotten.'

Cassie swallowed before replying and tried taking a deep breath to clear her thoughts. 'I'll deal fairly straight for most of the evening,' she gasped. 'Either Marion or Sarah will be in the role of candleholder and they'll give me a signal when it's time to end the game.'

Faye nodded.

She rolled the leather belt she had been holding into a loop and dropped it onto Cassie's tray. The additional weight was further torture.

'If they decide to end the game too early Brandon may elect to use another candle,' Faye explained. 'If they leave it too late, the candleholder might not have a say over when the game should end. What signal are they going to give?'

'They're going to say the words "Please Master Brandon",' Cassie remembered.

'And why will that be different to anything else they might say?'

Cassie racked her brains for an answer. Thinking past all the distractions was nearly impossible but, after a heroic struggle she said, 'Normally they would just say, "Please Master," or "Please Sir". "Please Master Brandon," will be subtly different and shouldn't arouse suspicion.' She finished tossing out the last of the cards and slammed the deck face down on the table.

'What do you do when you hear those words?' Faye asked. She moved her hand away from Cassie's breast and slapped Sarah's finger so the redhead would stop teasing.

'When I hear the words "Please Master Brandon", I do the main deal of the night,' Cassie replied.

'And what is the main deal of the night?'

Cassie drew a shivering breath. Now the two women had stopped tormenting her nipples she felt more able to concentrate on what was expected of her. Remembering the plan Faye had outlined, mentally visualising every detail of the scenario they had set up, she said, 'I throw Brandon three of a kind – kings. When he changes cards I give him the fourth king.'

'Why do you need to do that?' Faye asked.

'Because, the better his hand, the more likely he is to start gambling his staff.'

'What will you give to Stephen?'

'Stephen will get two pairs. That will keep him in the pot until the call, but he'll fold early in the bidding once he's changed cards.'

'And what are you going to give to John?'

Faye's questions were coming thick and fast and Cassie was able to answer without thinking. They had been over this so many times she didn't need to concentrate on what was expected of her – she only needed the opportunity to put the plan into action.

'John's going to get three aces at first,' she grinned. 'He'll be worried that Stephen is holding onto four cards but the two jokers I give him should assuage his fears.'

Faye studied her solemnly. 'And, do you think you can manage to do that deal while you're being teased and tormented?'

Cassie returned the woman's stern frown. 'Look at your cards.'

Faye glanced at the hand she had been dealt, and smiled at the three aces and two jokers.

'She bloody did it!' Sarah exclaimed gleefully. 'I've got four kings.'

To Cassie's right Sarah and Marion exploded in a fit of elated giggles but she kept her gaze fixed firmly on Faye. The blonde's verdict on whether or not she was capable was the only opinion that mattered to Cassie.

'You've learnt well,' Faye decided. 'I just hope escape is what you really want.'

Cassie frowned, ready to ask how Faye could say such a thing. Before she got the chance to speak, a draught from the door opening extinguished the room's candle. Brandon stood silhouetted in the frame, his tawse held threateningly in one hand.

'What the hell is going on here?' he demanded.

Cassie stammered to find a response but her thoughts were too jumbled. Before she could reply Marion was collecting the cards while Sarah deftly uncoupled the clamps from Cassie's breasts. The darkness hid what they were doing but, just in case there was a chance of him seeing something he shouldn't, Faye stepped forwards to meet the master.

'You said I was allowed to teach the newcomer how to deal,' she reminded Brandon. 'I've been preparing her for Friday evening's game.'

Brandon glared at Faye. 'I want you to go over to Stephen Price's office and relieve Laura from her secondment there.'

Faye started to protest but Brandon pushed her to one side. He snapped his fingers and pointed at Sarah and Marion before saying, 'You two. You're needed in the kitchens.' Stepping closer to Cassie he said thickly, 'And, as for you, there's no need for you to learn how to deal. I have another duty that you're going to perform. Come with me.'

Without waiting for her acquiescence, he pulled Cassie from her chair and dragged her out of the poker room.

Eight

During the short trip through the house, Cassie didn't know what was going to happen but Brandon managed to confound all her expectations. He took her along the main corridor, past the house's double doors, and into his office. He pushed her into the room, slammed the door closed and said, 'Sit down.'

She was amazed to see he was pointing at a dining table. Covered with a starched white linen cloth, laid with polished crystal, delicate crockery and gleaming silverware, it looked like the setting for a romantic meal for two. The lighting was sedate and a fluted vase in the centre of the table held a single red rose. The development was so totally unexpected Cassie had to be told a second time before she did as he instructed. Even then she wasn't entirely sure she wasn't dreaming.

She could see the table was set for only two people and she watched with growing unease as Brandon settled himself into the seat opposite. He had said he had a duty for her to perform and she wondered how unpleasant it was going to be. Considering the trouble he had obviously gone to in preparing such an ambient setting, she suspected it was likely to be bad.

'Dinner will be served shortly,' Brandon said gruffly. 'Would you care for a glass of wine before we begin?'

Unable to think clearly, not sure this could really be happening, Cassie could only nod. She watched him pour two Rieslings and, still unable to believe the comparative luxury of her surroundings, she took a tentative sip from the glass he handed her. The sweet taste, and the warming effect of the alcohol, served to remind Cassie it had been several days since she last enjoyed the simple pleasure of a glass of wine. She wondered what else she had forgotten since her imprisonment.

'You've been my property for more than a week now,' Brandon said, leaning back in his seat. When he wasn't shouting the gruffness of his accent mellowed and Cassie found she could understand his Celtic dialect with perfect clarity. 'You've been my property for more than a week and we still haven't found a use for you, have we?'

Cassie said nothing. She was loathe to agree that she was his property and she guessed he was building to a point. It seemed safest to wait and listen to what he had to say before embarking on any sort of confrontation. Sipping the wine slowly, hoping the drink wasn't going to affect her judgement, she regarded him coolly and waited for him to continue.

'You know what the rest of the staff do for me here, don't you?'

While his tone was light and carefree, Cassie noticed he was watching her with meticulous scrutiny. She believed his casual attitude to be false and guessed he was acting to lull her into a false sense of security. Determined she wouldn't reveal anything about herself, she maintained her silence.

'I suppose you could work as a relief when one of my staff needs a break,' he said, 'but I think you're capable of a more stimulating, individual role. I wonder if you might have a job skill you've been keeping secret from me.'

She stiffened in her chair and tried to remember the sanguine mask she had worn while dealing cards. More than any moment before, Cassie realised this was the time when she needed to be wearing a poker face.

'When I first interviewed you, you told me you had no useful abilities,' Brandon reminded her. 'Perhaps, now you've had a chance to see how I can find a use for anyone, you might have re-thought your initial judgement.'

'Why won't you just let me go?' Cassie asked. 'You can't seriously believe I'm your property, can you? Why don't we just apologise for inconveniencing each other over the last eleven days?' She put down her wine glass and extended a hand across the table. 'We can shake, tell each other this has been a silly misunderstanding, then you can let me leave and I can go back to my life in the real world.'

Brandon ignored her offered hand. Instead he held up a silencing finger and shook his head. 'Your leaving here is a moot subject,' he said crisply. 'Faye has harangued me long and hard about your suitability and I've declared a moratorium on the entire subject. She seems to think you're not a natural submissive and this environment is causing you genuine distress.' A dry smile curled his lips as he added, 'I know differently.'

'But –' Cassie began.

He held up his finger again and she knew there was no point in pressing her luck. Cassie slumped back into her seat.

A knock on the door heralded the arrival of dinner and Cassie wasn't entirely surprised to see it being served by Sarah and Marion. They were both dressed in the revealing uniform Brandon insisted his waitresses wore: fishnet stockings with a short black skirt and a snug fitting top that left nothing to the imagination. Neither seemed troubled by the way the costumes exposed them and they went dutifully about the task of serving the dinner. Cassie supposed she could almost comprehend their lack of shame because she was sitting at the table naked and was no longer bothered about covering herself. In Brandon's home, gratuitous nudity was just another aspect of everyday life.

Playfully, Brandon slapped Sarah's backside when she stood beside him to straighten his serviette. Rather than berate the master, she smiled warmly as though grateful for his attention. Brandon's hand remained on Sarah's buttock and Cassie was sickened to see him crudely caressing between her legs. She watched him penetrate the redhead, sliding his fingers deep into her hole, and heard Sarah sigh with obvious satisfaction. When Brandon withdrew his fingers they were sticky with remnants of her excitement. He raised both fingers to Sarah's mouth and, as the pair maintained eye contact, the redhead licked her wetness from his hand.

Appalled, Cassie wanted to look away but the exchange was riveting.

'Don't offend him,' Marion whispered in Cassie's ear.

Cassie held herself rigid, aware the brunette had manipulated herself so she could discreetly pass on the warning. She knew how much the woman was risking in talking to her so covertly and she was almost choked by a wave of gratitude.

'If Faye isn't here to sway the master's opinion we can't guarantee you'll be dealing on Friday night. It's vital you do whatever it takes to make him let you deal.'

Cassie understood what was being said but it was difficult to keep her mind on the importance of the words. She was mesmerised by the pleasure Sarah was receiving from licking her own juices. Her ripe lips worked their way up and down Brandon's fingers and she released soft, grateful moans each time he let her suck. She wondered if Sarah was deliberately distracting the master, so she and Marion could talk, but the interaction between the pair seemed so natural Cassie was more inclined to believe they always behaved with the same lurid affection.

'If you don't manage to deal this Friday you might have to spend another week here,' Marion hissed, 'and we're all aware you don't want that.'

'You're not talking to my dinner guest are you, Marion?' Brandon asked. The clipped authority in his voice implied a lot more than was actually spoken. Cassie realised that, if Brandon did think the brunette had been breaking his rules, he would make Marion regret her transgression.

Sarah stepped back as though she had been stung. She passed a nervous glance between Brandon and Marion.

Marion flushed guiltily and showed Brandon the platter she was serving from. 'The kitchen staff said you were entertaining a guest,' she explained. 'I was asking her if she wanted any of the vegetables.'

Brandon looked sceptical. 'Leave the meal, piss off and wait outside for when we're finished,' he growled. 'We are in the middle of an important discussion and you two are proving to be an unnecessary distraction.'

Dutifully dismissed, both women rushed from the room.

Cassie felt her spirits plummet when she heard the door slam closed behind them. The meal looked sumptuous and inviting but her appetite had gone. After all that had happened that morning, the unprecedented excitement in the poker room and now her arousal at watching Brandon and Sarah, the desire to eat was low on her list of requirements. Far more importantly she needed to know why her thoughts had become so wayward and what it was about the environment of Brandon's home that was fuelling her lascivious appetite.

'I can't keep you around just for decoration.' Brandon spoke around a mouthful of steak and gestured with his fork for emphasis. 'I have prettier possessions who could fill that role far more ably, but I do intend keeping you. All we need to establish is what position you're going to have.'

She thought of making a glib comment, suggesting she should test drive his vehicles, or be trusted to do the shopping for the house, but she didn't think the flippancy would do her any good. Remembering her escape plan, and still conscious of Marion's hissed warning, Cassie tried to sound casual as she said, 'Faye's taught me how to deal. I could do that.'

He waved the suggestion away with his fork. 'Faye's a good enough dealer. She doesn't need an understudy.'

'But –'

He raised a finger and Cassie was disgusted to find herself responding to the gesture. She wondered how he had managed to wield such control over her.

'There's a choice of two positions open to you,' Brandon said quietly. 'I'll leave the final decision up to you but I know which one I'd like you to assume.'

'What positions are those?' she asked, staring at her untouched plate.

He grinned and cut another chunk of steak from his dish. 'The first choice is: you can become one of my house sluts. You can become a piece of my property that's there as a sexual plaything for the use of me, or any of my guests.'

Cassie shivered at the idea, disgusted to realise the suggestion sparked an excited warmth.

'Try not to look so revolted,' Brandon warned her. 'Pretence doesn't really suit you.' She opened her mouth to argue but he raised his finger again and it silenced her rebuttal. 'Did you know the mirror in punishment room three is a two-way glass?' he asked innocently. 'Did you know I went in there after tying you up last Friday night? I spent a fair time watching you and do you know what I saw?'

'What did you see?' Cassie asked stiffly.

He studied her with obvious meaning. 'I saw a woman who was enjoying her bondage. I saw a woman

128

whose one outstanding regret was that she hadn't been lucky enough to receive the enema she'd had to give Faye. I saw a woman who would revel in the role of being a house slut.'

'I don't think so,' Cassie sneered. 'What's the second option?'

He reached beneath the table and pulled out something that had been hidden on the floor. 'The second option is that you can work on this proposal for me.' He threw a bulky folder on the desk and it landed heavily enough to make the crystal glasses chime.

Cassie suspected he was presenting her with the paperwork for a development proposal. The curled corners of folded architectural designs, the faded pink copies of council NCR sheets, and the stiff green cover of a listed building folder were all familiar enough to afford instant recognition. Seeing the paperwork laying on the dining table was like being shown a glimpse of her former life. 'What proposal is this?' she asked.

'It's the same paperwork I showed you before. These are the plans for the Harwood property.'

Cassie wrinkled her nose in distaste.

'I take it you've heard of the Harwood property? If you've been working in John's office I don't doubt he's mentioned it before because he knows it could be the most lucrative deal he ever signs. This is all the relevant paperwork along with my notes and suggestions for the development proposal.'

Even though she knew the contents were vile, Cassie was tempted to reach across the table and see what they were dealing with. After eleven days without access to her normal line of work she hadn't realised she missed the familiarity of something so superbly mundane. Like the glass of wine she still sipped, the chance to go over a development proposal was a pleasure she hadn't even realised she had missed.

Deliberately, she kept her hand on the wine glass and fixed her gaze on Brandon's commanding stare. She suspected there was a lot more going on at the table than he was telling her and she wanted to be sure of all the facts before she made a decision one way or the other. Cassie didn't know if Brandon had discovered the position she held in John's office but he clearly suspected she had something to do with the preparation of proposals.

While she felt sure she could have worked her way through the proposal with comparative ease, she didn't think it would be wise to let Brandon know the true extent of her talents. If he thought she was an able developer, she wondered if that might reduce her chances of escaping from his home. 'What do you think I could do with that?' she asked.

'You're not still trying to pretend you were just John's office girl, are you?'

His twinkling smile reminded Cassie of the expression Faye had used while trying to execute a bluff during the practice poker games. She wondered if the master knew he and his principal servant shared so many characteristics, then decided the observation was nothing more than a frivolous distraction. The important thing, she told herself, was to remember not to prepare his proposal.

The worry that he might decide to keep her as his property was only one of the factors that made up her mind. Cassie was also worried about John or, more exactly, the future of J & C Property Developments. She knew her partner didn't have her knack for shaping a winning proposal and she didn't doubt that any submission she put forward would beat his. The thought of creating a proposal that consigned her own business to the liquidators was something she couldn't bring herself to consider.

She swigged back the contents of her glass, then shook her head. 'I'm not doing that,' she said flatly. 'I'm not even looking at it.'

Brandon's smile was cold-blooded. 'Are you sure? I gave you two options.'

'I'm not working on that proposal.'

'Then that must mean you want to be one of my sluts.'

She watched his face for a sign of humour but his features were inscrutable. He stood up and, before Cassie knew what was happening, Brandon had wrenched the tablecloth away. Her uneaten meal was thrown to the floor as he brushed all the cutlery, crystal and crockery aside. In the confines of his office, the clatter was deafening.

'What the –'

'If you want to be my slut,' he began, 'then I may as well start using you properly. I may as well start using you now, just as I mean to continue.'

His features were flushed and it only took a glance for her to see he was deadly serious. She raised a hand to protect herself but, rather than helping her resist him, it simply meant he had a convenient place to hold. Gripping one wrist tightly, he hauled her from her chair and lifted her onto the table.

Cassie had almost forgotten about her nudity but now, the vulnerability of wearing no clothes struck her with renewed force. He was able to maul her breasts, press his mouth over one while groping the other, and touch her in other more intimate ways. She screamed for him to stop, insisting this wasn't what she wanted but he was deaf to her cries. As much as she struggled to resist, his strength was formidable and, as he continued to keep her in his embrace, she began to realise she wanted him.

She tried to shake the idea from her mind but it was intractable. Her need for him was apparent in the way her body bucked up to meet his and the way her pulse quickened with burgeoning excitement.

Scared by her own response, Cassie tried to find some reason to justify what she was doing. She tried telling herself it was an effect of the wine; or a result of spending so much time in the company of semi-naked nymphomaniacs; or simply a ruse to make Brandon accept her as a dealer. But, although she could have accepted any one of those explanations, Cassie knew the truth was far simpler.

She was surrendering to him because she wanted to.

Brandon pinned her against the table, holding both her hands above her head. Her legs dangled over the edge and she realised her pelvis was on the same height as his. Cassie stared meekly up at him as he opened the zip on his trousers.

'What do you think you're going to do to me?' Cassie whispered.

'Only what you want,' he laughed.

Exposed, his erection was as large as she remembered from her first night at the house. The end gleamed a dusky purple and the shaft pulsed with an urgency she could easily understand. He stepped between her legs and the end of his length pressed at her pussy lips. She thought of screaming, or refusing him completely, but she knew she didn't really want him to stop. On a primal level she had never discovered before, Cassie needed him to take her.

'Tell me you want this,' Brandon growled, rolling his length against her labia.

It was a cruel tease because he seemed to know exactly where to touch and inflame the greatest need. The slippery contact of his shaft against her pussy ignited an irresistible urge.

'Tell me you want this, and you can have it.'

She groaned and shook her head. Rather than try to pull herself from his grip she attempted to writhe her body down the table and impale herself on him. It was the sort of coarse behaviour she would have ascribed to any of Brandon's other property but she never believed she would catch herself acting on such a base desire.

Nevertheless, Cassie struggled to get closer and feel the glorious thickness of his penetration.

'Not until you've asked for it,' Brandon laughed. Without any apparent exertion he stopped her attempts to get closer and pushed her back up the table. Lowering his face over her chest he caught one teat between his teeth and began to gnaw.

Cassie wondered if she was still sensitive after what had happened during poker practice because the response he evoked was like nothing she had previously known. He didn't suckle on her areola, or tease her with his tongue. He simply caught her nipple between his teeth and chewed on the aching bud of flesh.

Cassie groaned with elation.

'Go on and ask for it,' Brandon urged. 'If you don't give in soon I might demand that you beg me.'

She willed herself not to give in but resistance was no longer within her abilities. Cursing whatever weakness was to blame she met his eyes. 'All right,' she gasped. 'I'm asking for it.'

He laughed in her face and shook his head. 'Ask me properly. Tell me what you want me to do.'

She didn't want him to humiliate her like this but Brandon left her no choice. He moved his mouth from her breasts and stroked his shaft against her sex again. The sensation promised a bliss she craved and Cassie found she couldn't resist the temptation. 'I want you to fuck me,' she groaned. When he continued to tease she raised her voice to a demanding scream. 'I want you to fuck me,' she insisted. 'I *need* you to fuck me!'

He responded with a swift thrust that left her breathless. One moment she was laid on the table, desperate to have his heat inside her. The next, he had buried himself deep in her confines, his thickness filling her and sending her emotions on an upward spiral.

With staccato force he ploughed into her, his thick weapon bruising her pussy lips as each thrust plunged deeper and more forcefully. Holding her by the hips, Brandon repeatedly lurched forwards and she realised he was pulling her down on the table as each entry banged into her. The observation was only peripheral because the majority of her thoughts were caught up in the wonderful world of bliss he had created. Her sex was brimming with potential satisfaction and her inner muscles convulsed with the promise of orgasm.

'You've been desperate for this since that first poker game,' Brandon growled. He spoke the words as he pushed himself into her and she could feel the echo of each syllable trembling through his shaft. 'You've been desperate for this, and so I'm going to make sure you properly enjoy it.'

She didn't know what was happening when he pulled himself out of her and she wanted to protest that he hadn't finished what he'd started. Before she had the chance to complain, Brandon had turned her over and pushed her face down against the table. She was able to place her feet on the floor and, as soon as she had spread her legs apart, he entered her for a second time.

They groaned in unison, the sound of their pleasure echoing from the walls. Cassie wondered how the tight hole of her sex was able to accommodate such a big man. He had seemed large when she had laid with her back on the table but, in this position, his girth felt enormous.

'You could do the job of a house slut quite well,' Brandon told her. 'You seem to have a natural ability.'

She knew it was an insult but that didn't stop the words from fuelling her arousal. His hands rested heavily on her back but, as he rode in and out with increasing speed, he moved them to clutch her buttocks. She was aware of him tracing an exploratory finger against the weal Faye had inflicted and then she was astounded to feel him touching her anus.

She tried lifting herself up from the table but Brandon had complete control. Placing one hand in the centre of her back he held her rigid as he continued pushing in and out of her sex. Tentatively, he pressed his finger into the puckered ring.

Cassie wanted to shout for him to stop but she couldn't voice the words for fear that he might obey. Whatever mad impulse had allowed her to surrender to him still held her in its thrall. Just as she had known she wanted to lie down beneath him, she now knew she wanted to feel him fingering her forbidden hole.

The digit slipped easily inside, its broadness stretching her so much that Cassie coughed back a scream of euphoria. Tears of joy spilled onto the table and she knew he was on the verge of transporting her to a blissful release.

'You'll be an accommodating house slut,' Brandon informed her.

His fingers probed deeper as he carried on riding back and forth. She could feel herself teetering on the brink of climax and only half heard what he was saying.

'I can imagine you'll be able to satisfy more than one lover at a time,' Brandon said dryly. 'I should put that to the test.'

The implication of what he was suggesting struck her as the orgasm erupted. She didn't know if it was the friction of his quickening shaft, or the lurid idea of what he was proposing. Whatever the cause the effects were undeniable and she sighed as the bliss shivered to every nerve ending.

'I was right that you wanted it, wasn't I?' Brandon laughed.

He continued to slide back and forth, his repeated entries sparking new and fresh sensations from the hypersensitive flesh of her pussy. Each time she thought she had reached her pinnacle he managed to plunge a fraction deeper and transport her to another realm of euphoria. By the time she had convinced herself she was inured to his skills as a lover, Brandon's rhythm had become erratic and she knew his climax was about to strike.

He snatched his thumb from her anus and plunged deep inside.

Cassie knew he had penetrated her fully because she could feel his scrotum pressing against her pussy lips. The end of his shaft nuzzled the neck of her womb and, with a handful of spasmodic twitches, his seed exploded.

The sensation was enough to spur her on to one final, devastating orgasm.

Brandon held her for a moment, seemingly unaware he was burying his fingers into her buttocks. When he began to withdraw she was tempted to hold him and savour the sensation of his flailing length as it wilted inside her pussy. Before she could act on the impulse, common sense made her think better than to try and control him. She allowed him to step away and turned over on the table to enjoy the pleasurable aftermath of their passion.

'Marion,' Brandon called. 'Sarah!'

Cassie considered telling him her name wasn't Marion or Sarah, then realised he wasn't addressing her. He was shouting for the two servants to enter the room and, whereas once Cassie believed she would have cringed at the prospect of another woman seeing her in such a used and dishevelled state, on this occasion she felt too drained to care.

Marion took in the scene without blinking.

Her expression was so calm Cassie wondered if she had half expected this outcome. She saw Sarah raise a curious eyebrow but it was the closest either of them came to registering anything that resembled surprise.

'Laura is away on secondment,' Brandon said, slumping heavily into his chair. 'So you two will have to take her place as cleaning girls.'

With a curt nod, Marion whispered, 'Yes, sir.'

Sarah smiled for him, then bent down on her knees in front of his chair.

Cassie half turned, trying to see what was happening.

She caught a glimpse of the redhead's tongue lapping against Brandon's spent shaft, then the woman's Titian tresses were covering the exchange. Not that it would have mattered because, at that moment, Cassie felt the slippery warmth of Marion's mouth against her sex.

While she wanted to be repulsed by what was happening, Marion's mouth was too delicious a sensation for Cassie to tell her to stop. She lay back on the table, enjoying the fading embers of her climax, and wallowing in the blissful sensation of Marion's tongue cleaning her sex. The intimacy was so satisfying Cassie could have happily enjoyed another orgasm if there had only been a little more stimulus to accompany Marion's attention.

'Enough,' Brandon said curtly. He replaced his shaft in his pants and clapped his hands for Sarah and Marion to tidy the room. The pair collected the broken crockery and wasted food from the floor, then exited in an obvious hurry to escape the threat of their master's wrath. He turned to Cassie as she pulled herself from the table. 'Is that your decision made?' he asked.

His eyes were sparkling with an honest lechery that made her wonder if he might take her again within the next few moments. The idea was so appealing she could feel the muscles of her sex clench hungrily in anticipation.

'Have you decided you want to become one of my house sluts?'

'If that's what you want me to be, then that's what I'll be,' she said defiantly. 'But the card game . . .'

'The card game?' he asked dourly. 'What about it?'

She struggled to find the strength to meet his solemn frown. 'I want to deal for the card game on Friday night. I'll be your obedient house slut if you let me do that.'

His eyes twinkled with barely concealed mirth. 'Dealing is a privilege,' he explained. 'If you really want to deal, you'll have to do me a favour first.'

Hope rose in her chest. 'What favour?' she asked. After all she had done for him so far Cassie believed she would be prepared to do almost anything if he said it would allow her to deal at the Friday night poker game. 'What favour do you want?'

His smile was grim with triumph. 'I wouldn't expect much from you,' he laughed. He snatched the Crystal file from the floor and threw it against her bare stomach. 'I'll just ask you to prepare those notes into a winning proposal.'

Nine

Vicky couldn't help but feel overawed in Laura's presence. Not only did the woman have a commanding beauty, and a style that was complemented by whatever she wore, but she also had a gift for handling people that went beyond anything Vicky could hope to achieve.

'Fuck off,' Laura told the blonde at the door. 'Two words. One meaning. No ambiguity. How much clearer can I make it. Fuck off!'

Vicky raised a hand to her mouth to hide her grin. Laura stood in the doorway, blocking the woman's entrance to Stephen's offices and Vicky thought it was clear the blonde would concede to Laura's superior presence. It was difficult to imagine anyone defying Laura when she was in such a commanding mood.

'Brandon sent me to relieve you,' the blonde said quietly. 'He's terminating your secondment. I'm here to take your place.'

Laura didn't move but, if Vicky hadn't known her better, she might have thought the brunette looked momentarily worried. Her frown tightened and her eyes narrowed to dangerous slits. 'I'm not going anywhere, Faye,' she hissed. 'I'm enjoying this assignment.'

Faye produced a mobile phone from her jacket pocket and held it out for Laura. 'Call the master and tell him,' she said flatly. 'Press that button there and say "Master", into the mouthpiece. It should get you straight through.'

Laura glowered for a moment and then seemed to change her tactics. She ignored the phone and tested a sycophantic smile. 'Can't you do this as a favour for me?' she asked. 'I've seen you doing favours for Brandon's other girls, but you've never put yourself out for me before. Can't you give me a break on this one occasion?'

Faye's features remained unreadable. 'I occasionally do favours for some of the other girls,' she agreed. 'But I limit the help I give to people who don't tell me to fuck off.'

Laura pursed her lips, making no attempt to suppress her growing irritation. 'Do a favour for me, and I can do one for you,' she suggested.

'I don't think that's a good idea,' Faye returned. 'I'm sure neither of us wants to be indebted to the other. You know you can't stay here indefinitely. Why don't you just do as the master has asked and let me relieve you now?'

Laura remained blocking the doorway. 'Do you really want me to go back to Brandon now?' she asked sweetly. 'If I saw him today I might feel compelled to tell him what happened on Friday night.'

For an instant, Vicky thought she saw a flicker of doubt in the blonde's sanguine features. 'Nothing happened on Friday night,' Faye said quickly. Vicky wondered if the woman had said the words too quickly.

Laura smiled in agreement. 'Of course nothing happened on Friday night,' she agreed. 'But I remember you telling the girls who work on the front door that they were to take a long break at teatime. And didn't you suggest they should leave the main doors unlocked?' As though she was changing the subject Laura asked, 'How's Brandon's latest acquisition settling in now? There haven't been any inexplicable escapes recently, have there?'

Vicky wasn't sure what had happened but she could see Laura had resumed control of the conversation.

Faye's eyes had thinned with contempt and she glared at Laura with a loathing that had to be borne from defeat. Nevertheless, the blonde seemed determined to make some stand. She continued to hold out her phone and said, 'If you're that determined to stay here, call the master and tell him what's happening. Tell him whatever it is you think you have to say to him.'

'I believe Stephen wants me to stay,' Laura said confidently.

Faye pushed the phone closer to her face. 'Then call Brandon and tell him that.'

Laura's shoulders slumped and Vicky wondered if the unthinkable had happened and her mentor had finally been beaten. When the brunette stepped back from the door, she realised Laura wasn't ready to give in yet. She grinned, pleased that her faith hadn't been misplaced. Her smile wavered when Laura grabbed hold of her wrist and dragged her from her chair.

'You're coming with me,' Laura said abruptly. Turning to glare at Faye she gestured at the reception and said, 'Wait in here. I'm just going to get Stephen's confirmation that he wants me to stay, then you can fuck off back to your precious Brandon.' She didn't bother waiting for a reply, hurriedly dragging Vicky down the corridor towards Stephen's office.

'Where are we going?' Vicky asked.

Laura spat her reply without looking. 'We're going to see Mr Price.'

'Does he have my winning proposal?'

Laura stopped and pushed Vicky against the wall. 'No one has your winning proposal yet because I'm still waiting for someone to submit something,' she hissed. 'As soon as the winning one arrives, I'll see the amended proposal is made out in your name, along with the award of the contract.'

Innocently, Vicky asked, 'Does Mr Price know all this?'

Laura studied her with undisguised contempt. She shook her head with obvious disgust and pressed her face closer. 'Stephen doesn't know what I'm planning,' she said quietly, 'and we're going to keep things that way. When we go into his office I don't expect you to talk. Leave that to me, and just do exactly as I say. Can you manage that?'

Vicky hesitated. After their last encounter she knew some of the things Laura was likely to say and a host of reservations sprang to mind. The woman had a devilish streak and Vicky was reluctant to put herself in the vulnerable position of just agreeing to do as she was told. 'I'm not sure that –'

'Do you want that contract making out in your name,' Laura asked, breaking through the confusion of Vicky's thoughts, 'or would you rather your business partner discovered how truly inept you really are?'

'Of course I want the contract,' Vicky said quickly.

Laura resumed her hold on Vicky's wrist and began dragging her toward Price's office. 'That's all the answer I need,' she growled. 'If you want the contract made out in your name, then you're going to do everything I say.'

Mumbling consent – anxious to do anything that would please Laura and secure the contract – Vicky hurried in her wake. Unconsciously she had tried to emulate the style of dress Laura wore for the office. Since their first meeting Vicky had made it her business to pay a couple of polite social calls on Stephen's office, easily finding some pretext or another to see the brunette again. She had noticed Laura favoured a distinctive cut of business suit: long line jackets worn with a medium length sleeveless dress. Invariably she went for charcoals and the darkest of navies and Vicky had dressed herself in an identical outfit cut from pinstriped black. Glimpsing their reflection in a passing pane of glass, she thought it looked as though she and Laura belonged together.

'Remember,' Laura hissed, pulling Vicky closer as they paused outside Price's door, 'you don't say anything unless I tell you to. And you don't do anything unless I tell you to. Do you understand?'

Vicky grinned, enjoying the thrill of being near Laura and her volatile mood. 'I understand,' she grinned. 'What are we going to do?'

Laura didn't answer. She knocked twice on the door and, without waiting to be invited, she twisted the doorknob and pushed her way inside.

Price glanced up from a pile of notes as the pair of them stepped into his office. He looked set to reprimand Laura for interrupting him when he noticed Vicky standing behind her. His smile turned briefly lascivious as he asked, 'And to what do I owe this pleasure?'

Laura glanced at Vicky then shook her head. 'Don't bother being courteous,' she said curtly. 'She's no one. Only a developer. I'm here to tell you that Brandon's sent someone to replace me.'

Stephen tilted his head to one side and made a sympathetic sound. He was handsome, in a swarthy way, but Vicky thought he didn't possess Laura's commanding presence. It seemed odd that the man she answered to was nowhere near as imposing as the woman who was his subordinate but Vicky supposed the same contrast of styles could be observed between her and John. It wasn't a thought she would ever have shared with anyone because, she suspected, the majority of people would treat the concept with ridicule.

'Brandon's sent someone to replace you,' Stephen repeated.

Watching him Vicky wondered why he seemed to be a conflict of emotions. His tempered frown and sympathetic voice gave the impression that he would be sorry to see Laura go but Vicky sensed he was also relieved. 'That's a shame,' Stephen went on. 'I was beginning to enjoy having your –'

'I don't want to go back just yet,' Laura broke in. 'I want to stay here and see the Harwood contract through to its award.'

Stephen spread his hands as though preparing to let her down gently. 'I'm sorry,' he began, 'but you are Brandon's property and, if he's –'

'You and I are on the same wavelength,' Laura said quickly. She moved closer to his desk and sat down on one corner.

Vicky could see the brunette was displaying an indecent amount of thigh and she wondered if the revelation of bare flesh was accidental or deliberate. From her position by the door it looked like Laura was trying to sway Stephen's decision by exploiting his interest in her. Vicky grinned to herself, sure he didn't stand a chance in the face of Laura's plentiful charms.

'I heard what you wanted to do with Harwood Manor,' Laura told Stephen, 'and your ideas are so close to mine it's almost as though we share the same thoughts. Aside from a couple of small details, you're trying to organise exactly the same pleasure palace I would have wanted.'

'It's very flattering you've taken such an interest in what I'm doing,' Stephen started diplomatically, 'and I'm pleased we share the same qualities of taste but, if Brandon's sent a replacement, then –'

'This is Vicky,' Laura said. She didn't bother looking in Vicky's direction as she made the introduction. She held Stephen's gaze and simply waved a hand behind her. 'If you tell Brandon you want me to stay here, I'll get Vicky to suck your cock.'

Vicky stared at her, bewildered Laura could have made such an outrageous offer. She considered pointing out that she would do no such thing, then remembered Laura had already extracted a promise from her prior to entering Stephen's office. Scowling unhappily, she wondered if there was a way for her to get out of the arrangement she had made.

Stephen seemed unaffected by the coarse suggestion. He cast a cursory glance over Vicky's smartly dressed frame then turned his attention back to Laura. 'That's very good of you but –'

Laura placed a silencing finger against his lips. The tip of one scarlet nail rested lightly against his cupid's bow. 'Let me stay until the contract is awarded, and we'll both suck your cock,' she promised. 'The blonde Brandon's sent doesn't like to lower herself to such chores but, if you keep me in your office, I can do this for you every day. If it's to your pleasing, I can also get Vicky to come along and help whenever you like.'

Stephen still looked as though he was going to decline and Vicky watched in awe as Laura exercised her able control over him.

'You don't know if we're serious about the suggestion, do you?' she giggled. Teasing open a button on his shirt, she pushed her fingers into the thatch of curls covering his chest and seemed to relish the contact with his masculine torso. Lowering her hand, reaching for the swelling lump at the font of his pants, she chuckled throatily and said, 'What do we have to do to prove we're both serious?'

Amazed by what she was watching, Vicky's eyes opened wider as Laura released Stephen's shaft from his trousers. He was thick with an arousal he had been trying to hide but, after only moving her wrist back and forth twice, Laura brought him to a state of full erection.

'A cock like this needs to be sucked regularly,' Laura enthused, lowering her face. 'A cock like this needs to be savoured.' As she spoke she dashed her tongue against his erection.

Stephen reached down and grabbed a fistful of her hair. Without showing any emotion he dragged her mouth away from his stiffness and turned her head until she was facing him. 'You must really want to stay around until the award of the contract,' he observed. 'I wonder how much you're prepared to do to remain in my company.'

Laura glared and Vicky couldn't decide if the brunette was angry because she was having her hair pulled, or if she simply didn't like Stephen having control. Tugging herself free, she stood up and snapped her fingers for Vicky's attention. Hurrying to obey any instruction, Vicky knelt where Laura had been and began to work her mouth against Stephen's erection. His shaft glistened with the brunette's saliva and Vicky's guts were twisted by a marvellous squirming arousal. She worked her lips around his stiffness and accepted him into her mouth.

'You don't really want to know what I'll do to stay here,' Laura observed. She resumed her seat on the corner of Stephen's desk.

Glancing slyly up at her, wondering if she might be graced by the brunette's approving smile, Vicky dared to move her head fractionally away from Stephen's length. She glimpsed the crotch of her mentor's panties and saw the white cotton was dark with spreading wetness. The sight confirmed Vicky's belief that Laura was just as excited by what was happening as she was. Then her face was pushed back to Stephen's erection.

'You're not interested in what I'll do to stay here,' Laura pressed. 'You know I'll satisfy any appetite, no matter how depraved. You just want to know *why* I want to stay.'

Stephen nodded. 'It seems you and I are on the same wavelength,' he agreed.

His tone was bland, as though he was indifferent to what Vicky was doing, but his apparent lack of interest only made her struggle harder to evoke some response. She traced the tip of her tongue beneath the rim of his swollen dome, then sucked gently on the end. Taking her time, she lapped around his broad girth, using her tongue and her lips to give the greatest tactile pleasure she could bestow.

'So, are you going to tell me?' Stephen asked.

'I already have told you,' Laura replied.

She reached down and raised the hem of her skirt to expose the sodden crotch of her panties. Pushing the gusset to one side, revealing the glistening split of her sex, she continued smiling for him as she guided Vicky's head away from Stephen's erection. Gently, but firmly, she tugged on Vicky's hair until her desires were made obvious.

Vicky pushed her tongue into the moist haven of Laura's sopping hole.

'I want to see the contract through to its award,' Laura breathed.

'But you still haven't said why.'

'I think I have,' she smiled. 'I think I told you that you and I are on the same wavelength. We both want to see the dream of Harwood Manor being properly made into a reality and I would hate to think any aspect of it wasn't realised to its fullest potential because I hadn't been here to assist.'

Stephen yanked on Vicky's hair. He continued pulling until she moved her mouth back to his shaft. Unwilling to leave Laura alone, relishing the flavour and scent of the woman's musk, Vicky teased a finger against her labia as she sucked and licked Stephen's shaft.

'I don't think you're being entirely honest with me. You're obviously interested in what I'm doing with Harwood Manor. But I think your desire to stay here might have a more selfish motive.'

Laura laughed. Vicky wasn't concentrating on the sound but she suspected the mirth had a nervous quality. 'You do me an injustice,' Laura told Stephen. 'You really do have a suspicious nature, don't you?'

'Can you blame me? What do you want, Laura? Do you want me to take you away from Brandon? Is that part of it?'

147

Vicky couldn't follow what they were saying and keep them both satisfied. She thought it was unreal that they could continue a conversation while being pleasured and she wondered if this sort of thing happened often in the world the pair seemed to inhabit. She could tell they were both aroused – Stephen's erection was twitching on the brink of climax and Laura's pussy muscles clenched at her tongue each time she penetrated her – yet neither seemed concerned about the pleasure they were receiving. Bizarrely, Vicky thought, she was the only one in the room not receiving pleasure and yet she was the only one being distracted by it.

Laura caressed her chin. At first Vicky thought the woman was affectionately reassuring her but she realised that assumption was misplaced when Laura grabbed her jaw. Firmly, she lifted Vicky's face away from Stephen's erection. With uncompromising force, she urged Vicky's tongue back between her spread legs.

'Lick my clitty,' she said quietly. 'You do that quite well when you put your mind to it.' Raising her head, speaking directly to Stephen, she said, 'I must admit, I'm growing tired of my duties at Brandon's house. But it's not a crime to want a change in life, is it?'

Vicky rested one hand against the top of Laura's thigh. The skin was like silk beneath her fingertips and merely touching her was worth the humiliation of her current predicament. Not that she begrudged Laura for the position she had put her in. Being used by both Laura and Stephen, savouring the taste and texture of their arousals, Vicky couldn't recall a time when she had enjoyed so much sexual excitement. She could feel an awakening appetite in the pit of her stomach and knew, when the mature version of that excitement finally kicked in, it would be an avaricious need that demanded satisfaction.

As that thought was going through her mind, Stephen grabbed hold of her by the ear and dragged her back to his erection. Vicky had time to place a last, loving peck against Laura's pussy, then she was working her mouth around his hardness again.

'What specific change do you think you'll get from me?' Stephen asked Laura. 'Are you expecting to be given the position of acting manageress at Harwood Manor? Is that what you think I'll give you?'

Laura giggled. 'You overestimate my desires,' she said dragging Vicky back to her sex. 'I don't think I have the necessary skills to be an effective manageress.' She tugged a fistful of hair and thrust her hips forward so Vicky's mouth met her sex in a wet, suffocating kiss.

Nuzzling against the slippery folds of flesh, greedily devouring the febrile skin, Vicky continued to stroke Stephen's trembling erection while she ate Laura's sex. If someone had touched her at that moment, placed a solitary finger against the pulsing nub of her sex, she would have exploded in a blissful orgasm. The idea was frightening because she knew, if she gave herself over to that pleasure, she would never be able to go back to the normal world as a mere office drone.

'I don't have a knack for people management,' Laura continued. There was a slight breathlessness to her voice, as though she was finally relenting to Vicky's persistence and accepting her pleasure as inevitable. 'To run a place like Harwood Manor you need to have a manager or manageress who can properly control subordinates and I don't think I completely fit that description.'

Stephen glanced at Vicky and said, 'You don't seem to be doing too bad a job of controlling her.'

Laura sniffed, not bothering to conceal her disdain. 'Anyone could control her,' she said flatly. 'It's no sign of acumen or skill in getting this one to go down on you. All you need is a three word vocabulary and available genitalia.'

Stephen laughed dryly and dragged Vicky back to his erection. The end leaked a clear stream of pre-come and she could tell he was on the brink of climax. Licking his dome clean, teasing the tip of her tongue into the eye of his length and rolling her lips around his glans, she ignored their derisory comments and concentrated on trying to coax his orgasm. Increasing the pace of her sucking, trying madly to push him beyond the brink, Vicky wondered if she could squeeze the end of his glans against the back of her throat.

'So, what is it you want?' Stephen was beginning to sound tired. 'There's no way the award of the contract could benefit you financially. And I don't think that would interest you if it could.'

Laura nodded in agreement.

'And, if it's not money or power, then what is it you want? I'd be tempted to think you were trying to assure the contract was made out in Brandon's name but I don't think it's that.'

Smiling softly, clearly enjoying listening to Stephen's speculation, Laura encouraged Vicky away from his shaft. Her hole was sodden with excitement and the scent of her sex had become richer as her arousal grew stronger. Vicky rubbed her face greedily against the slippery lips and then began to trill her tongue against the nub of Laura's clitoris.

'You're right,' Laura assured Stephen. 'I'm not trying to win this award for Brandon. I don't care one way or the other who is finally awarded the contract. But you're right in suspecting I have an ulterior motive.'

Her voice wavered as she spoke and, glancing up at her, Vicky saw a reluctant smile on the brunette's face. Pleased that her efforts were finally gaining attention, she pursed her lips around the pulsing ball of Laura's clitoris and encouraged it from beneath its hood. As soon as the bead of flesh pulsed in her mouth, she held it tight and tormented it with the tip of her tongue.

Laura released a sigh then shook her head as though trying to clear her thoughts. 'I do have an ulterior motive,' she repeated, 'but, having said that, you know I'm not going to tell you what it is, don't you? I think, by now, you've worked out that it most probably runs parallel to your own goals, yes?'

From the corner of her eye, Vicky saw Stephen nod.

'Then, why don't you just wait and find out? Why don't you humour me. Let me stay in your service until the contract's awarded, then see what it was I wanted?'

'I'd be taking a gamble,' Stephen told her.

'Are you telling me you're not a gambling man?' Laura purred. She shook her head as though dismissing the question before he could reply. 'Besides, it wouldn't be that much of a gamble, would it? You have the ultimate control over what happens to Harwood Manor and there's no way I could compromise that, is there?'

Stephen pulled Vicky back to his erection and contemplated the question while she sucked him. If he had been close to coming before she wondered how he was managing to stave off his climax now. His glans leaked a seamless flow of viscous ejaculate and she had to lap avariciously to cleanse it all away. Vicky wondered how much of his seed she had already swallowed and how copious his final eruption would be. The knowledge it would spurt into her mouth, and that she would have to savour every last drop, threatened to push her beyond the pinnacle of orgasm.

Stephen came to an abrupt decision. He slammed his hand against the arm of his chair and stiffened in his seat.

Vicky wondered if he was about to explode and held her mouth around the head of his swollen glans. She sucked gently, expecting the eruption to happen at any second.

'Go on then,' Stephen conceded. He was glaring defiantly at Laura, not seeming entirely happy with the decision but obviously determined to stick to it. 'You'll stay seconded to me until the award of the contract. I can't see Brandon complaining because I'm sure he thinks your presence here is going to work in his favour. You can inform him of my decision as soon as we're finished here.'

Laura squealed with delight. She pushed Vicky to one side and straddled Stephen while he remained in the chair. Her pussy lips encircled his length as she rocked her hips back and forth over him. Then she was impaling herself on his girth and the pair were groaning in unison.

Watching, Vicky didn't know whether to feel cheated that she was no longer required, or proud that she had been able to facilitate their union. The mixture of emotions sat uncomfortably with the knot of frustration that tightened in her stomach.

Stephen and Laura were all but oblivious to her. Laura smothered Stephen's face with kisses, then half turned to Vicky as she rode herself up and down on him. 'Go and tell that po-faced slut in reception to fuck off back to Brandon. Tell her Mr Price has made a decision and he wants me working under him until the award of the contract.'

Vicky wanted to ask if she could stay, wishing she could do more to be a part of their intimacy. Guessing Laura wouldn't allow that, sensing the woman would be disparaging if Vicky as much as suggested something like that, she fled from the office.

The sound of their elated grunts and groans followed her down the hallway.

Faye stood up as Vicky approached. Her expression was unreadable but Vicky got the impression the woman was studying her dishevelled appearance and figuring out what had happened in Stephen's office. Although Faye neither smiled nor frowned, Vicky knew she didn't meet with the woman's approval.

'Mr Price has just confirmed what Laura said before,' Vicky said quickly. 'Her secondment here is to be extended and she'd like you to pass that message on to Brendon.'

'Brandon,' Faye corrected absently. She collected the bag she had been carrying and started towards the door. Pausing with her hand on the knob, she turned to Vicky and said, 'The manipulative bitch is plotting something, isn't she?'

Vicky tried to look innocent. 'I don't know what you mean.'

Faye frowned and shook her head. 'You'd better hope you don't know what I mean,' she said earnestly, 'for your own sake. When Laura starts scheming, she only does it for her own benefit.'

With those words, she slipped out of the office and Vicky was left alone to wonder what she might be involved with.

Ten

Cassie stood before Brandon's desk feeling like a naughty schoolgirl in front of the headmaster. She was wearing the fishnet body stocking, her contours obscenely visible through its sheer fabric and, in spite of what had happened between them, she still felt as though she was exposing herself to a virtual stranger.

A kind word might have helped, she thought bitterly, or even a friendly acknowledgement. Instead, Brandon kept his head bowed over the proposal and, aside from occasionally scratching notes on a pad close to his hand, he simply read each page, turned it over, then moved on to the next.

Cassie stood on the spot he had indicated, hands behind her back and nervous butterflies churning through her stomach. The room was so quiet she could only hear the hastening thump of her heartbeat and the relentless tick of the wall clock. The atmosphere was thick and oppressive.

'This is professional,' he decided eventually.

Cassie said nothing. She was pleased with the praise but she knew if she said thank you, he would expect her to call him sir or master. Even though the day marked the end of her second week as his property, Cassie wasn't prepared to flatter him with either salutation. She remained defiantly mute.

'This is *very* professional,' Brandon amended. 'I think Stephen will like this. You've incorporated everything he said he wanted and managed to work the trickier elements so we're not infringing on the technicalities of the Listed Building Consents. I'm impressed.' He glanced up and said, 'It seems to me as though you've dealt with this sort of work before.'

Cassie remained silent.

The proposal had been a demanding challenge but she knew she had risen to it with aplomb. After everything she had seen and endured over the previous fortnight the document's references to sadomasochism didn't trouble her too greatly. She understood what was needed, tackled potential restrictions and problems with tried and tested solutions, and worked diligently to complete the paperwork. She had treated the less palatable elements as simply being parts of a whole package and felt sure the completed proposal was a viable and potentially lucrative prospectus.

Brandon appraised her with a dry smile.

His gaze lingered on hers until Cassie had to look away. The memory of what they had done two days earlier still burnt fresh in her mind. She didn't know what had possessed her to succumb to him but she hoped the streak of madness had now been well and truly spent. Ever since their liaison she had found her mind returning to that moment and wishing they had done more. She chastised herself for the wayward thoughts but, regardless of her own disapproval, they refused to go away. Brandon was a master of perversity, skilled in every act of degradation and it was impossible not to wonder what else he would have done if she had given sufficient encouragement. Trying not to let her thoughts follow that avenue, and nearly turning crimson with the effort, she tapped an impatient foot against the floor and glanced at the ticking clock above his door.

'It's a solid proposal,' he said, settling back in his chair. 'I'll have it sent over to Stephen's office this evening. I don't know where you got your figures from but I feel quietly confident you've just won the award of the contract for me.'

The clock edged closer to five-thirty.

Cassie knew the poker game was going to begin at half past seven. If Brandon allowed her to deal that meant she had two hours to help with the necessary preparations and get herself ready. The last time she had spoken to Faye the blonde said they were still hoping to help execute her escape plan and, more than ever before, Cassie wanted to get out of Brandon's home. She thought it was vital she escaped soon before her willpower crumbled and she found herself surrendering to him for a second time.

'Does this mean we've found your milieu?' he asked.

She frowned, not sure she understood.

'We've been searching for the role you can fulfil while you're my property,' Brandon reminded her. 'Is this the post you're going to take. Laura's the cleaning woman; Sarah's the entertainment staff; Faye's the dealer and you're the –'

'You agreed that I could deal tonight,' Cassie broke in. She could see he wasn't happy with her interruption but she didn't let the observation slow her down. 'You told me, if I prepared that proposal to your satisfaction, I could deal tonight. You promised.' To her own ears her voice was beginning to rise and become strident and she forced herself to calm down for fear he might suspect her motives. 'You promised,' she grumbled belligerently.

Slowly, Brandon rose out of his chair. 'I promised,' he agreed, 'and it's a promise I intend to keep.' He was pacing around her, circling like a predatory animal. As ever, the tawse was casually held in his left hand and he snapped it idly against the thigh of his trousers with every other step.

Cassie flinched from each crack as though it had scored her flesh.

'I get the impression you don't care for me,' he said quietly.

Cassie kept her lips pressed tight together.

'Are you aware that I don't just punish my property? Did you know I also reward desirable effort and behaviour.'

She considered making a sarcastic comment about how enlightened he was, then decided it wouldn't help her cause. While there had been times when he had exhibited some signs of humanity, Cassie didn't think his humour would stretch to snide remarks about the discipline of his regime. Shivering beneath his gaze, not daring to speak for fear of saying the wrong thing, she continued staring blindly forwards as Brandon repeatedly circled.

'You want to deal?' he barked.

Cassie nodded.

'You're aware of what's involved in dealing? It isn't simply a matter of throwing the right number of cards across the table, or being able to shuffle without dropping half the deck on the floor. You need to know –'

'I'm aware of what's involved,' she broke in coolly.

He studied her with a deepening frown.

She could see he didn't like to be interrupted and she cursed herself for again running the risk of antagonising him at this important stage of her escape plans. Despising herself for having to sink to such depths, shaping her words so they were spoken without too much contempt, she held his gaze and said, 'I'm aware of what's involved.'

He reached for the neckline of her body stocking with both hands. The gesture was brusque and came out of nowhere. One moment he was standing calmly in front of her, the next he was ripping the fishnet fabric into two halves. Her breasts spilled from their confines: they were now fully exposed.

She drew shocked breath and, in the claustrophobic atmosphere of the room, it sounded like a terrified gasp.

Brandon cupped one orb and caught her nipple between his finger and thumb. Squeezing the bead of flesh, rolling it to and fro as he held her, he shook his head and tut-tutted softly. 'How do you expect to deal at my table when you haven't had your nipples pierced? How do you expect to do something as simple as that when there isn't any steel through these taut buds?'

She held herself still, wishing she could distance herself from the sensations he inspired. He seemed to be able to hold her with sufficient pressure to make her discomfort only border on the unbearable. The difference between pleasure and pain was subtle enough to be indistinguishable and she was tormented by a rush of unwanted delight. The temptation to submit returned and she tried not to dwell on how much she wanted to experience his domination again. The pulse between her legs pounded greedily and she knew, if he gave the slightest indication that he wanted her, she would happily yield.

'You know how Faye wears the dealer's tray.' Brandon's voice was soft, almost cajoling as he continued to tease her breast. 'How do you expect to wear the dealer's tray when you don't have nipple rings?'

'There's a second tray,' she reminded him. She struggled to keep her voice even and unaffected, loathe to let him know he was exerting any influence over her responses. 'There's a second tray and it's fitted with clamps instead of clips. I intend to wear that one.'

He nodded sagely. 'Aren't you worried the clamps might hurt?'

Not trusting herself to reply, Cassie said nothing.

'Aren't you scared they'll bite hard and tug down until you want to scream? Do you think you can cope with that? Do you think you can cope with this sort of torment?' Roughly, he grabbed a nipple with each hand and squeezed.

The pain was infuriating and made worse as he dragged down on her breasts. She stared at him in amazement, blinking back tears that had come from surprise or pain. The temptation to slap him away was almost irresistible but, determined not to jeopardise her escape plans now the chance was so close, she clasped her hands firmly behind her back so she didn't inadvertently try to retaliate.

'Do you think you can tolerate this sort of punishment?' Brandon demanded. He pulled down fiercely, his grip remaining hard and unrelenting. A bitter smile twisted his face as he glared into her eyes. 'Do you think you can tolerate it for an entire evening?'

Her breasts were spiked by bolts of anguish and her body grew clammy with sweat. The torment was humiliating but Cassie could feel herself craving more. 'I think I can try to tolerate it,' she breathed.

He released his hold on her and wiped his palms on his thighs. Stepping away, resuming his predatory circle, he began to snap the tawse against his leg again. 'You prepared a very good proposal,' he said quietly. 'You managed it effectively and efficiently so you obviously have some ability in that direction. Why do you have an interest in dealing?'

The question caught her off guard and she wondered if her guilty flush might incriminate her. Glancing back towards the clock, annoyed to see the hands had barely moved, she tried to think of the best way to placate him.

'Why do you have an interest in dealing?' he repeated. 'Answer me, or I'll use the tawse to get you talking.' To show the threat was made in earnest, he raised the strip of leather to eye level.

Cassie glared at him amazed she could loathe and desire someone in such equal measure. 'You want to know why I'd rather work at your card table then slave in your office?' she barked. 'The answer's simple and I don't think you'll like it.'

Brandon raised a single eyebrow, encouraging her to continue.

'I'd rather watch you lose money than earn it for you,' Cassie told him.

Brandon's reaction caught her off guard. Instead of being offended he threw back his head and laughed. It was the sound of genuine merriment and the echo of his mirth bounced from the walls and shrilled interminably in her ears.

'You're a pigheaded bitch, aren't you?' he grinned. 'I can see now you're not the sort who'll let a little thing like a fact prove you wrong. What an asset you're going to be to my entourage when you finally come to your senses.'

She curled her upper lip into a sneer but didn't say anything. She wasn't sure she knew what he was talking about and felt certain she didn't want to know. On an instinctive level she suspected he was telling her things about herself that she was reluctant to acknowledge and, if her escape went according to plan, Cassie hoped she would never have to.

Brandon pushed his face close to hers and grinned lewdly. 'You're a natural submissive and the only person in this building who hasn't realised it yet is you. I'll let you deal tonight; I'll let you deal every Friday night if you think it will give you pleasure; but, when the truth finally sinks through your thick skull, I expect you to apologise to me in the only way a submissive knows how. Do you understand what I'm saying?'

She understood him only too well and wanted to recoil from his menacing scowl. Holding herself defiantly she asked, 'Are you telling me I can go and prepare for the card game?'

He grunted with exasperation and turned his back on her.

Deciding she was dismissed, and anxious to get her plans underway, Cassie fled from his office. She wished she had a better understanding of the forces that had been working on her since she found herself in Brandon's company. Her responses to him, and the depravity of his existence were mystifying. Everything he did and stood for repulsed her sensibilities but, on a level she was reluctant to contemplate, she also found there was a lot about him that excited her. While it might have been easy to ignore that response, with each passing minute she found herself being tempted to indulge in the sinister pleasure that could be gleaned beneath his sadism. Anxious to find company, needing to talk with anyone rather than brood on the chilling elements of self-discovery she was making, Cassie hurried to find the others.

Marion, Sarah and Faye were cleaning the games room and they huddled around her in a conspiratorial group as soon as she burst through the door.

'Do you remember your deal?' Faye asked. Her voice was lowered to a soft whisper and her gaze kept flitting towards the closed door. 'Do you remember what to do? And have you been keeping up your practice?'

'Of course,' Cassie told her. While she had been preparing the contract Cassie had held a deck of cards in her right hand and repeatedly gone through the motions of palming and dealing fixed hands. Her knuckles ached with the weariness of overuse, and her fingers felt interminably stiff, but each whisper of pain reminded her she was close to making her getaway. 'I've practised so much over the last seven days I've been seeing playing cards in my sleep.' Frowning to show her sincerity she put a hand on Faye's arm and said, 'I can do the necessary deal this evening. I can do it and no one will know I've cheated.'

Faye looked as though she was trying hard to believe everything Cassie said.

'Do you remember the sign Marion will be giving?' Sarah asked.

Cassie grinned at her. 'Marion will say "Please Master Brandon." As soon as she's said that, I deal John his winning hand and then she'll turn the lights out.' She paused, breathless with excitement and daring and wondering why the other women didn't seem to share her enthusiasm. It was still a mystery how they could enjoy their lives as Brandon's property but Cassie didn't want to broach the subject in case it soured their last moments together.

'Marion. Sarah. You two can finish getting this place ready for the game,' Faye instructed. Taking hold of Cassie's hand she said, 'I'll start getting you ready for your ordeal.'

Cassie frowned. 'What do you mean? I only have to sit there naked and deal, don't I? It's not like I've got to squeeze myself into a slinky little number, is it? What lengthy preparations could there possibly be?'

Faye shook her head sadly and led Cassie out of the games room. She took her through the main corridor and into one of the utility rooms in the east wing. Cassie recognised they were in an annex to the kitchen and she obligingly did as Faye told her, stripping off her torn body stocking before sitting on the counter.

Idly she wondered when she had overcome her anxiety about being naked in front of the others, then decided it was immaterial. Once she had escaped from Brandon's home Cassie was looking forward to returning to a life of prudish celibacy where only her doctor would have the privilege of seeing her nudity. She intended confining herself to private cubicles in the public swimming baths and, if she ever did meet a man with whom she wanted to go to bed, she would make sure that whatever happened between them occurred beneath the sheets, without any lights on, and most probably while he was wearing a blindfold. It didn't promise to be the happiest of futures but, because it would be a million miles away from her existence as

Brandon's property, Cassie told herself it was bound to be an improvement.

'You need shaving,' Faye said, pointing between Cassie's legs, 'and I can show you a couple of tips to make the clamps more bearable.'

'Why do I need shaving?' Cassie asked.

Faye placed her hand against Cassie's pubic mound and grabbed a swatch of curls between her fingers. With a vicious jerk of her wrist she pulled so hard Cassie was almost dragged from her makeshift seat on the counter. A squeal of pain erupted at her groin and she stared at Faye with wide-eyed disbelief.

'What the hell did you do that for?' she demanded.

Faye maintained her hold on the tangle of hairs, not allowing the tension to lessen. 'I'm showing you why you need to be shaved,' she explained innocently.

The flesh over her pussy was being grossly distorted and a handful of follicles were threatening to tear from their roots. Cassie hoped they would give up their fight before the pain became too much. 'Do you need to make the demonstration so uncomfortable?' Cassie complained. 'Couldn't you just tell me why, rather than hurting me like this?'

'If the players see this much pubic hair on your pussy they'll use it to torment you,' Faye explained. 'Didn't we tell you that players will make your life hell while you're dealing? Didn't we explain that clearly enough? They'll use your pussy hairs to drag you around the room, they'll pretend to set fire to them and they won't stop taunting you until you're in tears.'

Cassie glared at her, hating the rise of sick excitement Faye's words evoked. The pain in her sex had become a dull ache and she was revolted to realise it wasn't entirely unpleasant. Additionally, the idea of being teased and humiliated in such a way inspired a thrill she didn't want to understand. 'Shave it all off,' she decided. Her voice was thick with an emotion she could never name. 'Shave it completely bare.'

'I intended to,' Faye said, selecting a brush and razor from the nearby sink. She found a bar of carbolic, ran the warm tap, and worked up a lather. Daubing the soapy wetness between Cassie's thighs, spattering suds and sponging the liquid into her curls, she tested a sympathetic smile. 'Don't be surprised if you find this enjoyable. It doesn't mean you're a pervert because you like the sensation.'

Cassie was about to berate her for making such a foolish suggestion when Faye took her first swipe with the razor. A path of bare flesh was exposed beneath the lather and, as much as she didn't want to accept it, she had to admit the experience bordered on being enjoyable. Again, there was the mixture of pleasure and pain – the dull tug at her pubic hairs and the intimate caress of the blade – and she wondered why her appetites had suddenly become so depraved. Guessing Faye would be able to do a more effective job if she made herself more accessible, Cassie leant back and spread her legs wide apart.

To distance herself from the niggle of embarrassment, Cassie started talking about the proposed hands she would have to deal throughout the night. Faye had told Cassie she would need to balance the gameplay and make sure there were no big winners or losers by the time she dealt the final hand.

While she felt sure they were both earnestly involved in the subject they were discussing, Cassie couldn't shake the idea Faye was pleased she had a chance to shave her. It seemed like an irrational thought but Cassie felt sure it had the ring of truth.

Frowning with concentration, Faye worked between her legs. She swiped the blade down, rinsed it clean, readministered lather, then swiped the blade again. Each time the edge of steel brushed against her, Cassie stiffened and tried to ignore the excitement it evoked. She was congratulating herself on remaining almost unaffected when Faye caressed a finger against her pussy lips.

Cassie recoiled from the woman's touch, hoping she didn't look too horrified. She was on the verge of making a rash accusation – telling Faye she had known the woman was plotting this sort of intimacy – and acting with all the outrage she thought the familiarity merited. It was only with a massive exertion of self-control that she was able to restrain herself.

Faye grinned into Cassie's startled expression. 'I just need to trim a couple of stray hairs from the edge of your labia,' she explained. 'Hold very still while I'm doing this. I'm sure you don't want me to slip.'

Not daring to move, frightened to exhale for fear it might cause an accident, Cassie held herself rigid. She watched Faye lower her head to study exactly what she was doing and steeled herself against the feel of the woman's fingers teasing her sensitive skin. When the blade scratched her pussy lips, slicing the hairs from the flesh, she resisted the urge to writhe. The combination of fear and arousal were proving to be a heady blend and she knew she wouldn't be able to ignore them for long.

Faye stood up to rinse the razor.

Cassie drew a deep breath, not surprised to find her heartbeat hammering.

'Last one,' Faye smiled, returning to her position. She lowered the blade to Cassie's pussy, caught her outer labia between two fingers, then deftly swiped it clean. When she moved back towards the sink Cassie was stung by disappointment as she realised the ordeal had finally ended.

Cassie glanced down at Faye's handiwork and was mesmerised by the sight of her own sex. Shaved, it looked somehow different and she couldn't work out whether it seemed more exciting or simply bare and vulnerable. She touched the flesh and was disturbed to

166

find her skin acutely responsive. Each subtle exploration felt like an electric charge and, after tentatively caressing herself a couple of times, she mentioned her worries to Faye.

'It will be more sensitive,' Faye agreed. She spoke with forced patience, as though Cassie was stupid for not having worked out the simple fact for herself. 'It's bound to feel different. It's just been shaved.' Patting her arm reassuringly she added, 'By the time the card game begins your heightened sensitivity down there will be the least of your worries.'

The words offered little comfort but Cassie kept her reservations to herself. She slid off the counter and was disturbed to find the fresh responses from her newly shaved pussy didn't just occur when she was touched. Her sex lips bristled with each movement and she wondered if it was normal to be so blatantly aware of every sensation. Gingerly she stiffened the muscles in her thighs and was unsettled to find aftershocks of the tension shivering through her crotch. Repeatedly writhing this way and that, she marvelled at the wealth of new feelings she was enjoying.

'You'll be wearing the dealer's tray all night,' Faye said briskly. She had her back to Cassie and was bent over a freezer cabinet. 'What I'm proposing will help you adjust so you don't feel the bite of the clamps for the first half hour. After that, I guess a little discomfort might kick in but you'll have other things to occupy your mind by then. What I propose is *ice cubes*.'

She held one in each hand and pushed them both against Cassie's nipples. The shock was sudden and biting, stinging her with its frigid cold. Cassie tried to step away from the torment, but Faye followed and pressed the ice hard against each breast. She grinned, her smile shining with wicked enjoyment at Cassie's distress.

'Don't move them away. Keep them against your nipples until they melt, then you can get two more.'

'But they're cold.'

Faye regarded her with genuine disappointment. 'We don't keep a large supply of warm ice cubes,' she began sarcastically. 'Do as I say and it will make the night a little less traumatic for you. You do trust me, don't you?'

Shivering, Cassie cupped the ice cubes against her nipples and held them while Faye inspected her. She didn't want to answer Faye's question because she wasn't sure how honest a reply she could give. Instead, she asked, 'Why do I need to do this?'

'The ice cubes will numb your nipples for when the clamps are applied,' Faye explained. 'It's a bit of a double-edged sword really. They'll make accepting the clamp bearable but, once the effects of the ice begin to wear off, you'll find yourself a lot more responsive.'

'More responsive to what?' Cassie asked. 'Are you talking about pleasure or pain?'

Faye shrugged. 'I'm not sure there's a difference. Are you?' Not waiting for an answer, acting as though she didn't expect Cassie to understand, she said, 'Wait here while I go and get some make-up for you.'

Cassie was left to dwell on the remark, holding the freezing cubes to her nipples, and telling herself the nightmare would soon be over. When the ice cubes had melted away she delved into the freezer and got two more. Her nipples already felt numb but, because the start of the game still seemed a long way away, she thought it wisest to follow Faye's advice and continue applying the ice. She had changed the cubes a second time before Faye returned to the utility room carrying a large, old-fashioned vanity case.

'Let's make you look presentable,' she grinned.

Cassie smiled dutifully and returned to her seat on the counter. Faye went through the process of applying lipstick, eyeliner and blusher, barking instructions for her to lower or raise her head, and to turn this way and that. Cassie couldn't see what was being done and her only involvement came each time she had to tell Faye the ice cubes had melted. The feminine scents of powder and make-up reminded her of life before her incarceration at Brandon's and, like so many of the simple pleasures she kept noticing, Cassie wondered how she had been coping so ably without even registering its absence. She inhaled the sugary perfumes of the cosmetics and held herself still while Faye stepped back to admire her handiwork. It was comforting to think that the next time she breathed in the scent of perfume it would be as a free woman.

'The escape should be easy,' Faye said. She smiled approvingly and reached for a mirror. 'You'll blind them with your beauty and they won't know which way you went.'

Blushing at the compliment, but secretly pleased, Cassie took advantage of the opportunity to study her reflection. She had never been a great one for admiring herself and for an instant she barely recognised the woman staring back at her from the mirror. The lipstick was darker than anything she would normally have worn but it gave her mouth a fullness that was ripe and inviting. The eyeshadow accentuated the expression and colour of her eyes while the blusher gave her face a vitality she had never seen before.

From the corner of her eye she could see Faye was frowning.

'What's wrong?'

Faye shook her head. 'It's nothing. Nothing you want to hear.'

'Go on,' Cassie insisted.

'No.' Faye was adamant. 'You have your escape plans all set up and, before we hit midnight, you should be out of here. I'm not going to cock that up for you.'

Intrigued by the woman's manner Cassie asked repeatedly but Faye remained tight-lipped. 'We have to go and see if Marion and Sarah have finished in the games room,' she said eventually. 'Grab a fistful of ice cubes and follow me.'

Cassie wasn't comfortable with the idea that Faye was keeping something from her but she could see the woman wasn't going to be drawn. Dutifully, she followed her to the games room and was surprised by how much Sarah and Marion had managed to do in such a short time. The card table had been polished; clean ashtrays had been positioned next to the players' chairs; the bar had been re-stocked; and a buffet of canapés lined the trestle tables along one wall. A pile of gold chips sat beside each player's seat and Cassie remembered that at some point during her incarceration she had learnt each chip represented a thousand pounds. Honouring some senseless gentleman's code, Faye had said the players usually settled their debts with one another during the week between card games. Staring at the chips, Cassie was unmoved by the amount of money involved and worried only by the thought of all that weight dragging down on the tray she would have to wear.

For once the room was brightly lit but only by the glow of a dozen tea-lights; their sparkling flames leant a sheen of sinister glitter to the dismal surroundings and Cassie thought it looked like a dungeon at Christmas.

Marion and Sarah were exchanging a lingering kiss when she and Faye entered the room. They continued their embrace, as soon as they had assured themselves they weren't being caught by Brandon, allowing their caresses to become bolder and more intimate. Cassie watched as they stroked each other's buttocks and breasts.

'You're looking good, Cassie,' Sarah murmured.

The comment surprised Cassie because she didn't think Sarah had looked at her long enough to notice any change in her appearance.

'Faye's made you look the part,' Marion agreed. 'I especially like the shaved pussy. That's a nice touch.'

Cassie thanked them, inwardly squirming with embarrassment, but making sure none of them saw her discomfort. She double-checked everything was still set for her main deal of the evening and, barely breaking the lingering exchange of their kiss, both Sarah and Marion assured her they knew what was expected of them.

'We don't have much longer if we want Marion in place for when this game begins,' Faye said. Touching Sarah's shoulder she added, 'Do you think you can stop kissing her for two minutes while we get her in position.'

With obvious reluctance the two women parted. Marion stepped out of her body stocking, handed it carefully to Sarah, then stood in front of Faye and turned around. Her hands were behind her back and Cassie saw she had crossed them at the wrists.

Briskly, Faye snapped handcuffs on the brunette.

Sarah helped Marion to lie on the floor while Faye put the brunette's feet into ropes that trailed from the ceiling. She fastened the bindings securely, placing a spreader bar between Marion's ankles, before going to a pulley on the wall furthest from the card table. Continually watching the brunette, instructing Sarah how to hold her so the ascent was smooth and uneventful, Faye turned the pulley until Marion dangled above the floor.

Cassie watched the entire operation without daring to breathe. She released a soft sigh when Sarah stepped beside her and placed a platonic arm around her shoulders. 'Doesn't she look pretty there?' the redhead asked.

It hadn't been the only thought going through Cassie's mind but she had to concede Marion did look attractive in her suspended bondage. The rush of blood to her face gave her pallor a healthy flush. Even though she was firmly restrained and totally helpless, something about her expression gave an impression of vitality and passion.

'She looks enviable,' Cassie whispered.

Sarah released a puzzled laugh. 'Enviable?'

'Beautiful,' Cassie amended quickly. She was grateful for the faltering glow of the candlelight because she suspected it would hide her blushes. 'I said beautiful,' she insisted. 'You must have misheard me.'

Sarah shrugged as though the matter was of no consequence. 'Would you like to do the honours?' she asked, passing Cassie a long candle.

Marion grinned awkwardly at her from her bondage and nodded approvingly. 'Yes. Go on. Think of it as a going-away present.'

Cassie took the candle, not sure what they expected her to do with it. It was only when Sarah began leading her towards Marion's suspended frame that she realised where it was needed. Unnerved by the idea, she hesitated.

'Go on,' Sarah encouraged, nudging her closer. 'She's more than ready for it.'

Cassie hadn't needed the redhead to point out Marion's arousal because she could see all the symptoms clearly enough. The brunette's nipples jutted forwards, her pussy gaped eagerly, and her labia had peeled apart as though they were greedy to accept whatever Cassie wanted to plunge between them.

'It's not like it's a technical operation,' Sarah giggled. 'Just light the wick, then slide the base deep inside her.'

From the shadows of the room Cassie could see Faye was watching. Her features were stiff with consternation and Cassie felt sure the woman was trying to make up her mind about something. She strongly suspected she was at the centre of Faye's thoughts and wondered if the blonde was going to judge her on whether or not she responded to Sarah and Marion's playful cajoling.

Not wanting to seem reluctant, she lit the candle's wick from one of the tea-lights and then held the base over Marion's pussy.

'Aren't you going to lick it first?' Sarah teased.

Cassie frowned uncertainly, not sure where she was supposed to apply her tongue. She could see her hesitation caused all three women amusement because they each shared a knowing grin. Sarah plucked the candle from Cassie's fingers and with leisurely elegance took it in her mouth. She sucked obscenely on the end, then handed it back.

'No need to lick it now,' she said with a mischievous giggle. 'I've done it for you. You just need to wet Marion's pussy before you slide the candle inside.'

Cassie regarded her warily, wondering if Sarah was joking. Seeing no hint of mirth she realised what was expected and tried not to recoil from the prospect. Cassie didn't want to do what Sarah was suggesting but, because she was expecting assistance from the three women, she wondered how they might react to a straight refusal. She had invested so much in getting her escape plans to this stage she didn't want to spoil everything by refusing Sarah's simple request despite the depravity it alluded to.

Slowly, she lowered her face to Marion's sex. The scent of the brunette's musk was light and fragrant. As Cassie's mouth edged closer she could feel a heat generating from the gaping pussy lips and knew Marion was in a state of high arousal. That thought was confirmed when she buried her tongue into the slippery wetness of the woman's hole. She lapped deeply, tasting and relishing the intimacy as the brunette's inner muscles throbbed against her mouth.

'Now slide the candle inside,' Sarah said quietly.

Cassie moved her face away and took a breath. With her nerves feeling ragged, and her hand trembling unnecessarily, she placed the base of the candle over

Marion's sex. She had seen the end was rounded but still, careful not to inflict any needless suffering, she only pushed it gently inside. Marion's pussy lips yielded easily and, as she slid the base deeper, Cassie could feel tremors shaking through the thick stick of wax. When she realised the vibrations were caused by Marion's sex muscles squeezing around their prize she was touched by a whisper of the woman's arousal.

From beneath her, the brunette let out a lingering sigh.

Cassie matched the sound with her own grateful whisper and then heard Sarah applauding.

'Sarah said you wouldn't dare do it,' Marion explained. She was grinning up from her awkward position, her smile triumphant. 'I bet you would.'

Ignoring the pair, glancing over at Faye as she continued to watch, Cassie asked, 'Did you think I'd do it, or not?'

Faye secured the rope on the pulley and started blowing out the flames from the tea-lights. 'I think it's time to prepare for the guests,' she said firmly.

Her obvious disapproval was chilling.

Cassie faltered uncertainly and said, 'But –'

'Fasten the tray on her, Sarah,' Faye barked. 'Then go and wait by the front door in case you're needed.'

Cassie watched the blonde blowing out the flames, and wondered what she had done to upset her. She started to ask the question, then Sarah was distracting her by fastening the nipple clamps to her breast. As Faye had promised, the numbing cold inured her to the bite of the jaws and she was quietly grateful for the advice. Because Faye had almost finished extinguishing the last of the tea-lights, Cassie couldn't see enough of her to mouth a quiet word of gratitude. She was still wondering what she had done to offend the woman but, before she could resolve the matter, a man appeared in the doorway.

Even though there was only a solitary candle to illuminate his figure, she recognised him instantly. Her heart swelled with hope and, unable to contain the urge, she smiled wistfully.

'Cassie?' John grinned. 'Is that really you?'

Eleven

'Cassie?' John sounded incredulous. 'Is that really you?' He stared at her with his jaw slack and his eyes growing wider in lecherous amazement.

Of all the torments Cassie had been forced to endure, this was the most punishing. She hadn't expected the humiliation to hurt so badly but, standing beneath John's eager gaze, she didn't think it would be possible to sink any lower. She could see he approved of her nudity – judging by the swelling at his groin he was clearly aroused – but the experience was degrading and dehumanising. It was obvious from the lascivious sparkle in his eye that he no longer regarded her as his business partner: he was merely looking at her as an object of lust.

'You seem so different from the last time I saw you,' he said, struggling to sound casual. His gaze constantly shifted from her eyes, to the sight of her shaved pussy, over the swell of her exposed breasts, then back to her eyes. She could see he was intrigued by the clamps biting into her nipples but, because he was feigning an air of cool control, he didn't allow his attention to linger. 'I didn't think you'd settle down to being here so well,' he confided.

'It's not like you gave me much of an option,' she growled. Her voice was thick with vitriol as she struggled to keep a rein on her temper. 'When you used me as your ante the other Friday – because you thought four queens could beat four aces – you didn't ask me if I thought I'd fit into the new lifestyle you had planned for me, did you?'

Brandon appeared from behind John and raised his tawse. There was a frown of disapproval on his face and, after spending a fortnight in his company, Cassie knew the expression didn't bode well. 'Faye may have taught you how to deal but she clearly didn't instruct you on how to behave in this room,' he snapped. 'The dealer speaks to no one during the Friday night poker games. No one.'

Cassie opened her mouth to protest.

'No one,' he repeated. 'Is that understood?'

She blushed, wondering if his reprimand was hurting worse because she was suffering in front of John. Forcing herself to apologise, she tried hard to look humble as the third man, Stephen, entered the room.

'Price! It's good to see you again,' Brandon boomed. His upset with Cassie was forgotten as he welcomed his guest. 'I've just sent my proposal over to your office. I trust it will meet with your approval.'

Stephen shrugged, his smile tightening as he regarded Cassie. 'I'll look at it when I get back,' he said, dismissing the topic. 'Is this a new dealer?'

Despising her position as the centre of attention, Cassie raised her gaze to defiantly return their licentious inspections. She was naked and defenceless in the company of three boorish males and her heart hammered wildly. It was impossible to remember a time when she had ever felt more vulnerable or scared. Meeting the hungry gaze of each man she tried to decide if her anxiety came from a fear of what was going to happen, or her worry that they might do something worse than she was expecting. Faye had regaled her with an extensive list of the potential amusements she might have to suffer and, while Cassie hadn't thought any of them sounded appealing, she was prepared to endure anything if it helped her escape. Her growing worry came from her suspicion that the men might be able to come up with crueller and more vindictive torments if they thought the situation merited such initiative. Not letting herself dwell on that doubt, knowing she would panic if she brooded on it, Cassie tested a sanguine smile on Brandon and prayed he would simply want to begin the card game.

'Are we starting with cigars and a scotch?' Brandon asked, gesturing for the others to sit down. Treating their silence as approval he made his way to the bar and began pouring whisky into three glasses.

'Cigars?' John grinned quizzically as he settled himself into a chair. He laughed as though this was the most outrageous suggestion he had ever heard and flicked his gaze from Brandon to Cassie. 'Cassie won't light the cigars for you,' he said confidently. 'She's not that type.'

Brandon placed John's drink in front of him and looked down with mild contempt. The forced patience in his smile told Cassie the Scotsman regarded John as an ignorant fool and, for once, she found herself in perfect agreement with him. The only thing she couldn't understand was why she had never seen it before.

'You seem to forget she's been my property for a fortnight,' Brandon said smugly. 'Over the last fourteen days she's been trained to do as she's instructed or suffer the consequences. She'll light cigars for me if I tell her, or do anything else that's required.'

Although John was nodding agreement he didn't seem to accept what he was being told. 'You might have trained her to do as she's instructed. But she won't light your cigar for you,' he said emphatically. 'Not like Faye lights them. Not Cassie.'

Brandon exchanged a glance with Stephen before sitting down and snapping his fingers for Cassie's attention. She was loathe to obey the wordless summons but, knowing it would take her one step closer to executing her escape plans, she went to his side.

'Yes?' she asked curtly.

John raised a sceptical eyebrow.

Brandon pulled three Havanas from the breast pocket of his jacket and dropped them on her tray. The excess weight tugged a little but, because her nipples were still numb, Cassie wasn't bothered by the discomfort. She remained motionless, waiting for his instruction. 'Light those for our guests,' he said. 'I believe you know what's required of you.'

She could feel her reservations mounting and wondered if there was any way to simply run for the door now and try to make a getaway before any of them realised what she was doing. The idea didn't last for long because, as appealing as it was, she knew the building would already be locked and secure and she suspected Brandon wouldn't let her leave the room before catching up with her. Hesitantly, she reached for one cigar and began to remove it from its protective tube. Her fingers shook with nerves and she glanced from one face to another hoping one of them would tell her they were only joking.

No one spoke and, following the instructions Faye had given before the evening began, Cassie placed one foot on the table in front of Stephen. The position exposed the sight of her freshly shaved sex but it was easy to ignore the inquisition of his penetrating stare. Not hurrying, knowing she was less likely to look nervous if she simply took her time, Cassie pushed the end of the cigar between her legs. The stub was as thick as a finger but, when she pressed it into the centre of her pussy, it felt a lot broader. She twisted it lightly, allowing the end to slip inside, until it was wetted with a smear of her arousal.

Stephen grinned approvingly.

Blushing furiously, aware of John's gaze searing into her back, Cassie removed her foot from the table and

180

walked over to Marion. She stooped to the candle burning between the brunette's legs and lit the cigar. Moving without haste, forcing herself to appear untroubled by their lecherous glances, she returned to Stephen and passed him the Havana.

He thanked her and tipped a sly salute to Brandon.

Cassie swallowed. She would rather have lit Brandon's cigar next, wanting to defer her contact with John for as long as possible, or ideally for ever. Because Faye had told her to cater to the guests first and the master last, Cassie turned to face her former business partner.

John grinned broadly up at her. Everything about his smile said he was enjoying her humiliation and she could see he wouldn't do anything to spare her blushes.

Cassie snapped the cap from a second tube and produced his cigar. As she placed her foot on the table before him her embarrassment was more crippling than ever. She knew Stephen had been watching intently but his interest had been nowhere near as avaricious as John's. Her former business partner grinned idiotically, not bothering to hide his hateful interest in her pussy. He stared at her as though he had never seen a naked woman before and his attention inspired a bitter shame that made her feel sick. Once Cassie had wet the end of the cigar she started to move away from the table but John stopped her by putting his hand on her wrist.

'You should have pushed it deeper,' he said sternly. 'I want you to make it wetter than that.'

She was struck by an irresistible urge to slap his face but, knowing there would be repercussions if she did, Cassie simply obeyed. She returned her foot to the table and suffered his leering curiosity. Arching her back, relaxing the muscles of her pussy, she eased the cigar further into her tight confines. Its girth grew thicker the deeper she pushed and, by the time Cassie had fitted half its length into her hole, it felt like she was being skewered on a decent-sized cock. The idea of being watched by John as she humiliated herself in such a way was so shaming she could feel the threat of tears pricking at her eyes. Twisting the Havana gently from side to side, trying not to think about the swirl of pleasure it evoked as it drew against the walls of her sex, she relaxed and withdrew the cigar slowly.

John's grin was infuriating as he nodded approval. She thought he looked set to applaud and quickly turned her back on him so he wouldn't see the loathing in her eyes. Stepping quickly to Marion's candle, despising the acrid taste of the cigar as she puffed it to life, Cassie tried to compose herself for when she had to hand the Havana back to him.

'I never realised she had such a nice arse,' John said conversationally.

Cassie cringed at his coarseness.

'I'll bet she handles like a TVR. Is that right, Jock? Have you given her a test drive yet?'

Cassie kept her back to the three of them, not wanting to see John's face when Brandon replied. She could imagine him recounting every detail of what they had done and she cringed from the horror of having her lust made known. She was still loathe to think about how she had surrendered to Brandon and it wasn't a memory she wanted to revisit under these mortifying circumstances. Her shoulders were stiff and she could feel the dull glow of her blush creeping round to the back of her neck.

'Handles like a TVR?' Brandon repeated thought-fully. 'Given her a test drive?' He laughed to himself and said, 'Jesus, Johnny. You display all the classic elements of a seriously displaced sex drive. Had you ever thought of seeking professional counselling? You'll be having me hang furry dice from her titties next.'

John told Brandon to go and fuck himself and, amidst the light-hearted exchange of crass banter and name-calling, Cassie realised the master wasn't going to answer John's question. Waves of gratitude washed over but, as she handed John his cigar, she warned herself not to feel too kindly disposed towards Brandon. It was easy to appreciate his one act of kindness but it had to be balanced against everything else he had put her through over the last two weeks. Aside from her imprisonment there had been the thrashing, the bondage, the purgatory of having to give Faye her enema, and a host of other inhumane torments.

The memory of each violation rang through her mind as she went through the ceremony of preparing Brandon's cigar. She could see he was watching intently, and knew he considered her indebted for not replying to John's blunt question, yet it was impossible to read anything else from his fixed expression. Her worry that he had something diabolical planned for her continued to grow as she finally passed him his lit cigar.

'I can't believe you trained her to do that,' John laughed. 'That's fucking amazing. Will she do that for me if I win her back tonight?'

Cassie closed her eyes and hoped no one would see her response. She wanted John to win her this evening – the success of her escape plan depended on him winning her – but she could see her future at J & C Property Developments was now over. He would constantly be expecting her to behave like the servile slut Brandon had trained and, no matter how many times she tried explaining she had assumed the role as a means to an end, John wouldn't be able to see past the argument that she had done it once so she could do it again. Miserably, she hoped the players' interest in her had begun to subside so no one would notice her tears.

Stephen leant back thoughtfully and blew twin plumes of smoke through this nostrils. Cassie glanced at him and thought he looked to be savouring the rank flavour of his cigar with more relish than was necessary.

'A woman is only a woman,' he quoted sombrely, 'but a good cigar is a smoke.'

John frowned and then sputtered laughter. 'What the fuck does that mean?'

'Johnny's not really into Kipling,' Brandon grinned.

'No,' John agreed. 'Johnny's into winning back his Gemballa. Are we getting on with the game, or not?'

Cassie glared at him. She was miserably aware that, even as a potential sex slave, she wasn't at the top of John's priority list. If the evening came down to a straight choice of him being able to reclaim his beloved car or her, she didn't doubt he would be driving home alone in the converted guard's red Porsche.

Brandon leant across the table and glanced from John to Stephen. 'Do you both want to get right into the game?' he asked. 'Or did either of you plan to start this evening in a more traditional manner?'

Cassie held her breath, waiting for their replies. She was anxious to get the card game underway. Knowing John would be an active participant in whatever humiliations happened next, Cassie wondered how she could have been so foolish as to believe this was the easiest way for her to forge an escape.

'We haven't initiated your dealer yet,' Stephen remembered. He nudged John and said, 'Don't you think we should get that detail over and done with before she starts handing out the cards?'

'Bonus,' John cried enthusiastically. His cigar was clenched between his teeth and this time he did applaud.

The patter of his hands echoed hollowly in the flat acoustics of the games room and Cassie wondered if it was possible to loathe anyone as much as she currently despised her former business partner. She drew a ragged breath and, at Brandon's command, she climbed onto the poker table and knelt on all fours. The tray swayed beneath her and its weight grew heavier with each passing second. The numbness had dissipated and the clamps were beginning to make their presence felt against her nipples. The relentless bite of the jaws forced a dull pulse to throb through each nub and every pendulous swing increased her agony.

'You're expected to deal honestly and fairly,' Brandon said, standing in front of her. 'Are you aware of that?'

Cassie didn't worry that he might have seen through her plans because Faye had told her this was a regular feature of the evening. She raised her head so she could meet the unreadable study of his stern expression. 'I'm aware of what's expected from me.'

'If we have any suspicion that you're not dealing properly we'll punish you soundly.' His words had the ring of a prepared speech but Cassie listened attentively, fearful of missing anything that might be important. 'What you're going to experience now isn't even a fraction of the misery we'll make you endure if you're caught cheating,' Brandon went on, 'but it should serve to remind you that we won't tolerate dishonesty.'

Behind her a hand slapped her buttock.

Cassie wanted to cringe from the contact, hating the way the smack of the palm evoked a pleasantly warming glow. She couldn't see which of them had struck her but she suspected it was Stephen. While she believed John would be eager for the chance to touch her, Cassie expected him to make the punishment far more intimate and she was dreading the moment when that happened.

The hand slapped again, this time reddening her other cheek. The tips of fingers brushed against her cleft, rekindling all the sensations she had enjoyed after being shaved. It was a disturbing feeling because, while she didn't want to have the hand landing against her backside, she couldn't honestly say it was without pleasure.

'Deal fairly,' Stephen said. 'Deal fairly, or I'll make you sorry.'

The curt tone of his voice told her that was all he was going to say and she sighed, grateful the first aspect of this ordeal was over. She heard the groan of his chair being dragged against the floor and, without needing to look, she knew he was resuming his seat.

'Why weren't you ever like this in the office?' John complained.

He slapped his hand against her backside with resounding force. The vibration shook through her and her dealer's tray swayed vigorously. While Stephen's touch had been light and suggestively sexual, John's blow was purely intended to hurt. Cassie didn't know if he was aware of his own strength and there was no time to dwell on the matter as he slapped her for a second time. His hand remained cupping her aching orb and his fingers crept closer to her pussy.

'You really could have brightened up our boring office,' he laughed, teasing against her wetness. He inched past her labia, sliding gently against her slit, until she was aware of her excitement facilitating his entry. A note of genuine irritation crept into John's voice as he continued to talk. 'But, instead of doing anything fun, you play the role of an ice-maiden for me, and then become a sex slut for this bald-headed bastard.'

She glared mutely at the table, thankful she didn't have to look at John while he fingered her pussy and berated her for what she had become. Rather than continue to explore her confines he clutched the flesh of her backside then wrenched his hand away. Before Cassie could come to terms with the anguish he wrought through her buttock, John was smacking his hand against the cheek with a raw, powerful clap.

Tears spilled down her cheeks and landed in wet droplets beneath her.

'I hope I get the chance to win you back this evening,' he growled. His voice was low, as though he wanted the words to stay between them and his tone was thick with unexpected menace. 'I hope I get the chance to win you back,' he repeated. 'Because, if I do, I'll teach you to perform a few tricks that Jock here wouldn't dare have taught you.'

The droplets of tears became a flood.

'Have you finished trying to tempt her to deal in your favour?' Brandon asked coolly.

Stephen laughed and, without being able to see, Cassie could tell John was embarrassed to be the subject of their mirth.

'I haven't quite finished,' he said loftily. Leaning closer, pushing his mouth near to her ear, he grabbed her lobe between his teeth and gnawed on the flesh. 'If you want to cheat tonight, throw a couple of royal flushes in my direction.' Laughing nastily he added, 'The others won't mind if you do that.'

Cassie bit back a retort, sighing with relief when he finally moved his mouth away. He delivered a parting slap to her buttocks, chilling her with the force he used, and then she was allowed to climb down and take her position in the dealer's chair. It was hard to adjust her aching backside to the seat and eventually she decided it would simply have to be another torment she suffered for the sake of her escape.

'You never used your tawse on her,' Stephen observed.

Brandon shook his head. 'I've got other punishments lined up for this one later tonight,' he explained. 'The secret is in knowing when to chastise them and when to reward them, isn't that right, Johnny?'

John glowered, drawing on his cigar and raising his middle finger in Brandon's direction. Cassie realised it was the same finger he had slipped into her pussy and she was mortified to see the end glistened wetly with the remnants of her arousal.

She waited until she was told to begin dealing and then threw each player five cards. Forcing herself to concentrate on the immediate future, rather than the suffering of the present, she went through the motions of dealing and silently reiterated her plans. Faye had said Brandon was most likely to include her in the stakes if his confidence was boosted by a winning streak. However, she had also added that, for John to match Brandon's call each time, he would need to believe he was enjoying a run of good fortune. Consequently Cassie intended to let them each win every other hand, allowing Stephen to fund their victories. It meant paying careful attention to what she was doing but Cassie preferred to occupy her mind with that rather than think about the other things happening in the room.

'It really is a shame you were never more like this in our office,' John said, squeezing her thigh.

Cassie didn't know he had managed to sidle so close but she wished he hadn't. His fingers were intrusive, touching high at the top of her leg, and she knew he intended to make the contact more intimate. Holding herself rigid, remembering she wasn't allowed to converse with him and thankful for that regulation, she dealt a fresh hand of cards to each player without replying.

'You seem very interested in my dealer,' Brandon observed. 'Do you want me to use her as my ante for this hand?'

Cassie flushed brightly. She wasn't sure if she had wanted Brandon to make this suggestion so early in the evening and couldn't decide if it worked to her advantage or against it.

'I'd prefer it if you got her to suck my dick,' John replied honestly. He drained his whisky glass and said, 'The sight of her like this has had me bursting to screw her since I came in here.'

'She's our dealer tonight.' Brandon sounded as though he was bored with John's vulgarity. 'If you want your dick sucking I've got other girls who can do that for you and no doubt they could do it better than this one would. Now, answer the damned question: do you want me to put her up as my ante for this hand?'

John seemed to consider his reply before responding. He left his untouched cards on the table, went to the bar to replenish his drink, then returned with a knowing grin on his face. 'Go on then,' he grinned. 'I'll take the bitch off your hands if that's what you want.'

Cassie felt her spirits sink as she listened to him. She was amazed to recall she had once hoped he might fill the position as the man in her life. While she knew this was neither the time nor the place for a bout of introspection, it was disheartening to discover she had been so blind to all of John's shortcomings.

John picked up his hand and grinned at the three aces she had dealt.

Cassie could see Brandon was solemnly regarding his pair of eights without giving anything away. Stephen glanced at his cards then threw them back onto the table. His curse of disgust was enough to let them all know he had folded.

'Go on then, Johnny,' Brandon encouraged. 'What are you going to put into the pot to match the current call?'

'I'll place five grand against Cassie,' he said, dropping a handful of chips onto her tray, 'and I'll raise you five more.'

Brandon smiled tightly. 'I have to pay another five to stay in? OK.'

Cassie watched the pair. She was chilled by the way they could calmly play cards in exchange for control of her life and wished she could decide on the best course of action. She wanted to let John win the game, desperate to have him take her out of Brandon's home so she could return to her normal life. But, seeing how eager he was to raise the stakes, she could imagine he would gamble her again before she had a chance to get out of the room and she wasn't sure she could continually sway the results to her advantage without arousing suspicion. She reminded herself it was safer to stick with her original plan, knowing she shouldn't do anything until Marion gave a signal. She waited for Brandon to call, then dealt John two worthless picture cards.

He continued smiling, seeming confident he held a winning hand.

Despising herself, Cassie dealt Brandon another pair of eights.

The games continued for an hour, pausing only so the players could replenish their drinks, or snatch something from the buffet table. Cassie monitored what was being lost and won, although the task was made difficult by the interminable presence of the tray. Each time the stakes were raised one player or another would toss a handful of the gold chips onto her tray. Towards the end of each hand she was able to concentrate on little else except the torment being torn from the ends of her nipples. If it had only been discomfort, Cassie supposed she could have tolerated what was happening but, because each increase in weight heightened her responsiveness, she thought it would soon become too much. Each teat felt as though it was smouldering with need and she didn't doubt it would only take the lightest of touches to have her in the throes of orgasm.

Not daring to think about that, she focused her thoughts on the games and tried to remain involved yet distant as the night drew on.

'Please, Master Brandon. Please, Master Brandon.'

Cassie had been listening for the words for so long she wondered if they had come from her imagination. She turned towards Marion, making her interest seem subtle so no one else would notice that she was looking. The brunette was thrashing wildly, the candle spluttering between her legs and Cassie wondered how she could tolerate such a burning heat so close to her cleft. She wasn't sure if Marion was acting to make her cries more believable, or if she had genuinely held on for as long as her body could cope with the growing discomfort. Rivulets of spent wax trailed down her body and one stream dangled from the tip of her breast. In the wad that was caked around her cleft Cassie could see the spatters closest to her sex glistened as though they were still warm.

'Please, Master Brandon,' Marion gasped. 'Please.'

Brandon glanced in her direction, sniffed disdainfully, then turned back to the game. Neither of the others paid her any heed and, knowing the chance to escape was almost upon her, Cassie dealt the final hand of the evening. As she had planned she threw John his aces, then passed Brandon the kings that would make him gamble everything. She held her breath as she distributed the cards, hoping no one chose this moment to notice how carefully she was dealing. A shiver bristled up her spine as she realised, within the next few minutes she might be away from Brandon McPherson and his hateful house forever.

The trill of a mobile phone broke the tense silence.

Both John and Brandon reached for their jacket pockets but it was Stephen who held up his Motorola, pacifying them both with a sheepish grin. 'I forgot to turn it off,' he explained. Pressing the keypad he put the phone to his ear and said, 'I told you only to disturb me in the case of an emergency. This had better be important.'

Brandon and John studied the backs of their cards, neither of them lifting their hands while Cassie continued to hold her breath. She wished Stephen would hurry up and conclude his call so they could get on with the game. Until the three of them had looked at what they'd been dealt she knew the hand hadn't properly begun.

'I know one of the proposals was due to land there this evening,' Stephen complained. 'If I'd been bothered about that I could have read a copy of it while I was here.' Not bothering to put his hand over the mouthpiece he glanced at Brandon and said, 'That girl you loaned me to work in the office is proving herself annoyingly diligent.'

Brandon smiled while John rolled his eyes.

Cassie glared at all three of them wishing they could get this distraction out of the way and play the final hand of the night.

'I'll look at it when I get back,' Stephen said, snapping his phone closed. He glanced at the untouched cards in front of him and shook his head miserably. 'I might as well go now,' he told Brandon sadly. 'The mood's been broken for me.'

'Don't go,' John complained. 'Brandon and I can't play five card draw if there's just the two of us.'

Cassie could have repeated his cry, and with an awful lot more passion. She could see the opportunity for escape was slipping through her fingers. The idea loomed that she would be trapped at Brandon's home for ever and she tried to work out why her plans hadn't allowed for a development like this.

Stephen shook his head. 'I've lost enough this evening and I'm really not in the mood to lose much more. I'll see you both next Friday.' Climbing out of his chair, he bade them all goodnight and left.

Marion shrieked and the room was plunged into darkness.

Sitting quietly at the table, Cassie stared ahead in stunned despair.

Twelve

The doors of Harwood Manor opened onto a majestic double staircase. Circling up and around the entrance hall, leading to an elegant, galleried mezzanine, it was one of the few original features that had withstood the ravages of time. The delicate spindles remained intact and, in spite of a little wear, each step had been polished and maintained to its original state of perfection. Even close to midnight, caught under the unflattering light of site illumination, it was easy to see the staircase had once made the entrance hall a magnificent spectacle.

'Isn't this house simply divine?' Laura giggled, swinging from one newel post. She wore her hair loose this evening and it bounced enticingly over the shoulders of her overcoat. 'Isn't this hall the most beautiful thing ever?'

Her ebullient mood and the enthusiasm in her voice went some way to appease Vicky's worries but they didn't entirely calm her. She wasn't comfortable visiting empty buildings, especially in the middle of a Sunday night, and Laura had yet to tell her why they had to have their discussion in the Harwood property. She had thought a restaurant or a bar might be more civilised and, when both of those suggestions had been declined, she had even said it would be all right if Laura wanted to visit the sanctuary of her bedsit. But, with typical belligerence, Laura had insisted they liaise at Harwood Manor.

Feeling like a trespasser, Vicky followed her new friend into the building and closed the door behind them. 'Who left the lights on?' she asked, nodding at the stark sodium bulbs illuminating the stairs.

Laura grinned. 'I had them put on. I didn't want you losing me in the dark.'

The words alluded to mischief and, because Laura followed her statement with another throaty giggle, Vicky felt sure the woman was planning something deliciously wicked. The last of her reservations began to fade and, as she linked her arm in Laura's, she decided the night wasn't going to be the disappointment she had feared it might be. If the speed of her accelerating pulse was an indicator, Vicky guessed the evening might prove itself to be very satisfying. 'What are we doing here?' she asked. 'What was so important that we have to discuss it now, and here, in this place?'

'First things first,' Laura grinned. She took Vicky in her embrace and kissed hungrily. After the cool of the night outside, her mouth was a warm, inviting promise. Lowering her voice to a husky whisper she broke their kiss briefly to say, 'When I tell you what I have to tell you, I want you as my captive audience.'

The pressure of the woman's body against hers was enough to dispel any argument she might have made. Vicky could feel the swell of Laura's perfect breasts pushing against her own and – when she moved a leg between hers, and excited a whisper of electricity from between their stocking-clad thighs – the last of Vicky's resistance melted. 'Captive, how?'

Stepping away from her, Laura shrugged off her coat and let it fall to the dusty floor. She was wearing a dark blue suit but this time it was accessorised with a silk, aquamarine scarf. Slowly, removing it as though she was performing a seductive strip, she slid the garment from her neck. Climbing onto the first stair, she encouraged Vicky to join her, and then made her place her hands around the newel post. 'I want you captive in this way,' she whispered, looping the fabric around Vicky's wrists. 'Trust me. You'll have a better appreciation of what I'm saying if you just let me fasten this properly.'

It was impossible to contain all her doubts – Vicky still didn't believe Laura was entirely trustworthy, and she wasn't overly keen to be tied to the banister of the deserted house – but intrigue and the promise of excitement lulled her into relenting. Not wanting to argue, and relishing the feel of the whisper soft fabric gliding over her wrists, Vicky allowed Laura to bind her. The silky frisson became firmer as Laura pulled the scarf tight. After tying a final knot she stepped back and her smile broadened.

Unnerved, but determined not to show it, Vicky asked, 'Am I captive now?'

Laura nodded. 'You're captive,' she agreed, 'but I think we need a little more preparation before the moment's just right.' Without asking, she reached for Vicky's jacket and began to unfasten the buttons.

'What do you think you're doing?'

'Nothing you won't enjoy,' Laura assured her. She pecked a small kiss against the corner of Vicky's mouth and added, 'Nothing that we won't both enjoy.' As she spoke her fingers worked nimbly over the buttons. She unfastened the jacket, released all the buttons on Vicky's blouse, then started to pull at the zipper on her skirt.

'You can't undress me,' Vicky protested. 'Not in here.' She struggled to find a plausible argument but the best she could come up with was, 'Someone might come in. Someone might come in *and catch us*.'

Laura laughed. She held up a bunch of keys and said, 'No one else is going to come in. The door's locked and I have the only key.'

The assurance did little to calm Vicky's doubts. She tugged again at the bondage but her wrists were firmly secured around the post. Glancing warily around, she asked, 'What about Mr Price? He owns this building, doesn't he? Doesn't he have a key?'

Laura nodded and tugged the zipper down.

Vicky's skirt fell to her ankles and left her feeling chilly and exposed. She had guessed Laura might want to play this evening, and had worn appropriate lingerie with that in mind. Her bra was black and lacy, hugging the swell of both orbs. The matching thong tapered off to a fine string that became invisible between her buttocks. She had thought the stockings and suspender belt would make an exciting accoutrement but Vicky hadn't expected to be displaying her finest underwear in the hall of the desolate Harwood Manor. 'You nodded,' she pointed out. 'Are you saying Mr Price does have a key?' she asked worriedly. 'Doesn't that mean there's a chance he might surprise us?'

'Of course Mr Price has a key,' Laura said absently, 'but he isn't going to surprise us. Mr Price is already here.'

Vicky stared at her, wondering if this was a twisted joke. It was only when she heard the creak of footsteps from above she realised Laura was being perfectly serious. Stephen Price was in the building and walking down the staircase towards them. The vulnerability of her position became suddenly acute and unwanted. She tugged fruitlessly at the scarf binding her wrists.

'Hello again,' Stephen smiled as he walked past her. He glanced at her bound wrists and his grin tightened with approval. 'I see Laura has been getting you prepped.'

With his swarthy complexion and dapper dress sense, he always reminded Vicky of an Italian mobster. She blushed as her eyes met his and familiar feelings of guilt and forbidden desire began to overwhelm her.

'. . . *a time and a place for everything . . . this is never the place for private behaviour . . .*'

The memory of Cassie's words echoed through her mind and Vicky half expected Stephen to recite them for her. Admittedly, the last time she had seen him she had held his erection in her mouth but, because his lecherous smile said he was also thinking of that moment, it seemed like more intimacy than she wanted to share. She hurriedly lowered her gaze and cursed Laura for putting her in such an invidious situation. Glaring at the brunette she said, 'I thought we were going to be alone.'

Laura raised her eyebrows in surprise.

Considering her appetites and habits, Vicky thought her new friend had a remarkable ability to feign naïvety and innocence and, once again, she was almost overwhelmed by adulation.

'I didn't say we were going to be alone, did I?' Laura asked.

'No. You didn't say we were going to be alone. But . . .'

'And this is Mr Price's property,' Laura added with meaning. 'So you would agree, he does have some rights to be here, wouldn't you?'

'I'm not disputing that,' Vicky broke in. She could hear herself beginning to grow exasperated, as often happened while talking to Laura. The brunette was exciting and daring but there were times when she could be the most infuriating person alive. 'I was just saying –' Vicky got no further with her sentence, rendered mute by the intimate touch of Stephen's hand against her backside. The tips of his fingers brushed the gusset of her thong, surreptitiously stroking her labia through the flimsy strip of lace. Unable to contain her reaction, Vicky squealed indignantly.

Stephen snatched his hand away. 'I thought –' he began.

'It's all right,' Laura assured him. 'Feel free to do whatever you like with this one. She only pretends to object. If we're all being honest, she really likes it.'

Vicky stared at Laura with disbelief but the brunette simply grinned in reply. Making herself comfortable on a convenient step, smoking another of the cigarettes she had stolen from Vicky's packet, Laura waved encouragement for Stephen to continue doing as he pleased.

His hands went to the waistband of Vicky's thong. His fingertips were warm against her bare flesh and, as he began to draw the panties down, her loins were stirred by a heightened sense of anticipation. Not daring to reprimand him, and scared of what else might be about to happen, Vicky tried to silently beseech Laura for assistance.

Laura tilted her head back and blew a trio of smoke rings towards the distant ceiling. 'Stephen's made up his mind,' she explained. 'He's decided which proposal he wants to go with and that's why the three of us are here.' When she lowered her head, her smile shone with enthusiasm as she added, 'This is like our own private celebration.'

Vicky had difficulty concentrating on the words.

Still behind her, Stephen had slipped the thong down to her ankles and was nudging her legs wider apart. She was aware of him standing close, the pressure of his erection thrusting through his trousers and rubbing against her freshly exposed cleft. Leaning over her he cupped her breasts and squeezed. After grinding himself dryly between her legs, he eased her breasts out of her bra so his fingers were able to tease her nipples. Without any discernible effort he took her from being reluctant and wary, to a state of feverish arousal.

Staring at Laura, trying desperately to appear unaffected by Stephen's touch, she said, 'Did you say Mr Price has made a decision?'

Laura nodded.

'And did you do as you said you would?' She lowered her voice to a pantomime whisper trusting that, if Stephen did hear what she was saying, he would be polite enough to pretend otherwise. Her hopes of securing the contract overrode her common sense and obliterated her concerns about the morality of whether or not she should be allowing him to continue. The only important thing was confirming she had achieved success. 'Did you do like you said you were going to?' she asked eagerly. 'Have you put my name on the winning proposal?'

Laura lowered her gaze. 'That was one of the things I wanted to talk to you about,' she mumbled. 'Maybe we'll get back to that in a moment.'

Stephen cupped Vicky's buttocks, spreading them apart as he roughly kneaded both mounds. The delicate flesh of her pussy and anus were stretched taut and the rush of her burgeoning excitement quickened. 'I don't know which to do first,' he growled. 'Should I cane your arse first, or just go ahead and fuck you?'

The coarseness of his suggestion filled Vicky with a desperate need. Trying not to show her arousal, uncomfortable with how he might regard her if he believed she was turned on by his ungallant manhandling, she turned to Laura in the hope her friend might find a way to spare her embarrassment.

'Do whichever you want, Mr Price,' Laura said sweetly. 'The choice is yours. Just remember: she's here for your convenience.'

Vicky stared at her in amazement. She couldn't believe her friend had given the man unconditional permission to use her and she wondered if there was anything she could say that might make him refrain. Feeling his fingers probe clumsily around her anus, she suspected he was now determined to use her however he desired.

Coolly, Laura returned Vicky's gaze. 'There is a selection of crops in the umbrella stand to your right, Mr Price,' she said carefully. 'Might I recommend you use the dressage whip? It does have an evil bite in its kiss.'

Stephen thanked her while Vicky glared. She tried tugging again at the scarf around her wrists but Laura had fastened it securely. Forcing her thoughts back to the most important matter, she lowered her voice to a hiss and asked, 'Have you put my name on the winning proposal?'

Laura stretched back against the steps and fixed her smile behind Vicky. Her eyes were lit with obvious appreciation, as though she was assuring Stephen of her approval. Vicky had a moment to wonder what exchange might be passing between the pair when the dressage whip struck. A thin line of fire branded both buttocks and she gasped with shock as the pain reverberated through her cheeks.

'Not bad.'

Stephen sounded to be grinning but, before that thought could properly register in Vicky's mind, he was delivering another blow to her backside. Scoring the tops of her thighs, possibly striking the stockings, although she couldn't tell for sure, a second wave of blistering agony blazed through her behind.

'Not bad at all.'

Vicky gripped the banister as he repeatedly smacked the dressage whip against her. The pain was debilitating but it preceded a more powerful response. Each searing bite evoked a raw and desperate desire. Every time he landed a shot, she could feel her arousal growing. Quickly, her need for satisfaction became unbearable. Not bothering to fight the reaction, happy to give in to the shameful pleasure of surrender, she tensed herself in anticipation of Stephen's next blow.

With a swift, unsettling whistle, it struck hard across both cheeks.

'Try the paddle,' Laura suggested. Vicky blinked her gaze clear and saw the brunette had shifted her legs apart. Still smoking the remainder of her cigarette, her other hand rested over her lap. She raised the hem of

200

her skirt and revealed a view of her knickerless cleft. Idly, she began to toy with herself as she smiled at Vicky. 'Use the *studded* paddle,' she called, savouring the word as she added the emphasis. 'It's got a sting in the tail that I'm sure she'll appreciate.'

Vicky had a moment to wonder which of them was in control – with Stephen, supposedly a master, who took instructions from Laura, allegedly a slave – and then he was slapping the paddle against her backside.

As Laura had suggested, it was exactly the right implement to use. Whereas the dressage whip had left a line of fire in its wake, this warmed each cheek it struck. The impact rekindled the embers of every blow and, after Stephen had smacked it against her twice more, Vicky understood what Laura had meant about the paddle having a sting in its tail. Where the studs fell against her skin her buttocks throbbed with a pulse that beat in tempo with her arousal. Relishing the delicious pleasure of her punishment, Vicky arched her back and raised her backside so Stephen had a better target.

Laura tossed her cigarette to the floor and stamped on it, before using both hands on her sex. She splayed her pussy wide open, licked her index finger, then teased the wet tip against herself. Her lips were a flushed, hungry pink and, as she rubbed with growing urgency, the dark centre of her hole opened and closed.

Mesmerised, Vicky couldn't draw her gaze away from the sight. She willed herself not to blink each time Stephen slapped the paddle across her rear cheeks and groaned as her body inched closer to the bliss of release. Grinning to herself through tears of joy, she saw Laura had been right about one more thing when she had given Stephen his instructions. Just as the brunette had said she would, Vicky decided she really was appreciating the paddle.

Laura rubbed the pulsing nub of her clitoris then gasped as though the self-pleasure was too intense. She looked surprised by her own responsiveness and met Vicky's curiosity with a knowing wink. 'Do you remember me saying I wanted to impose one condition on the proposal?' she asked.

She spoke in a sultry whisper and at first Vicky wasn't sure if the woman was talking to her, or merely thinking out loud. Trying to concentrate on the conversation, not letting herself be distracted by the weighty shots Stephen smacked against her buttocks, she growled, 'Of course I remember you saying that.' Every second of that fateful day was etched in her memory and she had revisited it repeatedly while alone in her bed. 'We were on the steps, just outside the door behind me. You negotiated our current arrangement.'

Laura nodded. She was chasing lazy circles against her sex and clearly enjoying herself because her hands shook with afterechoes of her passion. 'Do you remember asking what that condition was?'

'Yes,' Vicky hissed. 'But you never told me. You said you were going to tell me the next time we met but we've seen one another a dozen times since then and still you haven't said –'

'I'm willing to tell you now,' Laura breathed. 'If you still want to know, I'm more than willing to tell you.'

Stephen slapped the paddle against Vicky's backside.

Vicky bit her lip to contain an excited squeal. Staring solemnly at Laura, intrigued that the moment of revelation was growing closer, she said, 'Go on then. Tell me.'

Behind her, there was a clatter as Stephen threw the paddle to the floor. Vicky heard the unmistakable sound of a zipper being pulled down and then she felt the head of his erection pushing between her legs. His arousal was obvious and, as he rubbed the swollen end of his dome over her burning lips, she longed for him to stop taunting her and simply fill her with his thickness.

Not bothering to get up properly, crawling on her knees, Laura moved to Vicky's side. She kept one hand between her legs fingering her hole so greedily the squelch of her sex was clearly audible. Her perpetual sneer had vanished this evening and, in its place, was a smile of honest wonder. 'Isn't this hall beautiful?'

Vicky didn't need to look around the hall to concede it was spectacular and Stephen didn't allow her the opportunity. He placed his shaft over the centre of her sex, squeezed a tight hold on her aching buttocks, then plunged himself firmly inside. He entered with a brutal rush and spread her sex muscles wide apart. The scrub of his pubic hairs was abrasive against her glowing backside but the reminder of pain only served to heighten her appreciation.

'I fell in love with this hall when I first saw it,' Laura confessed. 'The splendour of the architecture; the majesty of the decor; the decadent elegance of the whole, marvellous building. I simply fell in love with it.'

Vicky didn't hear a word.

Stephen was pushing in and out, muttering coarse expletives that were both disparaging and exciting. He rode her with a controlled urgency that wasn't quite the frenetic pace she craved, but promised to get there eventually. His thrusts continued slowly and she knew he was using her solely for his own pleasure. Whatever satisfaction she did glean would be incidental to Stephen's intentions and, somehow, that heightened her excitement.

'Couldn't you just fall in love with this whole house?' Laura asked. 'Isn't it just divine?'

But Vicky was lost in the pleasure Stephen was bestowing and oblivious to Laura's question. With her hands bound to the post she was unable to participate in any way other than to squeeze her pussy muscles tightly around his shaft. Her sex sang with a growing bliss that promised to eclipse every pleasure she had ever experienced. She was torn between a desire to give in and let the orgasm tear through her, or briefly resist in the hope that waiting might make the pleasure even more memorable.

'You haven't answered me,' Laura whispered.

Her face was close to Vicky's and she pecked small kisses against her mouth and chin. The scent of excitement radiated from her in a tang of secret musk. When she lovingly caressed Vicky's cheek, her fingertips left a dewy residue of wetness in their wake. Greedy to savour every experience the night could offer, Vicky twisted her neck until she was able to lick hungrily at the brunette's sodden hand.

Laura chuckled and continued to frig herself, occasionally pausing so Vicky could lick her fingers. Repeatedly, her body was buffeted with tremors of burgeoning bliss. 'You still haven't answered me,' she whispered. 'Don't you think this hall is divine?'

Vicky blinked her vision clear and smiled to show her lack of understanding. She wasn't sure if she had passed out at some point but it was clear she had missed a lot of what Laura had been saying. The brunette had been on the verge of telling her something about the proposal, although Vicky couldn't remember if it was to do with her being allocated the contract, or the condition Laura wanted to impose. Struggling to think past the swelling pleasure between her legs, Vicky realised she hadn't heard Laura explain either of those matters.

'I really fell in love with this place,' Laura confided. Her mouth was close to Vicky's and she delivered soft kisses between every other word. 'Then, when I heard how Stephen planned to develop it, I decided I had to be a part of the project.'

Her words made no sense and Vicky shook her head. 'You wanted to be a part of the house?' she frowned. 'I don't understand. What do you mean?'

'That's why I've tied you to the stair, silly,' Laura laughed. 'I'm trying to show you how I'm going to be involved.'

'It's a shame your pussy isn't tighter,' Stephen growled. 'I wanted to ride something that really squeezed my cock this evening.'

He tugged his shaft from Vicky's sex leaving her feeling hollow and empty. She choked back a wail of disappointment, ignoring Laura so she could glance over her shoulder and try to encourage him to continue. He remained standing between her legs, one hand kneading her buttocks while he thoughtfully studied her cleft. His erection stood hard and ready and he idly stroked his foreskin back and forth as he looked down on her. Watching his face, Vicky thought he looked like a man trying to make a decision. When she realised what he was planning a sick thrill of excitement tore through her. She opened her eyes wide to show her reluctance but she didn't dare voice any resistance for fear he might do as she said.

'You know you want it here,' Stephen said, nudging the end of his shaft over her anus, 'and I know I want it here. Are you going to hold still while I slide it inside?'

Vicky held herself rigid. She didn't watch him as he entered, not wanting to spoil the moment by having to look at Stephen's unappealing face. The pleasure was spectacular and degrading and she felt the first sparkle of her climax begin to flow through her body as he pushed ever deeper. Her anus felt stretched to the point of bursting and shockwaves of elation rippled through every pore.

'You're not listening to a word I'm saying, are you?' Laura complained.

She continued kissing but stole one hand against Vicky's breast.

Caught on a rising tide of passion, close to the promise of release she was so desperate to achieve, Vicky relished the touch of the woman's hand. She was anticipating a subtle stimulation and it came as a shock when Laura squeezed and tugged. The pain was so bright it threatened to push her beyond the brink of orgasm and she shrieked, sure she had reached her pinnacle.

'Under the proposals Stephen will be working with, this place should be up and running within three months,' Laura explained.

Vicky heard her but the words meant nothing. She was revelling in her climax and oblivious to everything else around her. She was aware of her knees buckling – and as she fell to the floor she felt the rude withdrawal of Stephen's shaft – but it was all of tertiary importance alongside the magnificence of her pleasure.

'She's done,' Stephen growled. 'Let me use you now.'

Vicky guessed he was talking to Laura because, dangling from her restraints at the newel post, she realised she was no longer in a fit state to be spoken to. Her body still throbbed with the aftermath of her release and she collapsed completely on the stair when Laura unfastened her hands.

Boldly, almost challenging him with her arrogance, Laura threw back her head to clear the hair from her face. She bent over, pulled her skirt up to expose her bare sex, then grabbed the newel post with both hands. 'I'm ready when you are, Mr Price,' she informed him.

Stephen held her by the hips and plunged into her.

Watching the pair, Vicky realised all her arousal hadn't been spent. She could understand the visceral pleasure Laura had enjoyed from her position on the stairs and, not even realising she was still emulating her new friend, Vicky lit a cigarette and then began stroking herself while she watched.

'This place should be up and running within three months,' Laura repeated. She spoke in staccato sentences that were pushed out of her by each of Stephen's rough entries. 'That's when I should see my dreams come true. When the doors open, I'm going to be chained to this newel post and I'll be Harwood Manor's welcome mat. Doesn't that sound like the best thing ever?'

Vicky wasn't sure what it sounded like but she had to admit the idea was exciting. She had been rubbing languidly against her cleft but, listening to Laura's suggestion she slowed her pace even further, fearful she would ignite another orgasm too soon to enjoy it properly.

Grunting happily beneath each penetration, Laura giggled as she continued explaining her dream. To Vicky it looked as though the mere act of thinking about what she wanted was enough to take her close to the edge of her climax and she secretly envied Laura the pleasure she was enjoying.

'Any visiting master will be able to use me how he sees fit,' she gasped. 'Any visiting master can cane my arse if he wants to. He can screw me; he can have me swallow his come; I'll be here for the benefit of anyone and everyone who walks through that door.'

Vicky shivered. She couldn't explain why she found the image appealing – it should have sounded base, and vulgar and thoroughly unpleasant – but as Laura continued to talk, Vicky began to understand her friend's enthusiasm and wondered why she had never harboured such a glorious ambition herself. 'Is that what you want from this?' she asked. 'Is that what you've been after all along?'

'That's what I was born for,' Laura said enthusiastically.

Stephen pushed forward and she thrust herself back to meet his entry. If it was a struggle to see which of them was the more dominant lover, Vicky couldn't decide who was winning. Laura was in the submissive position, with her hands clasped around the newel post and her backside thrust out for his use, but Stephen looked to be struggling to keep up with her urgent pace.

'Won't it be marvellous?' Laura sighed. 'I'll be giving pleasure to every master who visits here. Even the ones who don't touch me; I'll be giving them pleasure because they'll have decided I'm beneath them.'

Vicky rubbed more briskly at her sex. She wasn't sure if her body was ready to cope with the explosion of another orgasm but she knew she had to find out. Gritting her teeth, holding one of the banister's spindles to steady herself, she masturbated frantically in a bid to expel the welling climax.

'And then there are the slaves . . .'

Laura sounded lost in the fantasies of her own imagination. Stephen was still riding her but his involvement was only peripheral to the true source of her mounting excitement. The brunette was staring into the furthest corners of the ceiling and her smile was tinged with a faraway quality.

'Every slave who gets dragged in here will envy me,' Laura explained. 'They'll all be jealous while their master's spend themselves inside me; they'll all be craving the humiliation I have to suffer and they'll all wish they were me. I'll have the most enviable position of any piece of property in this country.'

She groaned and, in that sound, Vicky could hear the woman was close to the point of release. Struggling to stave off the climax until she was ready to accept it, Laura gripped the newel post tightly and drew a series of ragged breaths.

'That's why I was so desperate to negotiate with someone about this contract. I meant to tell you sooner but I never quite got round to it. I've written myself into the proposal.' Her smile was etched with triumph as she added, 'I've written myself into the proposal and Stephen's agreed that I'll be the perfect asset for his intended leisure facility. Any development has to agree to use me as the welcome mat for the first twelve months of operation.'

Vicky gaped at her. She would have been able to relish the blistering release of a second orgasm if her mood hadn't been dampened by a worrying thought. Her doubts grew deeper when she studied Laura's flushed face because perfect realisation washed over her. 'You haven't put the proposal in my name,' Vicky said thickly. 'Stephen's accepted a contract and you haven't put my name on it, have you?'

Laura groaned.

Stephen continued riding her but his pace had quickened considerably. He looked on the verge of erupting and, judging from the way they were both gasping together, Vicky expected the pair to climax in unison.

'You haven't put my name on the proposal, have you?' Vicky demanded.

'I know I promised I would,' Laura began carefully, 'but I had to go back on my word to get my own way. You can understand that, can't you? I had to tell Stephen what I wanted, otherwise he would have just scratched the clause out of the contract, and then where would I have been?'

Miserably, Vicky took the hand away from her sex and began to straighten her clothes. The euphoria of the evening had been obliterated by this single revelation and she only wanted to go home and try to come to terms with the knowledge that she had failed. After fastening the last of her buttons, and pulling her skirt back into place, she turned her back on Laura and Stephen and started out of the door.

Stephen groaned as he climaxed. He held himself tight against Laura as he spent himself inside her hole. His eruption was obviously a satisfying experience because the brunette gripped the newel post more furiously and cried out with a sigh of unbridled joy. Vicky was watching her sadly when Laura regained control of her composure and finally saw she was about to leave.

'Where the hell do you think you're going?'

Vicky shrugged. In truth, she didn't know.

'Just because I didn't put your name on the proposal doesn't mean I wasn't thinking about you.' She shook her head as though unable to believe Vicky could have thought her guilty of such a lack of consideration. 'I've allowed for you to benefit from this arrangement as well,' she said, grabbing hold of Vicky's hand and leading her back to the stairs.

'How do you mean?' Vicky asked doubtfully. 'If you haven't put my name down as the person who submitted the proposal, how can you have allowed for me to benefit?'

Laura laughed and began to bind the silk scarf around her wrists again. 'The hall has a double staircase,' she pointed out. 'There are two newel posts and I told Stephen how much like me you are. He agreed it would make for a marvellous feature if there was a slave secured at each side of the entrance hall.' She kissed the puzzled frown from Vicky's lips and lowered her voice. 'Don't tell him I've told you, but he's already agreed that you can be secured to the second post.'

Smiling to herself, as the last of her reservations evaporated, Vicky was reminded of the haunting refrain from Cassie's words. There was a time and a place for everything, she realised.

And, thanks to Laura's guidance, Vicky knew she had found both the time and the place.

Thirteen

'What the hell do you think you're doing?'

The sound of the voice almost startled Cassie into squealing. The pair of tweezers she had stuffed into the lock flew out of her hand and clattered somewhere on the hall's unlit floor. She squinted into the darkness, still trying to work out who had caught her, when a hand fell on her shoulder.

'This is ridiculous. Come back to the cellar before you get caught. Brandon will thrash you senseless if he catches you trying to escape.'

Recognising Faye's voice, Cassie breathed a sigh. 'It's because I don't want Brandon to thrash me senseless that I am trying to escape,' she whispered. Her anger was mellowed by relief and, once she was over the shock of being surprised, it was easy to get back to the task of trying to break free. 'Help me find the tweezers, will you? I almost had the lock turning before you crept up on me.'

Although Faye was kneeling on the floor beside her, Cassie couldn't see anything more than the woman's silhouette against dark shadows. Her other senses seemed to be overcompensating for the loss of vision because she could detect the warmth of the blonde's nearness and the familiar perfume of her deodorant. The floral scent was almost lost beneath the aroma of fresh sweat and Cassie wondered what the woman could have been doing to cause such heavy perspiration. She didn't dwell on the possibilities for too long because a breast brushed against her arm and Cassie was disquieted to think the flesh might be bare.

'Help me find the damned tweezers,' she insisted, not wanting to think about the sensations Faye's nearness evoked. 'I know I'm pushing my luck staying out here too long and I won't be able to escape if I don't find the damned things.'

'You can't pick a lock with a pair of tweezers,' Faye scoffed. 'That's the sort of cheap trick they use in badly-written novels. It doesn't work that way in real life.'

Brushing her hands over the floorboards, Cassie sniffed indignantly. 'Of course I can't pick a lock with a pair of tweezers,' she agreed sarcastically. 'That's why I'm still in the dungeon. That's why I'm still chained to the cellar floor.' Her fingers fell against something slender and metallic and she grinned bitterly to herself. 'Found them!' she exclaimed quietly. 'Freedom beckons at last.'

'You unfastened your cuffs with a pair of tweezers?'

In the darkness it was difficult to work out if Faye was sceptical or impressed. She leant closer and Cassie was unsettled to feel something brush against her side. It was impossible to see in the blackness but she could have sworn she had been touched by Faye's nipple. The bud of flesh felt hard and excited and Cassie couldn't work out why her mind was torturing her with such vivid images. She tried to put the idea out of her thoughts and concentrate on the more important task of getting out of Brandon's home.

'Assuming you can pick the lock and get out of the front doors,' Faye began softly, 'what are you going to do then? Have you thought that far ahead?'

It was difficult to understand the point she was trying to make because her voice was infuriatingly neutral.

Regardless of how hard she listened, Cassie couldn't decide if Faye was about to offer valuable advice, or adding more doubts to the thousand and one reservations that were already making Cassie think she shouldn't be trying to escape by such a covert method.

'You do know we're in the middle of nowhere, don't you?' Faye pressed. 'You have no money, there's no public transport, and the nearest inhabited building is a good ten miles away. How do you expect to get back to civilisation armed with just your tweezers and wearing only your body stocking?'

Cassie made the effort to mentally distance herself from Faye's voice. She shoved the tweezers into the lock and began to wriggle the tips against the lock's tumblers. She wasn't entirely sure how she hoped they would work but, because the handcuffs had opened, she expected the same good fortune to stay with her for this lock. 'As soon as I've got through this door I'm going to get in John's Porsche and drive myself home,' she whispered. It was impossible to say the words without feeling a twinge of anticipatory excitement and an involuntary shiver swept through her. 'It doesn't matter how far I've got to travel. Money and public transport won't be an issue as long as there's petrol in the tank.' She smiled grimly to herself and said, 'That's how I intend to get back to civilisation.'

'It isn't a Porsche, it's a Gemballa,' Faye pointed out.

Cassie was about to argue that there was no real difference but Faye spoke over her.

'And, it isn't John's Gemballa anymore,' Faye pointed out. 'Since he lost it in the card game it rightfully belongs to Brandon. Everything that was won in that card game belongs to Brandon and you shouldn't be depriving him of property that is rightfully his.'

Cassie could tell Faye was hinting at something but she wouldn't let herself contemplate what it might be. Not wanting to be drawn into an argument, concentrating only on the tweezers and the lock, she said, 'Whoever it belongs to, I've stolen the key from Brandon's office, so I'll be driving it home. Whoever it rightfully belongs to can pay for all the speeding fines I'll earn in my hurry to put distance between myself and this place.'

Faye said nothing and Cassie took advantage of the silence and returned to trying to pick the lock. She was pleasantly surprised at the adaptability she had shown in learning so many new skills. Three weeks earlier she had known nothing about palming cards, picking locks or stealing keys. Now, after only a short spell in Brandon's custody, she realised she was showing all the talents of a promising petty criminal. She supposed it might have been more sensible if she had also stolen the key for the front door while she had the opportunity but that was only a small consideration and she wasn't going to let it sour her rising spirits. With a twisted brand of optimism she had never known before Cassie decided, if her position at J & C Property Developments was no longer tenable, there was always a chance for her to forge a career as either a burglar or a cardsharp.

The tweezers caught on something and Cassie was elated to feel the mechanism within the door starting to shift. Spurred on by the promise of success she pressed closer and tried to turn the slender length of metal in a clockwise direction.

'I'm surprised you're going through with this,' Faye said quietly. 'I didn't think you would really try to escape.'

'You're surprised!' Cassie could hear an edge of bitterness in her voice. She struggled to suppress her indignation, scared someone might overhear. 'How can you honestly say you're surprised? You know I've been trying to escape since my first night here.'

Her eyes had adjusted to the darkness sufficiently for her to see Faye shrug. 'I know you've been paying lip service to the idea of escape,' Faye conceded. 'I don't know if that's the same as actually trying to get away from here.'

There was something in the way she spoke that made Cassie hesitate. She didn't want to waste vital moments arguing with Faye but, since the previous Friday, the blonde had been making a lot of sly comments at Cassie's expense. Like this remark, none of her sleights had been so blunt they demanded a retraction, yet Cassie knew this would be the last chance she had to hear what the woman was trying to say. She held the tweezers firmly against the tumbler, determined not to lose the purchase she had made, then turned to regard Faye's silhouette.

'Are you suggesting I don't really want to get out of here?' she demanded. She realised her voice was in danger of raising above a whisper and controlled herself before she could alert anyone else to her presence in the hall. 'Is that what you're trying to imply?' she hissed. 'Because, if it is, maybe you should come straight out and say it.'

'I'm saying you're not adverse to being submissive,' Faye returned. 'You're certainly not as reluctant as you'd like the rest of us to believe. I'm even beginning to think I might have been wrong while Brandon was right. Maybe you are a natural submissive and maybe you're just too stupid to acknowledge the fact.'

The statement sat awkwardly between them.

Cassie reflected on what Faye had said and saw there were only two ways she could possibly respond: she could remain silent and let the woman believe she was right, or she could vehemently deny the outrageous slur on her character. Acting instinctively, Cassie swept her hand out. It was difficult to see her target in the dark but she felt sure she would be able to slap Faye squarely across the cheek.

The blonde reacted with surprising speed.

She caught hold of Cassie's wrist and threw herself forward in the same swift movement. Her agility served her well as she pushed Cassie to the floor and knelt on top of her. The tweezers bounced out of the lock and landed somewhere on the floor.

'Isn't this what you've been wanting all along?' Faye asked. Her voice had taken on a viciousness Cassie had never heard before. Growling from the shadows above, her tone sounded ominous and threatening. 'I'm right, aren't I?' Faye pressed herself lewdly down and demanded, 'Isn't this what you've been wanting since that first Friday night?'

Cassie made a valiant effort to push her away but Faye seemed able to counter every move: when Cassie tried to push to the right, Faye pinned her weight on that side; when Cassie tried sliding to the left, Faye held her firmly against the floor. 'I haven't been wanting this,' she growled angrily, 'and I'm not a natural submissive. I'm not a submissive of any description.'

'Keep telling yourself that and you might always believe it.'

Cassie continued struggling but Faye had positioned herself cleverly. She squatted with a knee over each of Cassie's shoulders, effectively fixing her to the floor. Cassie wriggled, trying to prise herself free, and her earlier fears were confirmed as she discovered Faye was naked. The revelation disturbed her because, as soon as she was aware she was touching a bare breast and a naked buttock, her body responded with a shiver of arousal. Along with her concerns that Faye might spoil her escape plan, Cassie was worrying about the agenda the woman might have lined up. She had found her situation unnerving when she was worried about how Brandon might exert his control. But the thought of submitting to Faye was even more disquieting because Cassie found the idea darkly attractive.

'Were you telling yourself you weren't a natural submissive when you gave me that enema?' Faye barked. 'Were you telling yourself the same thing when you fingered my anus then pumped me full of warm, soapy water?'

Each time she spoke her voice grew louder. Cassie wouldn't normally have noticed the increase in volume but, because she was anxious to keep her presence in the hall concealed, she was conscious of everything that might warn Brandon she was trying to escape. A part of her wanted to tell the blonde to be quiet but, because there were more important matters to clear up, she couldn't bring herself to mention that detail.

'I didn't want to give you that enema,' Cassie protested. 'You know what was happening and you know I had no choice. Brandon made me do it.'

Faye made a noise to convey her disgust and contempt. 'Brandon's good,' she agreed, 'but, while you've been here, no one could have made you do half the things you've done if you hadn't been willing to some degree. Were you telling yourself you weren't a natural submissive when you let Brandon use you? He screwed you senseless in his office, didn't he? Were you telling yourself you weren't submissive then? Were you telling Brandon the same thing?'

Unable to think of a response, Cassie made another furious attempt to push the blonde from her superior position. It was an impossible struggle and, when her fingers touched a length of bare thigh, she wondered if she really wanted to break free. The thought was shocking and unwelcome and she struggled to ignore it. But, once the idea was set in her mind, the concept of submitting sounded infuriatingly tempting.

'Brandon was right about you,' Faye said scornfully, 'and Laura was right about you as well. You're as base as the rest of us. Even now, while you're pretending you still want to escape, I'll bet you'd submit if you were given an instruction.'

Cassie shook her head but the gesture went unnoticed in the darkness.

'If I told you to tongue my hole, you'd do it, wouldn't you?' Faye taunted. 'You might tell yourself you were doing it to keep me quiet – or doing it so you could finally make your escape – but the fact is, you'd do it. You'd do it. And you'd love doing it.'

Chilled by what was happening, Cassie saw Faye was lifting herself slightly. Her knees remained where they had been, continuing to pin Cassie to the floor, but Faye was inching herself forwards. Without giving up her commanding position she pushed her cleft closer to Cassie's mouth.

'No,' Cassie whispered. 'I don't care what you think of me. I still say you're wrong. And I'm not going to do that. I mean it. I'm not going to –'

She didn't get to complete the sentence.

Faye thrust forwards and the lips of her sex engulfed Cassie's mouth. The scent of arousal filled her nostrils while her face was smothered by wet, pink lips. The labia squirmed over Cassie's jaw and nose and she was unable to tell if the movement came from Faye writhing against her, or because she was shaking her head. She was struck by the worry that Faye might inadvertently suffocate her and, on top of that fear, came the idea it would be a divine way to die.

It was a liberating moment and Cassie wondered how she had been able to resist this temptation for so long. Doing as Faye instructed, giving in to the impulse that gnawed deep inside, she began to tongue the blonde's wetness. The musk of excitement was intoxicating and, scared she might have coloured the experience with her own anticipation, Cassie tasted her again. The sweet flavour of the blonde's wetness was thrilling.

'You dirty little bitch,' Faye growled.

The words struck Cassie like a slap of arousal. She shook her head against Faye's sex, forced her mouth closer, then pushed her tongue into the sodden cleft. The pulsing nub of a clitoris throbbed against her upper lip and, revelling in her inferior position, Cassie nuzzled it lovingly.

'You filthy little bitch!' Faye exclaimed.

Her words were insulting but, perversely, they were carried by a tone of honest approval. Cassie couldn't understand why she found the scorn exciting but she was too involved in the moment to analyse her response. It was enough to know her arousal intensified every time Faye deigned to deride her.

'You nasty, cheap, little whore. You pussy-licking-slut-bitch.'

Miraculously, Cassie realised the woman was lifting herself away. Confused, she wondered if she was being given a reprieve but, rather than wanting to take advantage of the opportunity to escape, her overriding impulse was to continue tasting her gaoler. She stared helplessly up into the shadows wondering what she had to do to make Faye change her mind and carry on with the domination.

Taking her time, giving Cassie countless chances to slide from the floor and run away, Faye turned around. Slowly, seemingly oblivious to the urgent need she had inspired in her prisoner, she changed her position and squatted over Cassie's face.

'Tongue me,' Faye demanded. 'You know you want to and now I'm telling you to do it. Tongue me.'

Sure she no longer wanted to resist, Cassie did as she was told. She raised her head slightly, pushed her mouth over the gaping lips of Faye's sex, and slipped her tongue into the blonde's hole. The tip of her nose rested against the woman's anus but, instead of disgusting her on any level, Cassie found the intimacy exhilarating. She tasted the flavour of excitement and devoured her bristling lips.

With obvious pleasure, Faye groaned. She still remained a silhouette against the shadows but Cassie was able to see her arch her back and tremble as the first inklings of satisfaction began to cascade through her. Faye's hands fell against her thighs and Cassie could feel her legs being pushed roughly apart. Beyond the concept of resisting, determined only to relish every experience available, she allowed herself to be spread open. She was aware of a fringe tickling her legs – the sway of golden tresses stroking up from her knees to the top of her thighs – and then Faye was lowering her head closer and the weight of a warm, wet tongue brushed her labia.

'Keep tonguing me,' Faye insisted.

Eager to oblige, desperate to do everything and anything that was asked of her, Cassie obeyed. Between her legs, Faye delivered a wealth of pleasure Cassie had never anticipated. The woman's mouth was a soothing balm against the burning need of her pussy. The crotch of the body stocking still covered her sex but the flimsy fishnet was so sheer each kiss felt as though it was being applied directly to the skin. As Faye stroked her tongue over the tingling length of Cassie's labia a series of shivers engulfed them both. They embraced, each burying their face against the other's sex, and in that moment Cassie knew her fate and her future were decided.

'How long have you been wanting this?' Faye breathed.

'I don't know,' Cassie answered honestly.

'How long have you been resisting?'

Cassie spat her reply between kisses to Faye's sex. 'I've been resisting for too long,' she gasped ruefully. 'Far too long.'

Faye's hands stroked up her thigh. The tips of her fingers caressed Cassie's sopping gusset and then she was wrenching the crotch fasteners apart before pressing her mouth against bare flesh.

Cassie sighed.

Faye kissed and drank. Occasionally her teeth would tug on the labia – and when she did that Cassie was dizzied by a rush of delicious responses – but mainly her attention was focused on pleasure rather than pain.

Taking Faye's touch as direction Cassie tried nibbling and nuzzling in the same way she was being treated. It was dizzying to discover how much satisfaction could be gleaned from giving pleasure and she wallowed in the servile bliss of licking and sucking. Encouraged by Faye's sighs and groans, Cassie held the woman tightly as she inspired another wave of tremors.

'Leave my pussy for now,' Faye snapped, throwing her head back over her shoulder to deliver the demand. 'I want you to tongue my anus.'

Excited by the instruction, Cassie only hesitated briefly. The intimacy went against everything she had ever believed was right and proper but that didn't stop her from wanting to do as Faye had told her. Boldly, she squeezed her tongue into the woman's forbidden hole.

'Do you know where I've just come from?' Faye gasped.

She was panting her words and Cassie was elated to think she had made her gaoler breathless. Pausing from the pleasurable chore of using her mouth against Faye's backside, she extracted her tongue and said, 'No. I don't know. Where have you come from?'

'I've come from Brandon's bedroom.' There was a sly smile in Faye's voice and Cassie could hear the expression even though she couldn't see it. 'Brandon had me in his bedroom ten minutes ago and he used me mercilessly. I sucked his cock. He fucked my pussy. Then he came in my arse. That's why I want you to tongue my anus. I want you to lick his seed out of me.'

The words should have sickened Cassie but they worked in the opposite way. Rather than being repulsed, her arousal was hastened with a furious impetus. Her appetite became a carnal hunger that demanded satisfaction and she eagerly returned her tongue and buried it deeper. The idea she could lap the remainder of Brandon's spend from Faye's hole was so base it pushed her close to the brink of climax. She clutched the blonde's buttocks, pulled her nearer, then pushed her face between the peachlike cheeks. She squirmed as far inside as she was able and savoured the pulsing contraction of the ring of muscle clenching around her tongue. Not thinking about the volume of her cries, beyond caring if she alerted anyone to her presence in the hall, she gasped with delight as the first waves of pleasure began to buffet her body.

The hall remained pitch black and because of that Cassie supposed it was easier to see all the mental pictures Faye's words had painted. She could imagine Brandon riding the blonde, forcing her to suck him, pushing his thick shaft into her pussy and ploughing back and forth. In the darkness of the hall it was easy to envision their shared pleasure as he entered her anus and impaled her on his pulsing shaft. More than that, submitting herself to the blonde and savouring the second-hand version of her experience, Cassie found herself tingling with envy. Although she wouldn't let herself dwell on the emotion, she knew a part of her wished Brandon had been using her instead of Faye.

'Go on, you bitch!' Faye screeched. Her cries were choked with climactic emotion. 'Go on and lick me clean.'

The blonde's body was pungent with the sweat of vigorous lovemaking and Cassie savoured the acrid aroma. She made her kisses deeper while urgency threatened to overwhelm her. As her body began to tremble with mounting pleasure she knew release was only a whisper away and she struggled to inflict Faye's orgasm before succumbing to her own.

Faye lapped and nuzzled with renewed vigour. She nibbled at Cassie's pussy lips with painful bites that took her to the fringe of ecstasy then snatched her back.

Her hands had returned to Cassie's thighs and she gripped with a determination that said she was still in charge. Burying her thumbs deep into the flesh and holding with a cruel passion, she snatched her face from Cassie's sex and said, 'Clean me properly. I won't let you up from here until you've at least done that.'

It was the instruction that pushed her beyond the point. Cassie still had her tongue fixed firmly in Faye's backside where she could taste the mingled flavours of the woman's anus and Brandon's spend. Feeling the echo of Faye's voice trembling through her mouth, relishing all the blissful eruptions the blonde was sparking between her legs, Cassie gave in to the moment and let the orgasm flow through her.

The explosion came in a cataclysmic rush. It tore through her with a force that was both marvellous and frightening. She lay back against the polished floor-boards, sobbing elatedly and sniffing back tears of pure joy. Every nerve ending tingled as though she were an overcharged battery and the gloom of the hall seemed somehow brighter and surreally illuminated. The mad urge to giggle swept over her but exhaustion killed the mirth before it could escape her lips.

'You haven't finished yet,' Faye growled. 'I don't think you've cleaned me as well as you could.'

Only hearing the words through a haze of delight, Cassie smiled up at the buttocks above her face. She could make out enough of Faye's figure to see both her holes were gaping and sodden. The knowledge that she had been partly responsible for that arousal was deeply satisfying and she vowed to do everything she was told.

Faye levered herself away from Cassie's prostrate body and collapsed in a gasping heap. Taking advantage of the opportunity, Cassie climbed over her and smiled down. It briefly crossed her mind she still had a chance to escape but that thought was insubstantial and unimportant. Far more pressing was the need to squirm her tongue into Faye's pussy again. Now she was past her inhibitions, the chance to touch and enjoy another woman was an irresistible temptation. She caressed the unfamiliar swell of Faye's pierced nipples, delighting in the sensation of having a puckered areola beneath her fingertips. Lowering her mouth to the orb, savouring the pulse of the nipple against her lips, she knew the night's pleasures were far from finished.

'You're really making a meal out of that,' Faye sighed. 'I told you to make me come, not touch me up.'

Cassie had been inadvertently straddling Faye's face when the woman spoke and the whisper of her words tickled the bare flesh between her thighs. The fringe of her blonde tresses brushed Cassie's buttocks and then Faye was tonguing her cleft. The threat of more euphoria was a double-edged sword because, while she would have been happy to revel in the pleasure, Cassie didn't think her body could cope with another orgasm. Not sure whether she should be resisting or accepting, and happy to absolve herself from making the decision, she squashed her face against Faye's pussy and began to lick.

She wasn't sure how long they writhed on the floor but their passion only seemed to go from strength to strength. Faye stripped the fishnet body stocking from Cassie's sweat-soaked frame, lapping rivulets of perspiration from her skin. Properly naked, Cassie rubbed herself against Faye and was almost taken to the peak of another explosion as she explored the tactile bliss of their shared nudity.

She did as Faye told her and tongued her sex until the blonde was screaming with elation. Even while the dew of her climax was still dribbling down her jaw, Cassie continued kissing and licking in the hope she could feel a repeat of the woman's cataclysmic release.

Determinedly, Faye began to use her fingers. She toyed with Cassie's labia, tugging gingerly on the lips,

224

before spreading the pussy wide open. The attention bordered on discomfort, making Cassie feel as though she was being stretched instead of teased, yet the nuisance did little to quell her responses. Pain and pleasure blended into one as she gave herself over to each new thrill. The brusque penetration of Faye's fingers, and the squirming of her digits as they slid deep inside, were powerful stimuli. The gentle frigging had Cassie quivering with renewed needs for release and Faye didn't stop until the craving had been satisfied.

Each time one of them would orgasm, the other would force their way on top until they had climaxed again. For one insane moment Cassie wondered if they were involved in the sexual equivalent of duelling – a form of unclothed combat with no losers – destined to continue until they were both too tired to retaliate. She didn't know which of them was likely to win such a battle because Faye's voracious appetite matched her own. The only reason they eventually stopped was when Cassie rolled over and found the tweezers sticking uncomfortably into her backside.

'You loved every minute of that, didn't you?' Faye said softly.

Even though the darkness concealed them both, Cassie lowered her gaze to the floor for fear her blushes might be seen. 'It was more than I thought it could be,' she admitted.

Laughing bitterly, Faye pulled herself from the floor. 'I don't think Brandon was wrong about you,' she said, extending a hand to help Cassie up. 'I truly believe you're a natural submissive who's too stupid to see the truth. But you're still wanting to get out of here, aren't you?'

Cassie thought about the choice being offered to her and wondered why she was even tempted to accept the way of life Faye was suggesting. Admittedly the experience she had just enjoyed with Faye had shown a glimpse of something wonderful, new and exciting, but her home, career and life waited for her outside the door. In truth, she knew all she could expect if she remained as Brandon's property was an existence of servitude and sexual subjugation. Yet somehow, for some reason she couldn't understand, she found herself considering the choice.

Faye seemed to take her silence as a definitive response. 'Forget I asked,' she whispered. 'If you're still determined to leave, perhaps I should just unlock the door for you.'

Bewildered, Cassie realised her chance of escape was about to become a reality. She watched in amazement as Faye's silhouette reached to a shelf beside the door and retrieved a key from the shadows. She pushed the key into the lock and without any of the effort Cassie had been forced to employ, she began to turn it. Listening to the tumblers click into place and then hearing the bolt draw back, Cassie knew she was finally on the brink of escape.

The eruption of light was searing against her eyes. She glared around the hall, determined to admonish whoever it was who had flicked the switch and put her escape plans in jeopardy, but her reprimands stuck at the back of her throat.

'What the hell do you think you're doing?' Brandon demanded.

Cassie stared at him, unable to formulate a reply. A few seconds earlier she had thought she was escaping but now she could see that plan was no longer part of the night's agenda.

'What the hell do you think you're doing?' he repeated. He shook his head and stormed angrily towards her. 'Don't bother answering that question. I can see for myself.' With a twisted grin he grabbed her wrist. 'You're trying to get yourself punished, aren't you?'

226

She shook her head but he wasn't looking at her. He snapped his fingers for Faye to lock the door and return the key, then pointed for her to go back to the cellar.

The blonde obeyed him without hesitation. She cast an apologetic frown in Cassie's direction, then disappeared towards the rear of the house. Watching her fade into the shadows above the cellar door, Cassie realised she was going to have to suffer Brandon's punishment alone.

The thought left her terrified.

Fourteen

Punishment room number one was as daunting as Cassie had feared it would be. Whips, crops and canes decorated three of the walls and the floor was strewn with stocks, chains and all manner of manacles. Dimly lit, oppressive in spite of being spacious, it looked like Brandon had designed every inch to the specification of her nightmares. He pushed her into its midst, pausing only to lock the door behind them.

'Escape,' he grumbled as he marched past. 'There are only two types of escape attempt that happen here: successful escape attempts and punished escape attempts. I'm sorry to inform you that yours fell into the latter category.'

He pulled back the blinds on the wall facing the door to reveal full-length picture windows. Cassie had time to see her bedraggled reflection – a pathetic figure, naked and humbled – then Brandon was pushing the glass aside to expose the balcony.

'Come here,' he demanded.

She shook her head and trembled beneath the icy breeze that trailed into the room. Brandon was wearing a pair of tight leather trousers with a loose, silk shirt. The evening wind rippled the fabric against his muscular chest and pulled it taut over his brawny biceps. The room's light glinted dully from his shaved skull and his frown grew more menacing as she continued to defy him. It was impossible to see any aspect of his bearing that wasn't piratical or threatening.

'Come here,' he repeated, 'and don't make me come back into the room to get you. There's no need for you to make your suffering more protracted than is necessary. That's a chore I'm looking forward to.'

She thought of refusing the instruction in spite of his sinister tone but, knowing the door was locked, and knowing there would be nowhere to run even if it wasn't, Cassie decided defiance would serve no advantage. Hesitantly, forcing each step, she approached the balcony. Brandon watched her with a thunderous expression, never once relinquishing his dour gaze. Every apology and explanation she wanted to stammer fell flat beneath the severity of his frown.

'Grab hold of that handrail,' he said, pointing into the darkness above her head.

She glanced up into the shadows and saw – above the balcony and suspended from an overhang on the next floor – a shiny bar of steel. It was clearly a comparatively recent addition to the building because it glistened with a freshly polished lustre that contrasted with the ageing masonry.

'Grab hold of that handrail and wait here.'

She wanted to refuse. The night was chilly and, while she knew there was no one around to see her, Cassie felt uncomfortable exhibiting herself so obviously. Nevertheless she reached up for the handrail and grabbed hold.

'Use both hands,' he snapped, stepping behind her, 'and face away from the room. I want you looking out into the darkness.'

Unhappily, Cassie obeyed.

The position was demeaning and unsettling. Moonlight dusted the surrounding acreage, darkly illuminating the distant forests and fields. She was able to see the nightscape stretching for miles towards the horizon and, because she could detect no signs of anyone else in the vicinity, she felt more isolated and alone than ever. Holding both hands above her head, displaying her naked body to the night, she was stung by a profound sensation of vulnerability. With her back to the punishment room, she had no idea what Brandon was doing or planning behind her.

'Ordinarily I'd make this lesson short and sharp,' he muttered, 'but I can see you need a much more comprehensive instruction on the follies of trying to escape.' The statement was punctuated by the whistle of a descending whip.

Cassie had enough time to realise she was about to be hit when the bolt of pain struck between her shoulder blades. The force was almost sufficient to make her let go of the handrail but, on an intuitive level, she suspected Brandon would punish her further for this. Writhing against the searing line of fire, she cried out into the night.

There was a brief moment when she could mentally picture herself: her naked body struggling to cope with the pain as she stood helpless and naked with the night's breeze brushing at her hair. She could picture her mouth open in a wide, never-ending scream with every muscle pulled tight in response to her suffering.

The image disappeared when Brandon slashed the whip down again. It landed with the crack of a gunshot and she wailed as she was branded by its sting. He delivered a third and fourth blow, lashing haphazardly but never lessening the force. By the time he had hurled a dozen strokes Cassie expected her back was a criss-cross of blazing red weals. She tried not to think how disfiguring the ugly red marks would look against her smooth flesh because she knew the idea would generate excitement. Unable to stop herself, she screamed louder.

'Scream all you like,' Brandon laughed. 'There's no one around to hear – and no one around who cares.'

Again, he smacked the whip and the broad length of leather caught her side. The tip curled around her ribcage, nipping viciously beneath her breast. It spat a searing agony into the base of her orb.

'You have to understand I have three reasons for punishing your escape attempt,' he began. He spoke evenly, not as though he was wielding a bullwhip and punishing her but in a tone more suited to polite, after-dinner conversation. 'First, you need to be taught that escape is not permitted.' He cracked the whip and scored a direct hit against her left thigh.

The pain was a blistering bolt and choked off all logical thought. Her view of the night began to shimmer as tears filled her eyes. Even though the breeze was chilling her, Cassie's palms grew sweaty and she had to renew her grip on the handrail.

'And second,' Brandon continued blithely, 'I need to set an example for your contemporaries here, so none of them make the same foolish mistake you've just made.'

With another brisk shot he sliced a white line of agony across both buttocks.

Cassie drew startled breath and struggled to conceal how much suffering he had already inflicted. Working hard to make her voice sound neutral, she took two deep breaths before speaking. 'You said you have three reasons for punishing me,' she reminded him. Her voice was surprisingly calm and she wondered how she was able to talk without sobbing. Not thinking about that, concentrating only on their exchange, she asked, 'What's the third reason?'

He grunted sour laughter and said, 'My third reason for punishing you is probably the most important. I'm doing it because it gives me pleasure.' As though he was trying to punctuate his own droll wit, he slashed the whip twice more in swift succession; one shot caught her arm and the other smacked brutally against her buttock. The inrush of pain was enormous.

232

She tried twisting herself to lessen the discomfort, not sure if there might be a better position to withstand the torture, or if she was only excusing her body's anguished writhing. For several of the strokes she dangled from the handrail, sure her legs would fail her if she used them to try and support her weight. Yet, no matter how she contorted, the blazing expanse of her lashed back remained a constant torment.

'I've had all the nonsense I'm taking from you,' Brandon said gruffly, 'and I think it's time you accepted your position here.'

She was disturbed to hear his voice growing louder and she cast a fearful glance over her shoulder. From the corner of her eye she saw he had thrown the whip aside and was advancing towards her. As he stepped nearer she found herself wishing he would continue to thrash her rather than do whatever it was he was now planning. After all the punishment and pain he had managed to inflict, she expected this next phase of her ordeal would be worse than any whipping.

'Why are you fighting against this?' Brandon asked. He sounded genuinely puzzled by her defiance. 'Are you really so stupid you can't even acknowledge your own desires?'

Shocked by his nearness, she couldn't answer the question.

Brandon had stepped directly behind her and pressed himself lewdly against her back. His hands went beneath her arms cupping both breasts. With despicable accuracy he found her nipples and tugged on them. He held each nub without delicacy, pulling on the sensitive flesh and stretching the teats, before rolling them between his fingers and thumbs. Pleasure trembled from the core of her breasts and Cassie struggled to ignore the responses. Between her buttocks Brandon's exposed erection pushed rudely against her flesh. She didn't know when he had unfastened his trousers, or which part of her suffering had brought him to this state of arousal, but his hardness was undeniable. Her cheeks were awash with fire from the thrashing and that meant she was aware of every nuance shaping the shaft that nuzzled at her backside. She could detect the swollen end of his glans, the thickness of his girth and all of his formidable, desirable length.

'Why are you fighting against this?' he repeated.

She stared into the blackness of the night, not thinking about how she was responding and trying to distance herself from his hatefully inspiring touch. 'Maybe I'm fighting you because I don't want to be your damned sex slave,' she suggested. 'Has that thought crossed your mind?'

His laugh was infuriatingly condescending. 'That briefly crossed my mind,' he admitted. 'But we both know it's not true. You've wanted to be a part of our lifestyle here since you first walked into that poker game. You wanted that, and you're wallowing in every second of what I'm doing to you now.'

As if he was trying to prove a point, he lowered his hips and his shaft fell away from her buttocks. Cassie had a moment to think he might be relenting and leaving her alone, when he thrust himself forwards again. His erection landed against the centre of her need and, without any hesitancy, he pushed inside. The penetration was harsh and swift and they both groaned as he buried his entire length into her pussy.

'How dare you even suggest this isn't what you wanted?' he growled. 'I've never slid into such a wet, needy hole before.'

She silently cursed the excitement he spurred and gripped more tightly against the handrail. As much as she told herself she didn't want to be used, she couldn't resist pulling forwards then sliding back down on him. His thickness spread her wide and delightful tremors bristled from her pussy muscles. Each wave of pleasure sparkled through her body and carried her ever closer to rapture. After the satisfaction of being with Faye, Cassie had thought her appetite was spent but Brandon effortlessly filled her with an insatiable hunger.

'Tell me you're not loving this and I'll call you a liar,' he grunted.

His words were spat on an undercurrent of rising passion and Cassie suspected he was already close to coming. As he pushed deeper inside she could feel his shaved scrotum pressing against her buttocks. His sac felt tight, as though he was ready to release his spend, and the entire length of his shaft trembled within her confines. The thought of that impending moment, anticipating the pleasure of having him pulse repeatedly and fill her with his semen, sent Cassie dizzy with shameless need.

'What do you want me to say?' she demanded. She was no longer making the effort to appear unaffected, aware that an effective deceit would be beyond her abilities. Clutching the handrail tightly, she allowed him to pump to and fro and asked, 'Are you expecting me to tell you I won't try to escape again? Or do you believe I'm going to say I'm sorry?'

He pushed himself fully into her and held her on his length. Still tugging on her nipples, pulling the fat beads of flesh so they stretched to an impossible length, he said, 'I think I've told you what I expect before, haven't I? I only expect you to concede you're a natural submissive. That, and your apology for not facing up to the truth earlier. Nothing more.'

She squeezed her muscles around him, relishing the inability to clench herself fully closed. His girth was thick enough to border on the uncomfortable but, with the combination of her desires and his control over her, Cassie found his penetration unbearably satisfying. Riding up and down, wriggling her hips hard against him in an attempt to feel every available millimetre of his shaft, she languished in the thrill of his dominance.

'You'll do it,' Brandon mused. 'I swear that you'll do it.' He sounded almost reflective and not like a man who was on the brink of spurting his seed into her pussy. 'One day soon, I swear you'll concede you're a natural submissive. And you will apologise. But I think you'll make me struggle to get you there.'

She considered telling him that he had beaten the struggle out of her and that she was on the verge of accepting his superiority. The words were at the back of her throat but because she was also wanting to moan with pleasure, she couldn't articulate them.

Brandon moved his hands from her breasts and gripped her hips tightly. Holding her on his erection he inched himself fractionally deeper; it was a movement that pushed them both beyond the point of no return.

His shaft pulsed; it briefly thickened and sparked an untold wealth of joy inside her pussy. Cassie screamed, not sure if she was in the throes of pleasure or pain. When his length twitched again she was aware of his seed jetting deep within her. The meld of wetness, heat and satisfaction finally gave her the impetus to climax and she roared her jubilation into the night.

Again, she could clearly picture the image she was presenting. This time the romantic vision of her punishment was tainted with a delicious reality. She could see the sweat plastering her hair to her brow; smell the rich scent of Brandon's semen as it continued to pulse into her; and see the dark flush of her cheeks as she revelled in the bliss of orgasm. It was a less flattering self-image than the first one but she thought it was infinitely more exciting.

Brandon held himself inside her until he was spent. He cursed her as she trembled through her climax but he didn't withdraw until his shaft had released its last faltering pulse. When he stepped away he slapped a condescending hand against her backside as though he was telling her they had finished.

'Have you taught me my lesson?' she asked. The words came out as more of a challenge than she had wanted to make and Cassie berated herself for running the risk of antagonising him. Trying to rectify the situation she asked, 'Am I supposed to know my place now?' Only after she had spoken did she realise the question sounded as truculent and defiant as ever.

Brandon glared at her with dark fury. His normally smooth forehead was knotted with disapproval and he strode towards her with anger resounding in every step. Viciously, he grabbed hold of her hair and dragged her away from the balcony. Cassie knew he hadn't given her permission to let go of the handrail but, because he was pulling so hard, she decided she had no option except to relinquish her grip. She noticed he had pushed his spent shaft back inside his trousers, although the shape of his bulge was still disturbingly easy to observe through the front panel.

'You don't want to press me too hard,' he warned, pushing her to the floor. 'I've kept slaves like you ensconced in this room for days on end and there's a variety of tools I can use to ensure you never try and escape again.'

Looking around the floor, Cassie could see he was right. The stocks and manacles seemed like something from a museum of cruel antiquities although, rather than being coated with rust, they were polished and disturbingly serviceable. Many of the lengths of chains had cuffs on the end and, after the education of her stay at Brandon's home, she recognised the spreader bars for what they were. She understood the use of the cage that filled one corner; the purpose of the hoods and straight-jackets; and the reason for the crucifix and all the ropes that were lying around. With growing despondency she knew he could easily make good his threat and force her to suffer a different punishment every day for the best part of a fortnight.

'What are you going to do with me?' she asked thickly.

His hand remained in her hair and he tugged sharply until she stood up.

'You want me to tie you up, don't you?' he guessed.

Cassie couldn't meet his eyes and lowered her gaze to the floor. Glancing at the punishment apparatus in the room it was obvious Brandon would find some way to bind or restrain her. As loathe as she was to acknowledge the fact, the thought of being bound held a lurid attraction.

'You want me to tie you up so you can absolve yourself of any willing involvement in all this,' Brandon grinned. He tugged on her hair until she had to look into his eyes.

Staring into the black depths of his smile, Cassie wondered if she was really so transparent. Brandon had a mesmerising command over her and an ability to judge her motives better than she knew them herself. It took all her willpower not to nod eagerly and tell him he was right.

With a disdainful sneer, Brandon shook his head and said, 'I'm not going to give you the pleasure of absolving yourself in that way. Just like you weren't restrained when I had you standing on the balcony, I won't bother restraining you for the next item on this evening's agenda.'

She started to protest, asking him what he was planning and where he thought he was taking her. Brandon resumed his grip on her hair and started towards the door. Unable to break free and, realising she wasn't going to be able to ask her questions, Cassie had no choice but to fall silent and follow. Stumbling along the corridor as he led her out of the punishment room, she staggered in his wake until they reached a familiar door.

Encouraged by renewed terror she made a futile protest and tried to stand still. Pinpricks of pain exploded from her scalp and she could feel clumps of hair being torn from their roots. Unmindful of the agony, she stopped following him. 'Not in there,' she hissed. 'You can't take me in that room. I won't go.'

Brandon's chuckle was unnervingly void of sympathy. 'I think you'll find I can take you in there,' he told her, 'and I expect you to do everything I tell you while we're inside.'

She started to shake her head but he was tugging her hair again and pushing the door open. Unable to break free, Cassie could do nothing except follow him into punishment room number three. Memories of the last time she had visited the room washed over with disquieting clarity. She remembered that, when Brandon had brought her to this room before, he had left her bound and helpless for the whole of a Friday night. She also remembered, before he had tied her to one of the room's two stools, he had made her give an enema to Faye. This time, she realised glumly, Faye wasn't there to suffer the brunt of Brandon's wrath. With mounting dread, Cassie suspected she knew exactly how he intended to abuse her.

'There's the stool,' Brandon said, finally releasing his hold on her hair. 'I think you know the position you're meant to assume.' He turned his back on her and locked the door.

'What if I refuse?' Cassie asked. She couldn't believe she had said something so bold but the thought of subjecting herself to this humiliation was enough to help her make a stand. 'What if I say I'm not doing it? How do you propose to make me?'

'There are chains I can get,' he said simply, 'and I have enough staff here who could help me secure you to the stool, but I don't think it will come to that.' He produced his tawse and brandished it half-heartedly. 'I could threaten to stripe new red lines across your blazing backside,' he mused idly, 'or I could whip your tits with this until you were begging for me to stop and let you bend over the stool, but I don't think it will come to that either. I don't think I'll have to use force of any description.'

She shivered beneath the vile knowledge she could see in his eyes, hating the way he was able to look at her and make her feel simultaneously disgusted and excited. 'Why don't you think you'll need to use force?'

'Because you're going to do as I ask,' he said quietly. 'You're going to do as I've told you and simply bend over the stool.'

Surprising herself, Cassie did as he instructed.

She walked over to the stool, trying not to look at her reflection as she stood in the centre of the room, but unable to resist the opportunity to see if there was a change in her appearance. Since Brandon had made her stand on the balcony, since he had flogged her and used her, she had felt like a different woman. It was more a transformation in attitude than anything else: a spirit she had thought she had given into while she and Faye writhed together on the floor of the hall. Studying her reflection, ignoring the vicious red marks blazing against her back and sides, she decided there was a new confidence in the way she held herself. It was impossible to define the exact difference between what she had become and what she had been, and Cassie couldn't say when the change had taken place, but she couldn't deny that something had happened to make her seem altered. Comparing the woman staring back at her with the images she remembered from her life before this evening, she thought her new reflection looked more self-assured, more content and much more satisfied.

'When you've finished admiring yourself,' Brandon sneered, 'you do have an instruction to follow.'

Cassie fell to her knees and folded herself over the stool. She didn't bother watching Brandon as he made his way to the sink, concentrating only on the attraction of her reflection and the insight her new appearance afforded. She remembered the posture from her first visit to punishment room number three, pulling her ankles close to the stool's legs and pushing her backside as high as the position would allow. Holding herself in that pose, and preparing herself for the ordeal that lay ahead, was an unbelievably calming experience.

Wordlessly, Brandon went through the chore of filling the enema bag. He didn't hurry, and she assumed he was taking his time to get the temperature to the exact degree of warmth. A whisker of excitement tickled deep inside her and she wondered if every experience she now suffered would be made memorable with the same lewd anticipation. Trembling eagerly, she gripped the stool and braced herself as Brandon began to walk towards her.

'Are you going to admit I was right about you?' he asked.

He stood behind her and she had to glare back at his reflection. 'I thought you were going to make me admit that,' she challenged.

His smile faltered and, with growing doubts, she wondered if she had pushed him too far. His hands were occupied with the enema bag and its pipe but she knew the tawse was always within his reach. Her worries didn't abate when he extended a hand and squeezed her backside. Fresh eddies of discomfort rippled from beneath his fingertips as he traced the aching lines he had lashed against her flesh. Cassie sucked breath and steeled herself as he began to explore the mounds of her backside.

'May I ask for something?' she asked suddenly.

Her interruption didn't slow him. His fingers continued edging between her buttocks, reaching for the puckered ring of her anus. When he made contact with his goal – when he prodded the tip of his index finger against her forbidden hole – she stiffened and repeated the question.

241

'May I ask for something?'

'No. You're property and in no position to ask for anything.'

His belligerence rankled and she wondered if she ought to address him as *sir* or *master* to try and sway his opinion. Using either salutation still seemed like a sign of more commitment than she was willing to give but, if it got him to hear what she wanted to say, Cassie thought it might be a price worth paying. She was opening her mouth, ready to address him with the reverence she knew he expected, when Brandon slapped his hand against her backside.

'You can't ask for anything, and I don't want you speaking further until I ask you a direct question.'

His abruptness left her in no doubt that she was expected to do as he said. Humbly, she remained silent as he returned his fingertips to her rear and began to tease her hole. The intimacy was bewildering, exciting emotions she would never have anticipated. He traced the shape of her anus, lovingly stroking the flesh, before attempting to enter her. Even then she could feel him daubing a stream of the enema's warm, soapy water over her buttocks to add lubrication before he tried to slide a finger inside.

Her body's natural resistance struggled to prevent him and she wondered if she should be trying to relax. The wealth of pleasure was so sudden and intense she couldn't think past the sensations to make a decision.

'It's just as tight as I remember,' Brandon grinned. 'I'm almost tempted to forsake giving you this enema so you can suck me hard and then let me fuck your arse.'

Cassie groaned.

He spoke with such coarse desire she couldn't help but empathise with his arousal. She was beyond caring how he decided to use her – unmindful whether he wanted to give her the enema or take her as he had threatened – and only aware of a longing for him to do something to her and soon.

He pushed his finger further inside, exciting her with the alien sensation of the exploratory digit squirming in her rectum. She writhed against the stool, willing herself to remain still, but unable to fully obey that command. When he slipped a second finger alongside the first, she sighed happily.

'You're more than ready for this,' he observed. 'You're not even treating it as a punishment, are you?'

It was a direct question and she took the opportunity to speak while it was allowed. 'May I ask for something?' she whispered.

He pushed both fingers deeper. The rush of friction was sudden and unexpected and quashed her desire to repeat the question. Impaled on his hand, shivering with the rise of responses churning through her, she decided there would be plenty of time to make her request once Brandon had taught her this lesson.

He forced a third finger alongside the first two.

Cassie considered holding back her squeal then decided there was no longer any need to hide her responses. The sensation of one finger had been daring; two had made her feel close to climax; but the addition of a third took the experience to a new realm. Her anus was stretched and distended and the muscle felt on the verge of snapping because it was being expected to accommodate too much. She wanted to tell Brandon he was asking her to cope with more than her body could manage when he briskly snatched all three fingers away. Although she couldn't see, she could picture her sphincter slowly contracting around the hollow vacuum he had left behind.

'I think you're ready for this,' Brandon said.

Glancing at his reflection, she saw he was grinning. With mounting disquiet she watched him take the pipe, point it towards her backside, and then she was being soaked by the flow of the water. The tepid stream drenched her buttocks and cleft, dribbling over her pussy before trickling down her thighs. Knowing what he was about to do, and dreading that it might prove to be more than she was able to suffer, Cassie wondered how he would react if she chose this moment to hesitate. She considered moving herself away and telling him she wasn't yet prepared for such a level of submission but she never got the opportunity.

Brandon slipped the pipe into her anus and the warm, soapy water began to flow into her bowel.

She had noticed Faye enjoying the enema in a way which seemed obscene and perverted but now it was easy to understand why the blonde had reacted with such enthusiasm. The sensation was unlike anything Cassie had known and, because it was concentrated on such a forbidden aspect of her body, she couldn't help but associate every moment with unrelenting pleasure. The water flowed slowly: a smooth jet that continued to pump into her until she felt fat and swollen. While Brandon had been riding her, and while she and Faye had been writhing together, Cassie had been aware of her arousal rising in steps. But this was a sensation where her excitement just continued to grow and grow without pause. She could feel herself hurtling towards a climax and knew, when it did strike her, her body would continue to climb to new pinnacles of euphoria until she had experienced the greatest level of satisfaction.

Even when the stomach cramps struck – agonising pains that insisted her bowel wasn't meant for this purpose – she continued to revel in bliss. The pain was another aphrodisiac and it nudged her closer to the joy of release. 'Too much,' she whispered. 'You're pouring too much into me.'

His palm tapped lightly against her backside. 'You were instructed not to speak, remember?'

She chewed on her lower lip, renewing her grip on the stool's legs and bracing herself as the enema continued to flow. Every movement she made – adjusting her

244

posture over the stool, tensing the muscles in her legs – all served to remind her of the position she was in and the indignity she was suffering. Worst of all, and the shame of it was additionally thrilling, Cassie thought she had never felt so aroused in her entire life.

Brandon snatched the pipe from her backside and walked leisurely back to the sink. He dropped the enema bag and pipe into the basin and then walked back to Cassie's side. Towering over her, glaring down with his sullen frown still prevalent, he asked, 'Has this taught you anything?'

Her mind was a turmoil and she tried to think beyond all the distractions so she could answer him honestly. The stomach cramps were coming with increasing severity, urgently insisting she expel the enema, but also exciting her because they reminded her what she had just endured. The combined thrills of discomfort, humiliation and debasement were so intense that for a moment she couldn't think how to reply.

'Has this taught you anything?' Brandon asked, squatting down on the floor so he was at eye level with her. 'Or, do I need to continue with your lesson?'

'What do you want from me?' she whispered. She thought she knew; she felt sure he had said it often enough this evening but, with the distraction of so many other events, she needed to hear him say it again: 'What do you want from me?'

'I don't want much,' Brandon said softly. 'I only want you to concede you're a natural submissive and apologise for not accepting that sooner. Am I asking too much?'

She struggled to speak coherently, sure she was close to collapsing with the new discovery of pleasure she was enjoying. 'You only want those two things from me,' she hissed, 'and I only want two things from you.'

He regarded her without speaking and she wondered if he was allowing her to talk or composing a reprimand for her temerity. When he made no attempt to tell her to stay quiet she supposed he was letting her continue.

'I want to deal at Friday night's poker game,' she told him. 'I want you to let me deal.'

He blinked.

Cassie couldn't work out if he was surprised or acquiescing and, with the urgency tormenting her bowel, she didn't think there would be the opportunity for her to work out which. Stumbling from the stool, holding her stomach in an effort to stave the discomfort racking her body, she silently pleaded with him.

'You want to deal at Friday night's poker game,' he repeated.

Cassie nodded.

His expression remained noncommittal. 'And the other thing you want?'

She studied him guardedly, still wondering if he was allowing her to do as she had asked or preparing to refuse. 'Which punishment room did you take Faye to when you got her breasts and her pussy pierced?' she asked.

Brandon answered without thinking. 'I took her to punishment room number two. That's where I keep the sterilised piercing equipment. That's where I pierce all my property. Why? What's the other thing you want?'

She didn't allow herself to think before responding, scared she might back out if she thought about what she was doing. 'That's the other thing I want,' she decided. 'I want you to take me to punishment room number two.'

Epilogue

'You're here at last. About bloody time.'

Cassie glanced up on hearing the words, trying to see who Brandon was addressing.

Marion was in her usual position and struggled against the torment of her inverted bondage. Subsequently, the poker room's fluttering candlelight provided more shadows than illumination and Cassie had to squint through the smoky darkness to see which of the players was the first to arrive.

John stumbled towards the table looking more dishevelled and unkempt than was usual for him. Cassie knew he cultivated a slightly ruffled appearance, with either designer stubble darkening his handsome jaw or his tie loosened and askew, but this evening he looked more untidy than was normal. His shirt was crumpled and unironed, his jacket had a small tear in one sleeve and she noticed a stain on the lapel. As he stepped closer, she saw the whites of his eyes were a bleary, bloodshot pink.

'You look like shit, Johnny,' Brandon laughed. 'What's wrong with you?'

John glared at him as he fell into the seat facing Cassie. He nodded vaguely in her direction by way of a greeting. If she had been in a mood to dwell on such things, Cassie would have thought it incredible they could treat one another so casually. Only one week earlier John had been lusting over her like a horny schoolboy while she had been painfully shamed by his attention. Yet now, after the passage of a further seven days, he was treating her presence in the dealer's seat as an accepted norm and she felt no embarrassment to be naked in front of him. However, distracted by all the other considerations that weighed on her mind this evening, and still reeling from the events of the last few days, Cassie didn't have time to give John a second thought. She continued to shuffle the deck of cards and glanced down at the tray suspended from her breasts.

'What's wrong with me?' John moaned, glaring at Brandon. There was a petulant whine in his voice that Cassie found distinctly unappealing. 'You're asking what's wrong with me?' His voice grew more strident with every syllable. 'You're still holding onto my Gemballa, the dizzy little bitch I employ in the office hasn't turned in for work all week, and there's still no word from Stephen as to whether or not I've won the Harwood contract. My life is currently floating in a toilet bowl and I have a feeling someone is about to pull the chain.'

'What charming imagery,' Brandon mused. 'I'm grateful you didn't save that analogy until I was eating.'

John fixed him with a suspicious glare. 'The bastard hasn't awarded the Harwood contract to you, has he? Has that "brunette bribe" you planted in his office finally paid off?'

Brandon nodded in the direction of the bar where Faye stood awaiting instructions. As soon as she saw she was being summoned, she immediately began to pour a glass of scotch. She glided out of the shadows, placed the glass in front of John, then knelt down by his chair.

'Let's dispense with the usual formalities this evening,' Brandon decided. 'I don't think there's any need to tease the dealer or have her performing like a well-trained pet.' Not waiting to see if John agreed, he threw a cigar to Faye and she caught it nimbly.

Without indulging in the same ceremony Cassie had been forced to perform, the blonde lit the Havana for John before placing it in his hand. Still watching Brandon, taking all her instructions from her master, Faye waited until he had nodded before she unzipped John's trousers and took his shaft from his pants. While John sipped at his drink and smoked his cigar, she worked her lips and tongue over his flaccid length.

Cassie watched with only a mild stirring of arousal. She wasn't sure she should be gleaning any pleasure from Faye's punishment and resisted the urge to indulge in gratuitous voyeurism. This was the penalty Brandon insisted she had to pay for trying to help Cassie escape and, with her usual spirit of sanguine acceptance, Faye was obeying her master's instructions faultlessly.

'You haven't answered me, Jock,' John persisted. 'Have you been awarded that contract?'

'Stephen hasn't been in touch with me since last Friday night,' Brandon replied. He settled himself into the chair next to Cassie and lit his own cigar. The room was already rank with the sour smell of tobacco and the cloud he exhaled only added to the shadows. 'My "brunette bribe", as you call her, says Stephen has made a decision but she doesn't know what that decision is yet.'

Cassie was only half listening. She was still captivated by the sight of her fresh piercings and revelling in the wealth of new pleasures they gave. The steel ball closure rings penetrating her nipples held each teat in a state of constant erection. Every time she glanced down at herself she couldn't help but marvel that the metal was looped through her intimate flesh and the desire to touch the rings was almost irresistible. Because the piercings didn't squeeze as the clamps had done, she found the jewellery was constantly exciting and stimulating. She found the weight of the chains and the tray were an exquisite torment and she wondered how she had existed in her life without these delicious pleasures. The stimulation was so divine she occasionally rocked herself to feel a renewed twang of discomfort.

'He's pissing us about.' John's fraught mood remained in spite of the hospitality Brandon was affording him. Seeming oblivious to the fellatio he was receiving, he glared at his host and said, 'Your girl says he's made a decision. Don't you think it would be nice if the bastard would share that decision with us?'

'Well, the bastard's here now,' Stephen said softly. Cassie glanced at his silhouette in the doorway and wondered how long he had been standing there. 'The bastard's here,' Stephen repeated, 'and he's ready to share his decision.'

John gave an apologetic grin that sat uneasily on his face. 'No offence meant,' he said as Stephen joined them at the table. 'I've had a shitty week and I'm cursing every bastard at the moment.'

Stephen ignored him and turned to Brandon. He had an air about him that said he was in no mood for trivialities and only wanted to deal directly with matters of importance. 'I want to keep your brunette.'

Brandon's composure remained unruffled. Acting as though he had expected this development, he took the deck of cards from Cassie's hand and placed them in front of Stephen. 'Would you like to cut for her?' he asked. 'She's yours if you win. She's yours and I get the Harwood contract if you lose.'

'Not fair!' John protested.

Stephen and Brandon ignored him. Stephen lifted the top card and showed Brandon an eight. Brandon cut the deck and turned over a six. He shrugged lightly and drew on his cigar. 'Congratulations, Stephen,' he said. 'You've got yourself the brunette.'

Stephen nodded and turned to John. 'Are you prepared to do the same thing in exchange for Vicky? We each cut and the highest wins. I get to keep her if I win. I get to keep her and you get the Harwood contract if you win.'

Cassie saw a flicker of hesitation furrow John's brow, and then it was gone. She guessed he had no idea Vicky was even part of the equation but she could also see that wasn't going to stop him from gambling her against the opportunity of winning the Harwood contract. Watching the expressions work their way so obviously across his face, she wondered how she had managed to work alongside such a deceitful opportunist and not see him for what he was.

John leant forward, careful not to disturb Faye as she carried on sucking. Maintaining eye contact with Stephen, he cut the deck. He turned over the ten of diamonds and tested his smile around the table.

The smile faltered then disappeared when Stephen cut to the Jack of Hearts. 'You can have the little bitch if you can find her,' John grumbled. 'I haven't seen her all week.'

'I shouldn't have any difficulty finding her,' Stephen said, his smile briefly shining with genuine warmth. 'I left her tied to my bed, begging for me to whip her some more.' Reaching into his coat pocket he said, 'I won't keep either of you any longer this evening. I'm looking forward to getting back to the manor and telling my new acquisitions that I'm now their rightful owner. But I do intend to stay for one game of five card draw.'

Brandon encouraged him to continue and they all watched as Stephen placed a large envelope on Cassie's tray.

It was surprisingly heavy and she was startled by the way it pulled down on her. Whereas the clamps had tugged and hurt, the added weight on her nipple rings produced a different, more deep-seated response. She

251

was unable to describe the exact difference: it was the subtle change of having her flesh pulled from within rather than outside, but she couldn't deny it was a stimulating sensation. The pulse of her arousal began to hammer harder as she tried to accustom herself to the painful pleasure of the burden.

'That's the Harwood contract,' Stephen explained, 'and I'm betting it on this one game of cards.'

Brandon straightened in his chair.

John pushed Faye away and absently slipped his erection back inside his pants. His interest in what was happening was suddenly piqued and he made no attempt to appear calm or indifferent. 'You're betting the contract on this game?'

Stephen nodded. 'If either of you two win, you take possession of the contract I've accepted, and you'll be paid at fifteen per cent over the going rate. Does that sound fair?'

'But, what if you win?' Brandon asked.

Stephen shrugged. 'If I win, the pair of you will divide the work, and I won't have to pay a penny.'

Cassie glanced at their faces: John grinning eagerly; Brandon frowning over some internal doubt; Stephen waiting expectantly. This was a development she hadn't expected and she tried to concentrate on what was happening rather than the new-found joy of her own constant arousal.

'Are we all agreed?' Stephen asked. 'I'd rather we got this over with as quickly as possible.'

Brandon picked up the cards and pushed them into Cassie's hand. Taking John's eager grin as confirmation he told her to deal.

She only paused briefly before tossing out the cards and that was to glance at Faye. She knew her main deal was supposed to come at the end of the night but, from what Stephen had said, it didn't sound as if they would be playing for so long this evening. Faye seemed to read the source of her hesitation from her face because she surreptitiously nodded, as though giving a silent sign to proceed.

Trying not to let her hands shake, Cassie went through the motions of her carefully prepared deal.

It seemed unreal to think they were each looking at their hands – two pairs, three kings and three aces – each believing they were the only ones who knew exactly what they were holding. She had to chew her lower lip in order to keep a grin from surfacing on her face and even then she felt thankful none of them were looking at her face. Her breasts heaved with rising tension and she was grateful for the distraction that came when her nipple rings tugged fresh sensations through her breasts. The tingling pull was enough to take her mind from the knowledge that she was the one in control of who was going to win.

'I guess the ante's already in for the first round of betting,' Brandon observed, 'unless anyone wants to raise?'

John reached for his pile of chips and began to count through them. Slowly, as though trying to make some point, he dropped them one by one onto Cassie's tray. She felt ten of them bounce down, falling heavily on the contract's envelope and each additional tug nudged her one step closer to a point of release. She didn't know when her body had started on the journey to orgasm but she felt sure, if the torment continued to mount on her aching teats, it wouldn't be long before she was revelling in a blissful climax.

'John's raised ten grand,' Brandon observed. 'Stephen?'

Shrugging, as though the matter was of no consequence, Stephen dropped ten of his chips onto Cassie's tray.

She refrained from gasping and simply wallowed in the thrill of the extra weight. When Brandon had placed his ante onto the tray she was stung by a heightened response. It briefly crossed her mind the piercings might be too new for this sort of treatment but, as long as the sensuality continued to be so profound, she was willing to run that risk. Hardly aware she was doing it, Cassie began to breathe in the same short gasps that normally preceded her orgasms.

'Does anyone want to raise further?' Brandon asked, 'Or is that the current call?'

John glanced from his cards to the growing pot on Cassie's tray and seemed momentarily undecided. Eventually he slapped down two cards and snapped his fingers for Cassie to supply him with a pair of replacements.

She dealt deliberately, making it look as though he was simply receiving two random cards from the top. Stephen asked for one replacement and Brandon required two, just as she had known they would. Watching their faces, Cassie wasn't surprised to see both Brandon and John grinning broadly.

'Have you seen the Ferrari I came down in?' John asked innocently.

Brandon groaned. 'Christ, Johnny! I can't take another car off you. The garages here are already beginning to look like a used car lot because of you.'

John brushed the insult away. 'You won't be taking another car off me,' he said, reaching into his trouser pocket, 'because I don't intend losing. I just want you to know that's the value of the current call.' Without waiting to see if this was accepted or not, he threw his keys onto Cassie's tray.

She gasped, relishing the extra tug as the impact pulled on her breasts. Adrenaline pounded through her temples and she held herself perfectly still for fear the slightest movement might trigger her climax.

'I'm folding,' Stephen said, tossing his cards onto the table. He pushed his chair back and started towards the door. 'I'm sure one of you will let me know the outcome of this game. I have more entertaining things to watch than you two trying to better one another.' Not waiting for a reply, he disappeared out of the poker room.

'I'll call your Ferrari with my Gemballa,' Brandon growled. He glanced at his hand and added, 'And then I'll raise you to the value of my database.'

Cassie blinked back tears as the extra weight of car keys and a floppy disc were dropped onto her tray. She knew the moment of release was only a whisper away and she held her breath for fear that exhaling might cause the cataclysmic rush her body was dreading.

'If that's your database,' John said simply, 'then I'll raise you to the value of J & C Property Developments. That includes all the company assets along with each one of the ongoing contracts.'

'You're betting an awful lot on that hand,' Brandon observed. 'Is it really that good?'

John shook his head and smiled confidently. 'It isn't that good,' he said. 'It's even better.'

'What am I expected to put up to see you?'

'Put your business in as well,' John suggested. 'Put in this house, all your ongoing contracts, and throw in your staff for good measure.' He glanced at Cassie and gave her a lewd wink. 'I wouldn't mind reacquainting myself with the ice-maiden now you've got her properly trained.'

Cassie lowered her gaze in case he read something from her eyes. The idea of having John control her was so unwelcome it was almost arousing. Coupled with the bolts of ecstasy being wrought from her nipples the whole experience brought her close to a shuddering explosion.

'You want me to put in my entire business,' Brandon mused. 'That would make this an all or nothing kind of game, wouldn't you say? The loser might just as well shut up shop and head out of town.'

'I guess so,' John agreed. 'We could even throw that clause in for good measure, if you like. Are you up for it? Or should I just take it you've reached your limit and you want to back out now while you still have something left.'

Brandon seemed to think for a moment as he flicked the ash from his cigar. 'Go on then,' he said eventually. 'We'll make this a winner-takes-all hand. I'll match your business with my business. And I'll put in my house and all my property to see you.'

'All your property?' John sounded sceptical. He glanced at Cassie and asked, 'Does that include her?'

Brandon followed the direction of his gaze and frowned with disgust. 'That includes all of them. It includes Faye, Marion, Sarah and Cassie. All my property.'

Chuckling, John turned over his cards and laid them down on the table. Cassie could understand his jubilant smile and she felt right in sharing some of his pride as he placed his hand beneath Brandon's inscrutable face. 'You'd have to do really well to beat that,' he laughed. 'You'd have to do really fucking well to beat that.'

Brandon nodded and put down his hand. 'You're right,' he agreed, turning over one ace after another. 'I would have to do well. And I think I just have done.'

John's face fell as he regarded Brandon's two jokers and three aces.

'I cheated,' Cassie told Brandon.

They were alone in the poker room and, although John had gruffly departed after losing, Brandon had still made no attempt to take his winnings from Cassie's tray. He sat easily in his chair, contemplating the remainder of his cigar and sipping triumphantly at his scotch.

'I cheated,' she repeated, wondering if he hadn't heard her the first time.

He nodded. 'I expected as much,' he said eventually, 'but just repeating the words doesn't tell me why.'

She glanced at him, wondering if he was prompting her for an explanation or if he really didn't know her motivations. Daring to take the initiative, Cassie released the clips from her nipple rings and laid the tray on the table. Sliding out of her chair, kneeling on the floor beside him, she unzipped his trousers and removed the stiffening length of his erection. Holding her mouth millimetres above his glans, she whispered, 'I did it to prove a point.'

'And what point might that have been?'

'You said you were expecting me to acknowledge my desires and apologise for my stupidity,' she reminded him. 'I thought, dealing so you would win, might be a good way of apologising.'

He contemplated this as she lapped her tongue against the tip of his glistening dome. 'Does that mean you're ready to acknowledge your desires?'

Lowering her head over his shaft, Cassie smiled to herself and said, 'I'm more than ready. I'm more than ready, *master*.'

NEXUS NEW BOOKS

To be published in January

DEMONIC CONGRESS
Aishling Morgan

Eighteenth-century Devon. Old Noah Pargade is a wealthy yet cur-
mudgeonly miser who marries the nubile and game Alice Eden. As
anxious to avoid sharing his wife as he is his wealth, he makes sure she
is enmured in his desolate old house on the moors. Fortunately for young
Alice, there are enough young bucks in the vicinity whose advantage it is
in to take pity on her. Noah's fears are well-founded, as Alice is able to
continue her cheerfully sluttish goings-on. Especially when the swash-
buckling John Truscott returns from his foreign travels, and quack doctor
Cyriack Coke, replete with a cartload of bizarre colonic devices, visits the
county. When the truth becomes plain, old Coke is forced to take drastic
measures.

ISBN 0 352 33762 1

CHALLENGED TO SERVE
Jacqueline Bellevois

Known simply as 'The Club', a group of the rich and influential meet
every month in a Cotswold mansion to slake their perverted sexual
appetites. Within its walls, social norms are forgotten and fantasy
becomes reality. The Club's members are known to each other by the
names of pagan gods and goddesses, or those of characters from the
darker side of history. Two of them – Astra and Kali – undertake to
resolve a feud once and for all by each training a novice member. After
one month, the one who's deemed by the other members to have done the
best job will be allowed to enslave the other, finally and totally, for the
duration of the Club's activities and beyond.

ISBN 0 352 33748 6

PRIVATE MEMOIRS OF A KENTISH HEADMISTRESS
Yolanda Celbridge

Graceful young heiress Miss Abigail Swift founds a new academy to teach Kentish maidens discipline and ladylike manners. She meets the stern, lovely matron, already adept at the art of a young lady's correction; the untamed Walter, longing to become a lady; and the surly beauty Miss Rummer, who keeps the local gentlemen on their toes. Visiting Paris, Abigail learns from the voluptuous Comtesse de Clignancourt that English discipline makes for French pleasure, and triumphs at the masked ball in Dover Castle by introducing her perverse but well-tested methods to royalty.

ISBN 0 352 33763 X

To be published in February

JODHPURS AND JEANS
Penny Birch

Penny Birch is currently the filthiest little minx on the Nexus list, with 14 titles already published by Nexus. All are equally full of messy, kinky fun and, frankly, no other erotic writer has ever captured the internal thrills afforded by the perverse shamings and humiliations her characters undergo! In *Jodhpurs and Jeans*, Penny returns to the world of human equestrianism, and also takes part in a very bizarre game of paintball!

£6.99   ISBN 0 352 33778 8

LOVE-CHATTEL OF TORMUNIL
Aran Ashe

Powerfully erotic fantasy fiction by the author of *The Handmaidens*. *Love-Chattel of Tormunil* continues the tenderly written erotic epic of *The Chronicles of Tormunil*, which catalogues the exploits and odysseys of outlanders, body-slaves, milk-slaves and soldiers, all versed in the Tormunite ways of tender SM and bondage.

£6.99   ISBN 0 352 33779 6

THE CORRECTION OF AN ESSEX MAID
Yolanda Celbridge

Rescued from degradation, young and naïve orphan Sophia joins the House of Rodings, a maids' training school deep in the Essex countryside, dedicated to the worship and correction of the naked female rear. She meets a cast of submissive and dominant females, all adoring or envious of Sophia's voluptuous bottom, and thrives in the complex ranks, rules and punishments of the House's hierarchy.

£6.99   ISBN 0 352 33780 X

If you would like more information about Nexus titles, please visit our website at www.nexus-books.co.uk, or send a stamped addressed envelope to:

Nexus, Thames Wharf Studios,
Rainville Road, London W6 9HA

NEXUS BACKLIST

This information is correct at time of printing. For up-to-date information, please visit our website at www.nexus-books.co.uk

All books are priced at £5.99 unless another price is given.

Nexus books with a contemporary setting

ACCIDENTS WILL HAPPEN	Lucy Golden ISBN 0 352 33596 3	☐
ANGEL	Lindsay Gordon ISBN 0 352 33590 4	☐
BARE BEHIND £6.99	Penny Birch ISBN 0 352 33721 4	☐
BEAST	Wendy Swanscombe ISBN 0 352 33649 8	☐
THE BLACK FLAME	Lisette Ashton ISBN 0 352 33668 4	☐
BROUGHT TO HEEL	Arabella Knight ISBN 0 352 33508 4	☐
CAGED!	Yolanda Celbridge ISBN 0 352 33650 1	☐
CANDY IN CAPTIVITY	Arabella Knight ISBN 0 352 33495 9	☐
CAPTIVES OF THE PRIVATE HOUSE	Esme Ombreux ISBN 0 352 33619 6	☐
CHERI CHASTISED £6.99	Yolanda Celbridge ISBN 0 352 33707 9	☐
DANCE OF SUBMISSION	Lisette Ashton ISBN 0 352 33450 9	☐
DIRTY LAUNDRY £6.99	Penny Birch ISBN 0 352 33680 3	☐
DISCIPLINED SKIN	Wendy Swanscombe ISBN 0 352 33541 6	☐

Samplers and collections

NEW EROTICA 5	Various	☐
	ISBN 0 352 33540 8	
EROTICON 1	Various	☐
	ISBN 0 352 33593 9	
EROTICON 2	Various	☐
	ISBN 0 352 33594 7	
EROTICON 3	Various	☐
	ISBN 0 352 33597 1	
EROTICON 4	Various	☐
	ISBN 0 352 33602 1	
THE NEXUS LETTERS	Various	☐
	ISBN 0 352 33621 8	
SATURNALIA	ed. Paul Scott	☐
£7.99	ISBN 0 352 33717 6	
MY SECRET GARDEN SHED	ed. Paul Scott	☐
£7.99	ISBN 0 352 33725 7	

Nexus Classics

A new imprint dedicated to putting the finest works of erotic fiction back in print.

AMANDA IN THE PRIVATE HOUSE	Esme Ombreux	☐
£6.99	ISBN 0 352 33705 2	
BAD PENNY	Penny Birch	☐
	ISBN 0 352 33661 7	
BRAT	Penny Birch	☐
£6.99	ISBN 0 352 33674 9	
DARK DELIGHTS	Maria del Rey	☐
£6.99	ISBN 0 352 33667 6	
DARK DESIRES	Maria del Rey	☐
	ISBN 0 352 33648 X	
DISPLAYS OF INNOCENTS	Lucy Golden	☐
£6.99	ISBN 0 352 33679 X	
DISCIPLINE OF THE PRIVATE HOUSE	Esme Ombreux	☐
£6.99	ISBN 0 352 33459 2	
EDEN UNVEILED	Maria del Rey	☐
	ISBN 0 352 33542 4	

- - - - - - ✂ -

Please send me the books I have ticked above.

Name   ....

Address   ....

                ....

                ....

                .... Post code....................

Send to: **Cash Sales, Nexus Books, Thames Wharf Studios, Rainville Road, London W6 9HA**

US customers: for prices and details of how to order books for delivery by mail, call 1-800-343-4499.

Please enclose a cheque or postal order, made payable to **Nexus Books Ltd**, to the value of the books you have ordered plus postage and packing costs as follows:
    UK and BFPO – £1.00 for the first book, 50p for each subsequent book.
    Overseas (including Republic of Ireland) – £2.00 for the first book, £1.00 for each subsequent book.

If you would prefer to pay by VISA, ACCESS/MASTERCARD, AMEX, DINERS CLUB or SWITCH, please write your card number and expiry date here:

....

Please allow up to 28 days for delivery.

Signature ....

Our privacy policy.

We will not disclose information you supply us to any other parties. We will not disclose any information which identifies you personally to any person without your express consent.

From time to time we may send out information about Nexus books and special offers. Please tick here if you do *not* wish to receive Nexus information.   □

- - - - - - ✂ -